PRAISE FOR SATAN'S GAMBIT

"WOW! *Satan's Gambit*, Book One, will take the reader on a journey that will make you spit nails and distrust anyone in a position of power and influence."

- Cecelia T.

"Dr. Conti delivers a stunner of a novel. Replete with solid documented facts, it is punctuated with humor while educating and captivating the reader with whiplash strikes to the intellect, like a knife slicing through your neck and you don't realize it until you turn your head and it rolls off."

- Camille W.

"If this is fiction then only the names and maybe the abbey are. Excellent! Thought-provoking! Read it in one day; could not put it down. Answered two questions I've pondered for years. When are two and three coming out?"

- Roger V.

"Our country is heading into an epic storm of absolute destruction! *Satan's Gambit* will provide you with a frightening glimpse of what is to come if we do not change course."

- Sean W.

"Gene Conti has written a superb work on par with the likes of a William Forstchen novel, and completed with the action and military detail on par with that of the late Tom Clancy. This book is filled with unique facts that can be verified by a simple search. The novel is filled with adventure and action. As you follow Father Ed and Dr. Lucci on their epic journey you feel as if you are right there with them. Once you come back to reality and turn on the news you realize that perhaps the author may just be a modern-day Nostradamus."

- Craig P.

"This is spot on! It's a compelling well-put-together novel, and I can't wait to get Book Two. I have two friends that can't wait to read it, and I'm buying copies for several family members and friends."

- Ted L.

SATAN'S GAMBIT

BOOK ONE
Battle Lines Are Drawn

A Novel By

GENE CONTI, MD

SATAN'S GAMBIT

Copyright © 2018 by Gene Conti

DISCLAIMER

Many of the characters and individuals whom I have included in the novel are real; and in some cases, famous celebrities. In reality I do not know if they are in agreement or in support of any of the ideas, tenets or propositions I have put forth in my novel. I have included them only in the hope of making the novel more interesting.

Cover Design by Perceptions Design Studio

Library of Congress Catalog in Publication Data available upon request.

Paperback ISBN: 978-1-949021-09-7
eBook ISBN: 978-1-949021-10-3

Printed in the United States of America
16 17 18 19 20 21 LSI 9 8 7 6 5 4 3 2 1

DEDICATION

To the absolutely wonderful nurses I have worked with throughout the years in the emergency department. They truly have nerves of steel, hearts of gold and the patience of Job.

The women and men in the emergency department are the tip of the medical/nursing spear. They are the first to fight on the front lines and in the trenches. Do not be deceived. The emergency department of today is a war room of controlled (and at times not so controlled) chaos.

The entire medical system today is in free-fall. The meltdown commenced a few years ago. These women and men are the glue who are trying to hold it together. *Daily* they are subjected to ridicule, harassment, and physical abuse; being cussed, punched, spit at; and have their lives threatened by the very people who they are trying to care for. This is not your "ER" of twenty years ago, or even ten years ago. There is not an emergency physician or other health care provider today who could even begin to function without their support and assistance. They are more than deserving of your honor and respect.

CONTENTS

CONTENTS

PREFACE

We as a nation stand looking back on what has taken place over the past few decades. Many of us are confused as to what has happened to us, and why. This novel takes place just a few short years into the future and is an attempt to answer these very crucial questions.

I believe things will get worse before they get better. However, in order for we as humanity to have a brighter future, and we will, we must understand what exactly has transpired. Only then can we . correct our mistakes.

This new edition, hopefully, will allow you, the reader, to engage in the battle at some level to save our great nation.

ACKNOWLEDGMENTS

This novel could never have been written without positive constructive input and criticism from people whom I admire. There are several individuals who I would like to thank for their sage advice and comments: Ted Flynn, Colleen Flynn, Robert Keitzer, Dawn Bennett, R.N., Lucille Gross, R.N., Alanna LoGioco and, of course, my loving wife, Barbara. Also posthumously my parents, both of whom persisted in prayer for me to return to the straight and narrow way.

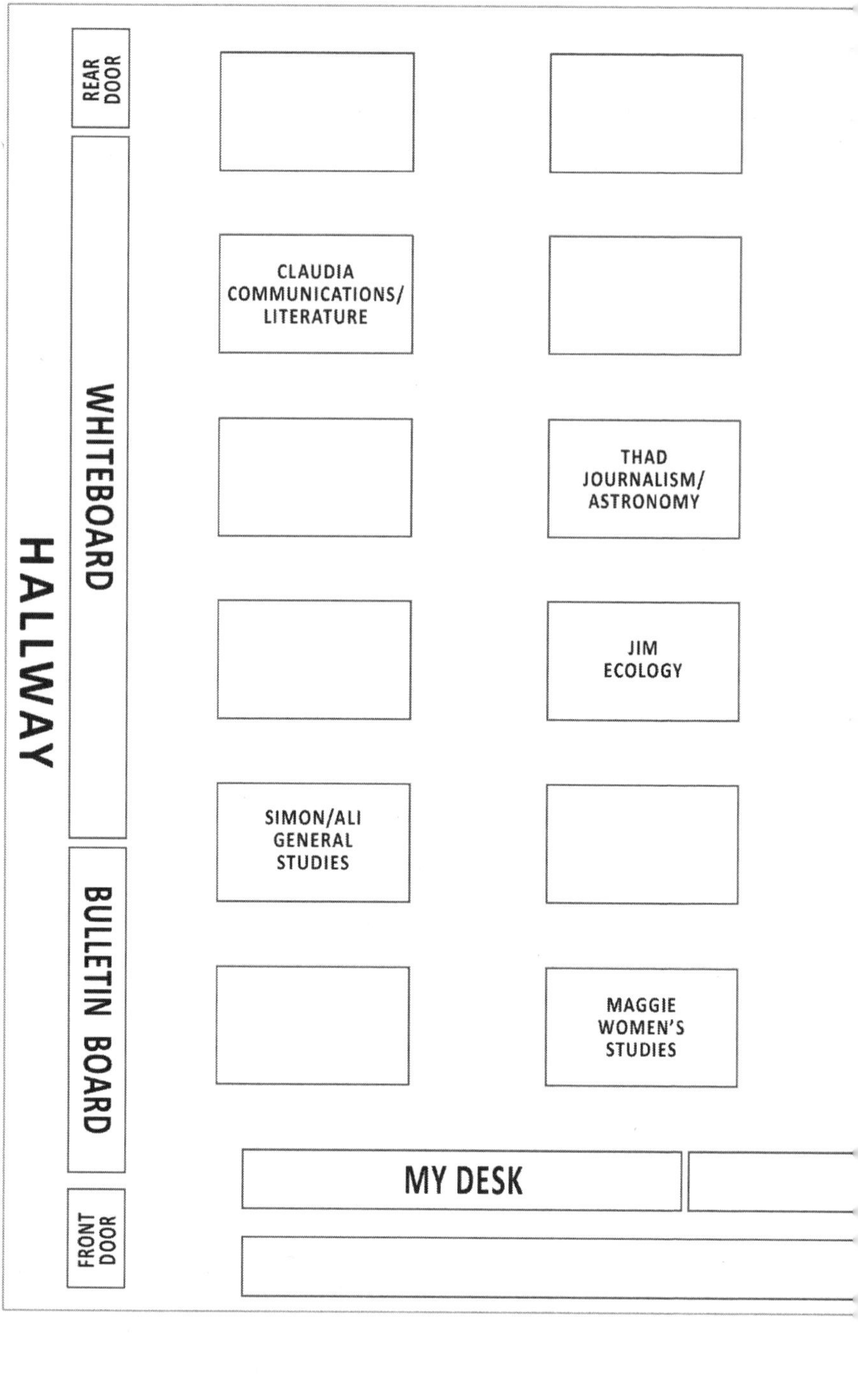

REAR DOOR

FRONT DOOR

HALLWAY

WHITEBOARD

BULLETIN BOARD

CLAUDIA
COMMUNICATIONS/
LITERATURE

THAD
JOURNALISM/
ASTRONOMY

JIM
ECOLOGY

SIMON/ALI
GENERAL
STUDIES

MAGGIE
WOMEN'S
STUDIES

MY DESK

PHILIP PHYSICS/MATH/ BIOCHEMISTRY		JUDE POLITICAL SCIENCE
	NATE BUSINESS/ COMPUTER SCIENCE	
ANDY ENGINEERING/ ARCHITECTURE	PETE GEOLOGY/ MARINE SCIENCE	MATT FINANCE/ MARKETING
	TOM HISTORY/ PRE-LAW	JUAN TEACHING/ PSYCHOLOGY
MARIA NURSING		SANTI SOCIAL SCIENCE

WINDOWS AND WINDOW LEDGES

LAB TABLE

WHITEBOARD

CHAPTER ONE

THE LAST DAY

The sun was shining through the classroom windows, providing warmth to the room; it was comforting and almost consoling after yesterday's cold rain. I could hear the birds chirping and singing outside, which brightened my spirits. The classroom was a standard size room, not like the classic lecture halls with theater-style seating as portrayed in most movie settings.

I had begun packing my personal books, science texts, DVDs, and reams of lecture notes that I had used for the course throughout the past two semesters. The fossils and other props I had shown to the students during the class lectures would have to be carefully covered with bubble wrap before boxing.

The events of yesterday still had my mind roiling. In retrospect, I'm surprised I was able to teach two semesters before the powers that be finally had to crush me. It was just a matter of time. I should feel grateful that I was able to accomplish the little that I did. Hopefully the kids got the message. The question is: did I impact them enough, enough for them to carry the torch?

The serenity of the classroom was suddenly broken when Maria, one of my students, rushed into the room. Exhausted and panting she is extremely agitated and stumbling over her words.

"Maria, calm down and breathe slowly; what has you so upset?"

"Someone has killed himself. Someone has killed himself." Confused and crying - her head and eyes wandering about without focus or direction.

"Maria," I grabbed both her shoulders firmly, "look at me! Organize your thoughts and tell me what has happened. Who has killed himself?"

"A few of us were inside the coffee shop when we heard some loud talking, almost screaming from someone outside on the patio."

"The outside patio of the coffee shop?" I asked.

"Yes, Yes, and then we heard a loud gunshot." As her breathing started to slow down, she looked and spoke directly to me. "There were a few students and faculty sitting outside on the patio and they began to scream . . . and . . . and everyone inside the coffee shop ran out to the patio."

Maria started to become flustered again. I gripped her shoulders once more and calmly asked, "Maria, when you got out to the patio, what did you see?"

"Nothing."

"Nothing?" I asked, repeating what she just told me.

"Well, some of the kids who were originally on the patio when the gunshot went off were still screaming when Father Flanagan ran up. He took charge rather quickly and began questioning those who were present."

"What did they tell him?"

"That some guy was standing on that little wall on the edge of the patio ranting and raving about something; then he took a gun out and shot himself in the head."

"And the body?"

"It must have fallen off the wall into that deep ravine below. Everyone ran to the wall, but couldn't see anything, probably because of all the trees and bushes and stuff way down there. Father Flanagan found the gun on the patio next to the wall where it landed after the guy shot himself. Someone heard him say something about blood on the gun and that he was going to contact the police."

CHAPTER TWO

BATTLE OF CHOSIN

I t was just over a year ago that Father Ed Flanagan talked me into doing the teaching stint at his college. He felt that I really had something to offer the youth and pressed me to meet with the dean as soon as possible, so as to get me on the fall roster. Of course, Father Ed paved the way for my meeting with Dean Avery, which went as smooth as silk.

Father Ed Flanagan was quite a colorful character. He was widely well known and respected by a broad swath of people from diverse backgrounds. I came to know of Father Ed through his books and articles. It may have been through the writings on WND that I was first exposed to him. I was drawn to his style, which revealed his character. He was definitely not the PC type. He told it how it was. More of a kick butt and take names kind of personage.

The more I read his books, the more I wanted to meet him. My wife, Emily, encouraged me to contact him. With some persistent prodding, I finally did. He was a bit cautious at first, but in short order we hit it off. We were two peas from the same pod. After that first luncheon at Clyde's, a well-appointed Washington restaurant, we both knew neither of us needed to put on airs. Early on we met frequently for coffee or beer at some local pub or bar and grill, in town, not far from Georgetown University. We would find a quiet corner and just talk for hours.

Father Ed wasn't always a Roman Catholic priest. His father was Irish and mother was Scottish. His accent and speech expressions are a mixture of both the Scottish burr and the Irish brogue with the requisite blarney thrown in occasionally for emphasis. When he was about fifteen years old he lied about his age and "snuck" into the marines. He went through basic training at Parris Island and then was immediately shipped to Korea as part of the 1st Marine Division.

Ed quickly saw action and was involved in the Battle of Chosin Reservoir in November to December of 1950. Temps dropped to minus thirty-five degrees Fahrenheit. Firing pins failed on their rifles. Blood plasma froze and was useless. The Navy Corsairs had no choice but to drop napalm on the Chinese hordes descending over and upon our marines, which ignited on our own troops as well.

Ed was near his commanding officer, Lt. Don Carlos Faith, when shrapnel from a grenade injured them both. Ed watched as Lieutenant Faith died from a mortal wound. Ed himself would have bled to death if it weren't for the freezing temperatures, which stopped him from exsanguinating.

Ed was one of the "Chosin Few" as they were called. He survived after a splenectomy, and losing a small finger and a few toes that had developed frostbite and subsequent gangrene. They had to be amputated at a mobile army surgical hospital (M*A*S*H*) — without anesthesia.

There are no atheists in foxholes, as Corporal Flanagan soon learned, and that the utopian Marxist philosophy of communism can only be established with bullets and bayonets.

CHAPTER THREE

FALL OF SAIGON

The tall, skinny, kid that had entered the Marines was honorably discharged a few years later, and was now a tough-as-nails man with the physique to back it up. He bummed around for a while after returning to the states, taking all manner of odd jobs from working in a lumber mill to serving as a bouncer in a dance club. But something was gnawing at him.

Ed attended college at Georgetown University and majored in philosophy with a minor in political science. After graduation, he worked in Washington as an entry-level bureaucrat at one of the alphabet agencies. Ed hated the mundane work, but loved meeting and networking with people. He made some good contacts higher up in the pecking order and saw how all the political intrigue of the Washington scene could be addicting. He developed some close friends he really trusted while trying to avoid the K Street boys, or ravenous human parasites as he called them.

Still something was yearning within him. His spirit was unsettled. One beautiful summer day he visited a Marine buddy who was undergoing some physical rehab at the National Rehabilitation Hospital off Irving Street. It was a great reunion. They laughed until they cried, exchanging old war stories, and then talked about family and work and things. Upon leaving the facility, that pesky feeling was bugging Ed again. He drove around McMillan Park and headed east on Irving Street, crossed over North Capitol Street, and began to head up Michigan Avenue when he spotted a beautiful building on his left. He double backed and pulled into the main parking area. The white marble structure glistened in the high noonday sun. It was the Basilica of the Immaculate Conception. It reminded him somewhat of Hagia Sofia Mosque which he had seen while on one of his bureaucratic jaunts to Istanbul, Turkey for the agency. The Hagia Sophia was originally a massive cathedral, built in the sixth century, in the former city of Constantinople, which was converted to a mosque with the fall of Constantinople by the Muslim Ottoman Turks in 1453.

An indescribable gentle force was lulling him to go inside. Once inside the basilica, Ed looked around, was suddenly overwhelmed, and dropped to his knees. He knew what was wanted of him. It still took him another year to work through all his conflicting emotions and desires that were pulling him in a multitude of directions. Deep in his heart and soul, he knew what was his true calling.

Five years later he was ordained a priest lying prostate before the Cardinal, a supplicant before God. He had attended the Theological College of the Catholic University of America, which was essentially on the same campus as the Basilica of the Immaculate Conception he had walked into several years earlier.

By the time Ed was ordained, the Viet Nam conflict was in full swing, and the new Father Ed wanted to be in the thick of it. He knew his Marines and others in the military, as well as the Vietnamese people, needed him—they needed God. He volunteered and was sent over as a chaplain with the Marines. Besides his pastoral care to the soldiers and civilians, he was helping establish orphanages and teaching the staff to raise chickens. The chicken business didn't always work out well as the starving urban civilians usually ate the chickens before there were enough eggs to repopulate the coops. It wasn't long before his buddies with the alphabet agencies got wind that Ed was in Nam, and he soon was roped into aiding "the cause" doing some covert work for the CIA.

Father Ed never trusted President Lyndon Johnson. He didn't think the president was prosecuting the war as a battle to be won but as a prolonged protracted minimalist campaign to benefit the military-industrial complex that President Eisenhower had warned about in his farewell speech. Initially Father Ed was the good Boy Scout and thought he could make a difference. But the carnage around him and the senseless deaths of American lives as cannon fodder for the elite took its toll.

Father Ed was at the fall of Saigon on April 29, 1975, when the Air America helicopters evacuated CIA personnel from the rooftop of Gia Long Street in Saigon. From a clandestine location, he watched in silent outrage as American flags were ripped down, burnt, and trampled upon. It had been only a few months since he had discovered that the events in the Gulf of Tonkin, which originally brought us into the war, was a false flag op. The incident was provoked so that the president would have an excuse to start a war.

Father Ed refused to just leave the Vietnamese people to a grisly fate. North Korea resounded in his mind. He knew firsthand what awaited these poor people. Slavery and starvation were certain. A quick death would be a blessing. The USA had sold them out. The Viet Cong captured Saigon the next day.

Not exactly Jungle Jim, Father Ed had learned a lot about survival from the rural Vietnamese people over those years. For them it was routine daily life to live off the land. Instead of Father Ed helping them, the Vietnamese who he could trust, were helping him. To harbor an American, and a priest at that, would mean torture and death for one's entire family. Word did get out that a CIA operative—Father Ed—was still at large.

CHAPTER FOUR

THE ESCAPE

After losing their pursuers in the wilds of the Mekong Delta, Father Ed and several families, who had been targeted by the new Communist regime for aiding the Americans, made it to the tip of the Vietnamese peninsula. Three families each lost a member when they disturbed the domain of a brood of swamp snakes. The entire band was exhausted, dehydrated, and bloated from innumerable mosquito bites and the blood-sucking leeches that had attached to every exposed body part.

It was there that they received a blessing from heaven—a Mekong Delta Freighter. It was owned by one of the families' relatives, and he hated the Viet Cong. They had killed his youngest son for not giving over his meager fishing catch and other supplies that they demanded. Classic communist "share the wealth" mentality.

As they were loading the freighter, Father Ed noticed a case of number 10 cans in a cardboard box with American military labeling on it. Stenciled on the side was CHOC PUD. He asked the freighter captain what that was all about. He said that some of the Navy swift-boat sailors gave it to him as a present. Told him it "fell off a truck." The captain said it was really "good stuff." They used it as bait to lure some of the small swamp animals into their cage traps. The animals loved it. With that Father Ed picked up the case and brought it aboard the freighter. He said, "The *kids* will love this stuff."

All the families bordered the vessel with Father Ed. Should they attempt to cross the Gulf of Thailand they would risk getting caught by patrol boats or swapped by a sudden squall, as it was early in the monsoon season. The captain suggested they hug the west coast and follow it up to Bangkok. They would travel only at night and anchor and sleep during the day in small hidden alcoves. The vote was for going up the coast.

They seemed to avoid the patrol boats easily enough, but they were almost captured by a group of North Vietnamese Army Regulars while moored one day in a tiny fresh water bay by a river outlet in Cambodia. The women on board were washing clothes and some of the men and boys who weren't sleeping were fishing.

The foot soldiers on the shore beckoned the vessel to come closer, probably with the intent of stealing the vessel's supplies and foodstuffs. Father Ed was sure the soldiers had absolutely no knowledge of the freighter's "real" cargo. They immediately pulled up anchor and high tailed it out of the bay under a fusillade of bullets. No one was hurt, but the freighter had a few holes that needed to be plugged up.

Eventually they made it to Bangkok, Thailand. Father Ed went immediately to the American Embassy, pulled out all the stops and called in all his favors. He presented himself first as an American CIA operative and then as a Catholic chaplain in the Marines. Father Ed could put on a stone face and a stare that would melt steel when he needed to. No shouting, just a strong presence and firm words to those low-life bureaucratic pukes at the embassy.

He had himself and all those families, who wished to go, on a flight back to the states in twenty-four hours.

CHAPTER FIVE

THE PRESIDENTS

He finished his tour of duty as chaplain stateside and was honorably discharged. He renewed his relationship with his alma mater, Georgetown University, and for the next several years taught as an assistant professor of theology and poly sci to the undergraduates.

One evening I was waiting for Father Ed, at the Tombs, a restaurant at the edge of the Georgetown campus, for one of our usual "blethers" as he called our chats. The Tombs, built in a Federal-style townhouse circa 1800s, was known for good food and as a great gathering place for students. While waiting I ran into one of Father Ed's former students. We shared a brewski together as he raved that it was the best two courses he had ever taken.

"Had I taken just theology or poly sci, the impact on me would not have been the same," as he waved and gave a thumbs up to one of the basketball players—probably regarding the big win Georgetown had the night before against Syracuse. The Hoyas were on a winning streak.

The kid said that about 60 percent of Father Ed's lecture notes were essentially the same for both classes. Very animated, he expressed, "I never realized how much theology and political science overlapped and dovetailed with each other."

I knew from reading Father Ed's books exactly what that kid was talking about: the fact that metaphysics and government are so intertwined. They are literally two halves of the same coin, which is why I had been "relieved," at least partially, of my professorial teaching duties.

By the late 1980s, the Reagan administration had the county's economy booming again. The media was still controlled by ABC, CBS, and NBC almost exclusively. They tagged it the "decade of greed." Perhaps they should have called years of the prior administration of Jimmy Carter the "decade of want"? Mortgage rates under Carter had skyrocketed to the high double digits, and inflation was rampant.

Father Ed perceived President Carter to be wishy-washy and inept. The 1979 takeover of our embassy in Iran by the Muslim extremists and the Ayatollah Khomeini was a travesty; and the disastrous failed rescue attempt in April of 1980 of our hostages by Carter humiliated the USA even more. The scenes of the twisted wreckage in the desert of a Delta Force helicopter and transport plane from Operation Eagle Claw, along with the deaths of eight servicemen, were splashed across the evening news. Carter's fate was sealed.

Father Ed said that we should have listened to our military leaders and squashed them like bugs immediately after the embassy takedown, instead of Carter's dilly-dallying for more than a year afterward.

At another blether, late one afternoon, after Father Ed had finished teaching for the day, we were having some java at the coffee shop across from the Georgetown University bookstore in the Leavey Center. The coffee shop had a checkered past, but was trying to really help the students. He educated me as to the time President Teddy Roosevelt went head to head with the Moroccan government in the early 1900s. A brigand Muslim terrorist had captured an American businessman, and Roosevelt was going to invade a sovereign country by sending in the Marines to rescue the American. Just the threat from Roosevelt made Morocco back down.

Hollywood made it into a movie called the *Wind and the Lion* with two attractive stars: Sean Connery and Candace Bergen. "The theatre-going public would rather pay to see Sean Connery as a debonair sheikh and the beautiful Candace Bergen as a damsel in distress than someone playing the role of a fat, pudgy businessman, and another as a fanatical wild-eyed crazed Islamic kidnapper," Ed declared as he downed the second cup of strong black coffee.

Then came the Clinton era. Father Ed had no use for either of the Clintons. Still maintaining his friendships with some close friends of the alphabet agencies, he and his buddies would occasionally bowl at Potomac Lanes at Joint Base Anacostia-Bolling (JBAB), just across the Potomac from Reagan International, and have some pizza with beer to wash it down.

Sometimes they would bowl against the team from the Defense Intelligence Agency (DIA) who were on the same base. "Those guys at DIA were smart as whips, but a little stiff, which may have affected their bowling skills, or lack thereof," he commented to me between sips of his third java brew.

The group that he seemed to have the most fun with was the guys of the Secret Service. Serious dudes when they were guarding the President and First Family, but they really knew how to cut up in their off time. Their fleet of black Suburbans was also parked at JBAB. The array of antennas that splayed from the roofs of the SUVs gave it away that someone of importance was being transported on "the train," as he said they called it, when they were all driving bumper to bumper at high rates of speed.

"Bill Clinton's code name was 'jumper' because any time he saw an attractive woman, he would want to 'jump her'. Clinton knew the code name the Secret Service had given him and he liked it. Hillary was another matter. Hers was 'broomstick,' for obvious reasons," Ed explained.

"A real life 'cailleach'," Father added. "She cussed like a trucker and could drink like a sailor. One never, but never addressed her.

You didn't speak unless she directly asked something of you. And the shorter the answer, the better. If you could respond with a "yes ma'am" or "no ma'am," so much the better."

"Cailleach?" I asked, wondering what that Gaelic term meant.

"A hag or witch - the code name 'broomstick' must have been someone's stroke of genius," as he struck a pose of the Wicked Witch of the West.

CHAPTER SIX

MR. PEN AND A PHONE

FBI Agent Gary Aldrich and Father Ed were close in those days. He was one of the first to blow the lid on the Clintons with his book *Unlimited Access*. On occasion, Gary invited Father Ed down to Blackwater in North Carolina. They would go with a few of the other agents during the summer months to hone their driving skills on the Blackwater track, and use the firing ranges and shoot houses to bone up on their marksmanship.

There were other facilities the FBI used locally in the Washington/Maryland area, but Virginia Beach was only a stone's throw from Blackwater. The lure of the strip and nightclubs was the summer draw, especially for the single agents. Father said he would retire to Star of the Sea Catholic Church in Virginia Beach and stay at the rectory with the pastor, who was a good friend of his.

"Both Bush I and Bush II, and their families," Father said at another of our coffee klatches, "took the office of the President seriously and were respectful of it, and looked upon their temporary stay in the White House—the people's house—with the admiration and courtesy that the old edifice deserved. That doesn't mean they were without their faults," he added. "Bush II and Cheney have a lot to answer for regarding 9/11."

"The Obama's were another matter," Father voiced. "They truly believed they were royalty and pranced around the White House as if it was their personal domain, all while treating the staff as servants to be bossed around. Both Barack and Michelle looked down upon the American people, with contempt and derision."

"Take the 9/11 Commemorative Ceremony in 2011 when she leaned over toward Barack and asked, 'All this for a damned flag?' pales in comparison to her earlier 2008 statement of 'for the first time in my adult lifetime, I'm really proud of my country.'" Father Ed adamantly added, "Look at her facial expression as she said it. That look alone speaks volumes and should silence the Obama supporters," getting so angry and red-faced that he almost totally spilled his coffee.

"Confirming her position as American Royalty, Michelle's travel junkets spent the taxpayer's money in a way that would have made Marie Antoinette feel like a penny-pincher. All while 43 million people were on food stamps and 95 million were out of work," Father fumed as he dabbed up the coffee from the table with a napkin.

Mr. Pen and a Phone, is what Father Ed called Obama. "A community organizer is simply a modern connotation for rabble rouser; which is exactly what Obama was. An extremely amiable, smooth-talking liar, whose divide-and-conquer skills he had perfected in the Chicago gangsta political machine. He was iron fisted in his attempt to destroy Christian America and a milquetoast internationally, with all his bowing and sucking up to the Muslim leaders."

By now, Iran, with Russian support, and Radical Islam had conquered most of the Middle East, save that one tiny island of democracy called Israel. The radicals had by now tortured, burned, beheaded, and crucified almost one in four Christians.

"The women and children who weren't killed, were raped and then sold as slaves and prostitutes," Father told me. "They're getting smart now, timing their executions to sell—cash only, of course—the transplantable organs to middlemen for transport to the highest bidders and thereby increasing their liquidity to purchase more arms and supplies. And our once-Christian country stands by silent."

Regarding both houses of Congress, and both parties, Father Ed said he prayed for them daily. With few exceptions, he said, "they were eunuchs who had sold their souls to the highest bidder. The K street boys would fund their re-election campaigns in exchange for favorable tax breaks, and EPA and OSHA passes for their firms."

"The politicians then promptly use their campaign war chests to pay for flashy ads offering their constituents more 'free stuff' than the other guy—who is a liar and a cheat—if the poor slobs would only re-elect them again for the umpteenth time. The 'free stuff' really came from the worker and small businessman who actually paid taxes."

The tables had tilted many years ago in favor of crony capitalism, warfare, and welfare. There were now more people, illegals, and counterfeit corporations in bed with the government and on the dole, than there were people actually working and contributing to the experiment called America. Even the stock market was rigged. Free enterprise was dead. We had lost our moral compass. Truth and the Judeo-Christian definition of right and wrong had been ripped from the lexicon.

CHAPTER SEVEN

COMPLIANT WEASEL

At another session, Father and I were at Froggy Bottom Pub somewhat near the Georgetown campus (you really needed to drive there). He knew the owners well. The Buis were both refugees from Vietnam. Hoang's cousin was saved on Father Ed's escape years earlier on the fishing trawler up the west coast of Vietnam to Bangkok. He and Hoang chatted a bit while Hien, Hoang's wife, brought Father his usual pint of Guinness Extra Stout and bowed slightly, as she placed it on the table before him. I hated the stuff. He took a long slow draught and proceeded to enlighten me.

"Sweet Mother Mary," he started off, "thank God that hooligan and shamus of a President is behind us."

He was speaking of course of Obama.

"Since he's been out of office, everyone and his brother has been writing books on how they knew from the very beginning, before he was elected, what a fraud and numptie he really was. Why on God's green earth didn't they warn us while he was first running in '08?"

"And a 'numptie' is?" I queried, blowing the head off the draft beer I had ordered.

"An idiot," he shot back loudly, just as some guy with one too many under his belt bumped into our table giving Father Ed a dirty look.

I had beer coming out of my nose with Father's weak maladroit attempt to explain his faux pas to the plastered patron.

"Aye, that fella's blootered," he half whispered to me. "And getting back to our numptie, it's not considered an ad hominem attack against someone, if you can back it up with evidence."

"Oh, kinda like a superstar ball player; it ain't bragging if you can really do it," I remarked as I stuffed some peanuts from a bowl on the table into my mouth.

He ignored my poor analogy and went on.

"Every President has had his share of wrongdoing. But Mr. Pen and a Phone, where does one start? The guy has a laundry list a mile long, and that's no exaggeration—the Fast and Furious scandal, the IRS scandal, the Benghazi scandal, the Bowe Bergdahl scandal with the Taliban Five scandal piggybacking it, the Associated Press scandal, the Solyndra scandal, the VA scandal, the Clinton e-mail scandal, and the Fort Hood scandal. Those are just some I can think of off the top of my head."

"Yeah, and no one prosecuted. Hey Father did you see *13 Hours*?"

"I know Kris Paronto. We call him Tanto. If it weren't for his team of six private contractors who disobeyed orders, all those civilian CIA pencil pushers would have died. And they may have even been able to save our ambassador. All one need do is watch the clock on the screen which silently indicts both Hillary and Obama with each passing second."

"I remember, in less than thirty minutes the Pentagon knew, which meant both Hillary and Obama knew," I exclaimed, slamming my beer mug onto the table. "What if one of those CIA personnel was your son, your wife, your brother?"

Father's eyes were getting red and started to tear. "We lost three good men in Tyrone, Glen and Sean. Obama sent no help whatsoever—even *after* thirteen hours! He and Hillary expected the whole lot of them to die." He wiped his eyes. "Marines don't cry, the eyeballs however sometimes sweat a little," he explained as he took another sip of his Guinness. "And the leftist media never pressed the issue with the public."

"Forty or fifty years ago, the press would have wanted them both impeached," I remarked. "And what's with the *new* President?"

"The current POTUS has been *selected*, as usual, by the international elites. The American people think they have a choice; they don't."

"Any and all honest candidates are eliminated early on by lies, guile and subterfuge, using a compliant media. Recall how they destroyed Dr. Ben Carson, and others, several years ago in the 2016 elections. The candidate of both parties is vetted in advance by the powers that be—the Council on Foreign Relations, CFR for short, the Bilderbergers, the Trilateral Commission, etcetera. The Bilderbergers pretty much make the final two selections."

"The election process itself is just a formality. The international elites usually watch and root with feigned admiration for the party who could rig the voter fraud in their candidate's favor, whether by sophisticated manipulation of the computerized electronic voting machines or just old fashioned stuffing of the ballot boxes with dead people's votes and/or voting multiple times at different precincts."

"It didn't make a wit worth of difference which of the two candidates the people elected. All U.S. Presidents are either a member of the CFR prior to election or must meet with them after being elected. If the newly elected President was to dispute their authority, they are read the riot act in no uncertain terms." He waved the waitress over and pointed to my empty mug for a refill.

Father reminded me of the talk that Hillary gave at a CFR meeting, which can still be seen on YouTube where *Hillary Clinton admits the CFR gives the orders*. She thanked the CFR for helping guide U.S. policy.

"In the run up to the '08 elections, Obama and Hillary slipped away from the press on June 5th only to be hosted at a Bilderberger meeting. Hillary dropped out of the race two days later; but as you know, in 2016, they gave Hillary her shot. Her moment had arrived to be coronated now; the globalists would want see to that. However, with her loss, rest assured they would not, and have not made the same mistake again - since they underestimated the populist turnout for Trump back in 2016. Hmm."

"That's right, Father. I recall one of Bill O'Reilly's interviews with Newt Gingrich, former Speaker of the House, when Gingrich stated, 'Bill you have to remember, Trump has not been initiated, he is not a member of the Secret Society.'"

Father tilted his head to the side, raised an eyebrow while nodding his head with a knowing smirk on his face; then he took another swig of his Guinness. "And Joe, do you remember on the Rachel Maddow Show when Chuck Schumer threatened Trump with the CIA saying, '...they have six ways from Sunday at getting back at you'; a veiled reference to what happened to JFK."

"That's right Father, I almost forgot."

"It gets better Joe. An old buddy of mine, Kevin Shipp, who was a former counterintelligence officer with the CIA, has turned whistleblower. I attended one of his connect the dots lectures. The CIA was formed post World War II."

"Yeah, I know that."

"But do you know who created it?"

I just gave Father a doltish stare, while shaking my head no.

"The CIA was created by none other than the CFR - Council on Foreign Relations."

My mouth dropped open as Father continued.

"And the CFR was formed in 1921 by the major banking families - the Morgans, the Rothchilds, etc."

I just sat there still shaking my head.

"My friend Kevin explains in his talks that at least 21 Directors of the CIA were also members of the CFR. That's one to check out on YouTube, if you don't believe me."

I was still in a daze, speechless and dumbfounded, thinking of these globalists.

CHAPTER EIGHT

KEY TO THE FUTURE

Father Ed has great foresight and vision. It was during the Nixon administration that Father saw the writing on the wall for the United States and the world, when Nixon closed the gold window and our government began to print un-backed paper. Father Ed saw Reagan as an anomaly. There were too many liberals and progressives gaining control in seats of power, whether it be in government, education, the media complex, or even the churches. He knew the only way he could make a difference was at a foundational level.

Day by day the nation was drifting further away from its roots, which our Founding Fathers had planted almost 250 years ago. Our public schools and public university system had been co-opted by the liberals many decades ago. Even many of the Christian and Catholic colleges and universities had become acolytes of the progressives, socialists, secularist, humanists—which are all just communism lite.

He explained all this to me one hot autumn afternoon as we walked under a canopy of red maples that lined both sides of our path on his new campus of Immaculate Conception College (ICC). I had just started to teach there several weeks earlier, with Father's influence and encouragement. The tree colors had just peaked, and the autumn reds were incredibly vibrant that year. The mountains in the distance were displaying a radiant rainbow of their fall foliage.

"He alone, who owns the youth, gains the future," Father Ed stated, quoting Hitler who understood very well that the youth are the key to the future. "The Hitler *jugend,* or youth, that Hitler had carefully fostered in the pre-war years became his most fanatical followers once World War II commenced," Father Ed continued as he pulled his handkerchief from his back pocket to wipe a bead of sweat that had started to drip from his forehead. "If one can train youth for evil, why not for good. As the Good Book says, 'Train up a child in the way he should go: and when he is old, he will not depart from it.' Seems ol' Hitler understood the Bible better than most Christians," he added as we entered the student center, which had vending machines, on the ICC campus. I sprung for some bottled water; and as I was putting my dollars in the machine, I turned and asked "Proverbs?"

"22:6, Solomon was no slouch," he immediately responded as he reached for the bottle I was handing him.

"I recall he was also quite the stud muffin, with what . . . seven hundred wives and three hundred concubines?"

Father didn't reply.

CHAPTER NINE

THE MONKS

I continued my packing. The books were finished. Next I had to pack the DVDs, and then the tedious job of wrapping all the delicate fossils, which I was *not* looking forward to. As I worked I reflected back to how Father Ed had come to start Immaculate Conception College.

He had great reverence for the Blessed Mother. It was her Basilica he was drawn to those many years ago before he became a priest. He often prayed to her to intercede for him when he was in some tough spot.

"Who do we run to first when we are in a jam?" he once asked me. As he answered his own question: "Your mom, she will always listen to you." He recounted the times he would approach his own birth mother when he really needed something or had a peccadillo to answer for. "Better me mamm than me tad, who meted out the more rigorous discipline if needed. We were required to go out in the field and cut our own switch from a shrub or tree."

I remembered it had been Father Ed's goal to save the country by helping the youth. He had been praying to the Blessed Virgin Mary (BVM) for what seemed like an eternity with no answer in sight. He had decided to get in his car and just drive. "Hey, it worked well another time and I became a priest," he confessed at another of our mastermind meetings over beer. He swore that a Guinness actually helped the brain to think better. Now I know that alcohol is a vasodilator, but think *better*?

He headed out on Interstate 66 driving west out of D.C. As he approached Front Royal, he decided to turn off and head into the Blue Ridge Mountains since it was such a beautiful calm day with just a hint of a mild breeze. Not caring what country roads he was taking, he had the windows down and the radio off and was just soaking in God's creation.

It was getting late and the sun was just above the crest of the ridges when he came upon what appeared to be a complex of old stone buildings, probably from the late 1800s. He drove through the entrance, which had an old, faded wooden sign identifying an abbey. He recalled he initially didn't even take close note of the name, as the paint was almost completely flaked off anyway.

The entrance took him to the main building, which was sorely in need of repair, as were the other buildings. Before he reached the top step an elderly thin monk, Brother Stanislaus, opened the main front doors, which were made of solid oak and massive by any standard.

Contrary to being quiet and sullen, Brother Stanislaus had a big smile on his face and greeted Father Ed with a big bear hug, which set him mentally off balance for a moment. Then Brother Stanislaus grabbed Father Ed's arm and virtually dragged him inside before Father knew what was happening.

The friendly old monk pulled a long, heavy, knotted rope that ran up into the tower, apparently attached to a large bell which was out of sight. The clanging that echoed off the stone walls was deafening and almost disorientating. Father Ed had to cover his ears. Several monks came running from different directions, appearing out of nowhere. They ran directly to the old man vigorously pealing the bell like there was a fire to be extinguished. Everyone was shouting at him and one another, wanting to know what the emergency was all about, totally ignoring Father Ed.

Once the calamity had settled down, Father Ed was invited to dinner. The monks wanted information as to what was happening in the outside world almost more than they wanted to know about their guest. These were Carmelite Monks and had a special devotion to the BVM. Their heads were shaved, save a small ring of hair that appeared like a halo on their heads called, a tonsure. They wore the classic tunic (habit) of brown wool with an attached cowl or capuche and leather cincture in lieu of a belt. On their chest was a large wooden cross with a metal corpus of the crucified body of Christ. Their feet were shod with sandals.

The food was excellent, grown by hand in their own gardens. No pesticides, no herbicides, no insecticides and no GMOs, either. I remember Father Ed chuckling that he didn't think they even knew what Roundup was. The various vegetable and fruit flavors virtually exploded on your taste buds, and he wanted to savor every morsel. There wasn't a course that he didn't relish, and he ate each one heartily.

These monks knew how to eat. But they also knew how to work. There wasn't a fat one in the lot. No junk food was consumed here. I remember Father Ed mentioned in passing that the monks brewed an excellent dark lager.

From sunup to sundown they were either praying or working the land or doing both. This sacrifice was a true labor of love, and it showed on their faces; they were by and large a happy lot. Relating this story to me, over his usual pint of Guinness and a very large corned beef sandwich, we both agreed that at the end of a work day, these monks had absolutely no problem sleeping—no need for a sleeping pill.

Contrary to many of my patients who do not work other than lift a bottle of booze to their lips or to snort some cocaine up their nose, and need a pharmacy of pills to function daily and still can't sleep at night. These are the same bad habits that put them on government disability and welfare programs in the first place. Only now they are using tax dollars, instead of their own money, to continue to feed their same destructive lifestyles. What a deal!

The head prior did most of the talking with Father Ed. It seemed that the main monastery for the order was located in the Rocky Mountains of Wyoming. This abbey was a branch of that Carmelite Order and was struggling financially. Ever since the government truly became secular, all religions were in effect outlawed.

The first amendment became "freedom of worship," rather than "freedom of religion." The difference being that one could practice their religion all they wanted, sing all they wanted, praise and worship all they wanted—but only within the confines of government approved buildings, facilities, or complexes, but not beyond them. Use of private homes as churches or for Bible study was expressly forbidden by law. To add insult to injury, all churches and religious institutions had lost their tax-exempt status.

Evangelizing, therefore, was taboo. Anyone caught proselytizing outside the bounds of designated worship centers was subject to immediate and indefinite detainment. The government was careful not to use the term "arrest." No trial, no legal representation, no judge, and no jury. The word on the street was you were processed directly to a FEMA camp; you do *not* pass GO, you do not collect $200. You were not heard from again. People had forgotten about the updated National Defense Authorization Act (NDAA), which was signed into law by President Obama in 2016, authorizing all of this.

As a result, contributions to many charitable causes went begging, the abbey being one of them. Yes, they were able to sustain themselves by growing their own food and fostering husbandry of livestock; however, land taxes for large properties and estates had increased dramatically. The government was constantly looking for ways to fill their empty coffers since the dollar and all fiat paper currencies worldwide had become essentially worthless.

The lapdog press that supported the government's decisions at every turn always bought into the "soak the rich" mentality. However, not all large estates belong to wealthy people. The abbey and many small farmers were hit hard. The small farmer had now reverted back to becoming a sixteenth century serf for the large agri-corporations that had gobbled them up.

CHAPTER TEN

A DREAM AND A PLAN

Father Ed listened very attentively to the prior as he laid out his woes. When he was finished, Father Ed presented a possible solution. "Let's create a college with the abbey being the central focal point of the enterprise." The name came to him instantly. "We can call it Immaculate Conception College."

"Student tuition will cover the operating funds. We'll find investors whose initial seed money will fund the restoration of the buildings and upgrades to the property. The operation would be small but sustainable enough to get it off the ground. The college could expand as net profits permitted. We could add additional buildings as we grow and prosper. St. John's University in New York, on Long Island, is a great example of how this will work."

The prior and other monks sitting around that rustic wooden dinner table were ecstatic and could barely contain themselves. They all admitted they had been praying to the Blessed Mother, their patroness, for a miracle. This was to be their last year, and they were mentally preparing themselves to close shop and sell off the abbey and its property. The name of the college, the *name* that Father Ed had proposed was perfect because it honored her as well.

The prior, being a bit more level headed than the younger monks, asked Father Ed with whom he expected to develop such fiduciary relationships to underwrite this project to get it started.

Father Ed, his mind racing with solutions, was already two steps ahead of the prior. He explained to all the monks that he had made many contacts throughout the years. He knew many men of integrity who despised what the government had devolved into and who would jump at the chance of establishing a biblical college. They were not stupid people who would just fork over money willy-nilly and watch it go down the drain. The time was ripe for this kind of investment. With every crisis comes opportunity—the yin and yang concept. Pagans had also been created by God and came up with some very profound concepts and ideas at times. Confucius had always maintained his popularity for sound reasons.

The rest is history, to use the hackneyed expression for what then transpired quickly. Father Ed was focused like a laser beam from then on. He plowed through all his contacts and sold his vision to the majority of them. He was pleasantly surprised by how many wanted a piece of the action. Other associates and investors of his were able to cut through the maze and morass of red tape to get the permits, licenses, charters, and a fog of other concessions that were necessary for the project to succeed. Father Ed didn't want to know the details of how they accomplished it; he just wanted to expedite the creation of the college. Within four years it was a reality way beyond his initial expectations. The entire abbey and property transformed into a beautiful campus, with a couple of new additional buildings designed to blend with the original European monastic ones. The grounds, walkways, and gardens all manicured with flora indigenous to the Blue Ridge. It felt natural and not overdone.

The students felt at home in this lush setting; sitting on the grass, others under shade trees, and some on benches that occasionally lined the paths and walkways.

The jewel at the center of it all was the abbey. Totally restored and refurbished inside and out, it was a beautiful place for the monks to continue to live and pray. A section of the land was set aside for them and the agricultural students to continue to labor.

The local Bishop dedicated the chapel, which needed to be almost totally rebuilt, to Our Lady of the Immaculate Conception on commencement day. Father Ed could have done without the pomp and circumstance put on by the numerous religious actors who were present that day. He would have preferred something more staid, solemn, and reverent. His dream was fulfilled, but not totally complete. The icing was not yet on the cake. He was on the board of directors, the executive committee, the course selection and approval committee, taught some courses, and worked alongside the monks and students in the fields to stay in shape. By then he was pushing ninety. Little did I know, but I was to be that icing on the cake.

CHAPTER ELEVEN

THE JOB OFFER

The sneaky dog invited me out to the campus the spring before I was to begin the fall semester. Father Ed had been giving me progress reports regarding the remodeling and alterations to the abbey, chapel, and grounds. He deliberately timed our meeting on campus when everything was in full bloom: the forsythias, mountain laurel, daffodils, rhododendrons, azaleas, and the Bartlett pear trees with their delicate white blossoms floating down on us like a gentle rain. It was a veritable Garden of Eden. The infinite spectrum of colors and fragrances just overwhelmed ones senses. The tour couldn't have been planned better. He must have placed an advance order for the picture perfect weather, which just added to the overall aura and ambiance of the entire setting. Talk about setting one up for the kill.

As we were walking along one of the pathways through the campus complex, he asked me straight out, "Joe, have you ever thought about teaching college?"

Now Father Ed knew I had taught high school science decades ago, prior to my going to medical school. I didn't answer him directly, other than to request he elaborate. I believe I simply said, "Why do you ask?"

By now we had entered the campus' main quadrangle, a large wide-open area of beautiful rosé colored paving stones. The quadrangle was like the hub of a wheel, with walkways radiating out from its center. One could turn in almost any direction and get a snapshot of the entire campus. At the very center of the quadrangle was a massive forty-foot gleaming white flagpole, the base of which was surrounded by a charming colorful bed of flowers encased by a circular stone wall of paving stones about two feet high. The bed compassed out about twelve feet or so from the pole's cement platform. The monks asked to be engaged in caring for the flower bed, as well as many of the landscaping projects.

The top of the pole was capped off with a golden globe and an eagle mounted on it. This golden eagle was positioned with its wings swept back in a dive attack mode. Old Glory was fluttering intermittently when a gust of wind would hit it.

"I have never seen an eagle on a flagpole like it Father," I commented. "Who designed it, who made it?"

"Great little story behind it," responded Father Ed, and he went on to unfold the tale. "One of our investors is former Air Force, as well as a design engineer. He is the one who came up with the idea. We found an artisan in fine metal work right here in Front Royal who actually fabricated it," he beamed proudly as he placed one foot on the ledge of the wall and lit up a Camacho Ecuador cigar, one of his few immoderate vices that he allowed himself.

He persevered with his little saga.

"Which direction to place the eagle? Facing down the path toward the abbey, down the walkway looking upon the chapel, toward the social sciences building, or gazing forth at the mountains? After some minor bickering, the squabble was settled. It would face down the path to the abbey."

"A myth was concocted, no one knows by whom, which spread like wildfire the first year. It was said that if ever one of the brothers performed a nefarious deed, the eagle would come alive, swoop down upon the errant monk, and carry him away to God knows where." Father Ed then gave a hearty laugh as he produced a perfect smoke ring.

To one side, on the edge of the quadrangle, a magnificent new pearly white marble statue of the Blessed Virgin had been placed on a pedestal surrounded by clusters of knockout rose bushes in a semi-circle behind her. The roses directly behind the statue seemed much taller and were attached to a trellis of sorts, which appeared to almost frame the statue. The statue, standing on a half hemisphere of the earth, including its stanchion, must have been about eight to nine feet high. She was standing in a simple prayerful pose, head slightly bent, and her hands together close to her chest and pointed toward heaven. We stopped momentarily to admire it.

I turned to Father and conjectured as I looked him straight in the eye, "I'll bet dollars to donuts that you were the prime instrument of having this statue commissioned to be carved and placed in this exact location."

All he could say is, "you win," as he smiled, chuckled, and gave me a wink. "Let's grab a cup of coffee and talk about your future," he said tilting his head in the direction we were to go.

In short order we arrived at the coffee shop, appropriately called Holy Grounds. Decorated as a medieval castle eating hall, the coffee shop was complete with heavy wooden straight-backed chairs and hefty tables. The windows were faux stained glass with heavy draperies. Coffee was appropriately served in ale-style tankards. The waiters and waitresses (working students) were clothed in period attire. The coffee was excellent, but not cheap.

Our conversation went on for what seemed like hours. I was developing quite a caffeine buzz after a couple of tankards of the rich brew. Father Ed learned to drink his cup of joe strong and black. When he was in Korea they didn't have the luxuries of cream and sugar most times. Little did I realize that this café would be where Father and I would spend many an afternoon after my class was over for the day.

His pitch for me to teach at ICC was straightforward, as I expected no less of him. We had many times before discussed the state of the nation and the world. We both came to the realization that we needed a grassroots effort, one that started with the youth. Our nation was pumping out little Marxists year after year from the socialist universities. Was our country magically expected to get back to its Judeo-Christian roots; and somehow, miraculously these young men and women would vote for conservative constitutionalists?

We both knew what the definition of insanity is: doing the same thing over and over while expecting different results. He planned to set up an appointment for me to meet with Dean Avery, so he could get me on the fall docket as soon as possible.

Before we parted ways, I asked him, "What should I call the course that I'm going to teach?"

"Faith and begorrah me lad, you'll come up with something catchy that will appeal to the kids, Joe." We were both standing by this time. He took his arm and put it around my shoulder and squeezed. No one would doubt Father Ed was still in good shape. Then he downed the last of his tankard and thumped the empty vessel on the heavy wood table.

CHAPTER TWELVE

THE MATRIX EXPOSED

I called Emily when I reached my car and gave her a heads up on when I would get home. Upon arrival, the sun had already set. There was just a remnant of afterglow in the mountains behind our home. I pulled "the tank," what I called my car, into the garage. The dang thing had more mileage on it than Methuselah, and you couldn't kill the beast.

A new car was not in our plans. I was happy the darn thing still worked properly. With the dollar's demise as the world's reserve currency, interest rates had skyrocketed, as well as the prices of vehicles and everything else under the sun. Apart from that, for almost two decades there had been a fight for the dashboard. The major electronic players—Sony, Google, Apple, Microsoft—wanted to control the flow of information on vehicle dashboards.

The government also saw this as a source of invading and amassing additional private info for their National Security Agency (NSA) computers. Things had come a long way since 2014 when it was revealed that Samsung's new "smart TV" could watch you as you were watching it. All TVs had advanced microphones similar to the noise and wind reduction ones that motorcycles riders use to communicate. Some viewers erroneously thought that by raising the volume, the NSA would not be able to hear if they wished to discuss something privately. The government selectively granted consent, like a king bestowing knighthood, on only those corporations who would comply with government "requests."

The newer dashboard monitor displays fed the government real time location of your vehicle whether you had the map feature turned on or not. And all the late model vehicles had a LoJack chip installed that the government could use to govern and slow your car to a stop if it wanted to. And most new car owners didn't realize that the onboard computers can also be remotely hacked to *totally* take control of the vehicle away from the driver.

Bluetooth devices incorporate the perfect mike and receiver that the various agencies tune into to listen to people's conversations live. All speech in your vehicle, as well as your travel destinations, are being fed and logged into the massive NSA computers in Maryland, Utah, or other undisclosed facilities, to be used against drivers and their passengers.

The public begged for this monitoring because they still could use their cell phones to call their carrier to unlock the car door if they had left the keys inside. They also could notify authorities if their car was stolen so they could activate the LoJack system and retrieve the vehicle.

During our dinner, which was ravioli with meatballs —what more could one of Italian extraction want—Emily and I spoke at length about Father Ed's proposal. She was all for it.

"You've put in over thirty years into the emergency room," her eyes dead-focused on me, "and it's taken its toll on you. This sounds like a great opportunity, *take* it!" she said.

Chewing on a meatball, it took me a couple seconds to respond. "Yeah, I like the idea, but—"

"But what?" she interjected.

"Okay, but I haven't taught in years," I replied still masticating my meatball. "Besides, I don't know what title to give the dumb course." I was getting frustrated with her, and a bit with Father Ed.

"I'll help you develop the name. Okay?" Her voice was sweet, and she looked at me lovingly, meaning what she said.

I avoided the topic for a while and asked her how her day went. She said she was worried about her raised-bed vegetable garden that she had just recently finished putting in.

"All I saw today were chemtrails crisscrossing the sky, pumping out their trailing clouds of heavy metals. How many more dead plants will I have this year? And the deer and raccoons seem to eat the good ones just as they ripen before I can pick them," she stated in a very frustrated voice.

"Crisscrossed?" I repeated.

"Yes, crisscrossed . . ." As she pronounced the second syllable slowly, she looked at me. I was still looking at her as we both smiled at each other, clinked our wine glasses and said at the same time: The Matrix. We promptly proceeded to give each other a quick kiss as we laughed.

Over the next half hour we worked out the particulars, calling the course The Matrix Exposed 101 and 102, for the fall and spring semesters. The Matrix Exposed 101 would be a required pre-requisite before a student could take 102 in the spring. It would be a three-credit course per semester. We'd meet three times a week—Monday, Wednesday, and Friday—for an hour each of those days. In the course, I would detail the how and why the Matrix we currently live in was formed. I would explain how science, religion, and politics had created it; and that all three would be needed to unveil and dismantle it.

By then we had almost polished off the bottle of Merlot and were feeling very happy with ourselves. I grabbed for the bottle and looked at the label. "Huh, Yellow Tail from Australia no less. Those Aussies can make a pretty good wine," as I took my last sip.

"Kroger," my wife added. "*And* we get the gas points."

I called Father Ed as soon as we finished dessert, which was a scrumptious chocolate pecan pie with whipped cream on it.

"Well, what do you think?" I asked him after giving him the skinny on what Emily and I had concocted.

"Praise be Mary and the Saints, you've really nailed it, Joe. I believe the topic will be something the kids will gravitate to. *The Matrix* film trilogy has always resonated with them. As a matter of fact, the student union showed it last year as part of their classic film festival."

CHAPTER THIRTEEN

THE PLEDGE

I had already printed my name—Dr. Joseph Lucci—on the whiteboard with a blue dry erase marker. As I waited for the students to arrive, I stood behind the long almost black soapstone-covered lab table which was to the right of my standard plain wooden desk. My back was to the whiteboard and the students' desks were directly in front of me. There was a bank of windows to my right, which looked out on part of the alluring grounds. One bushy poplar tree's branches almost touched the closest windows; and as I would learn as the semester progressed, would scrape against the windows during heavy winds and storms. We were on the second floor and were also graced with a commanding view of the Blue Ridge Mountains in the distance.

The wall on the left side of the classroom had a whiteboard with some bulletin boards on it, and a front and rear door that led to the hallway.

Each student had a desk, which had a retractable arm that folded up and down for appropriate writing, note taking, book or tablet placement, etcetera. These desks were actually fairly comfortable. The investors understood that the mind can only absorb what the backside can endure, and were willing to put their money into good quality classroom furniture for the students.

Brother Francis had come into my classroom a day earlier to see if he could help me in any way, and I readily accepted his assistance. He was fairly young, average height and robust from working in the fields. His skin was almost the consistency of tanned leather.

He suggested we arrange the desks in five rows of six chairs in each row. Each desk had to weigh at least seventy pounds, and he proceeded to move them around with ease. If it took him two minutes, that was a lot.

"There, finished," he exclaimed proudly observing his endeavor as an artist inspects his finished masterpiece. "There is ample room in front of your lab table for you to perambulate up and down in front of the first tier of desks, pontificating to these raw minds that you will mold and develop into critical thinking adults," he announced with a wide smile on his face.

Brother Francis' endeavor reminded me of an apologue I heard once about three common brick layers. A passerby asked the first one what he was doing, and he said, "laying bricks." He proceeded to ask the second what he was doing. "I'm building a wall," he said. When he arrived at the third worker, he asked the same of him. The third man stated proudly, "I am a master mason, and I am constructing a cathedral." All three were doing the same work, and all three had an entirely different outlook on life, which was reflected in their attitude and work ethic. I saw the same in Brother Francis.

He continued, "Also the margin between rows is appropriate that a student doesn't feel his personal space is being invaded from the student in the row next to them." He then added with a sheepish grin, "It will also make it difficult for them to cheat," he exclaimed with a smirk.

"Could I get an American Flag for the class room?" I politely asked. "One that has a bracket that can be attached to the wall close to the end of the whiteboard near the windows. The flag should be relatively small, probably about two feet by three feet and will hang at an angle from the bracket."

He knew exactly the kind of set up I needed, and it was magically in place when I walked into the classroom that following first day.

Before Brother Francis left he made a very astute observation. "Would you mind if I grew some plants all along the window ledges? It sure would brighten up the room, as it looks kind of sterile right now."

He was absolutely right. I cheerfully agreed and thanked him. "You are welcome to come into the class at any time."

***

It was getting close to 9 AM, and the students were starting to file in. I was getting some butterflies in my stomach. It had been decades since I had taught. Fifteen students had registered for the class—twelve men and three women. I guess that's not bad for starters as the kids had no idea of who I was or exactly what the course was going to be about. In the curriculum guide it was listed under philosophy, but I was teaching the course in St. Albert's Hall, the science building.

I recalled from my old high school teaching days that students tend to select a seat in a room where they feel comfortable, and it revealed a bit about their personality as well. This should prove interesting.

By my watch it was 9 AM sharp, and as I was closing the door, the last student rushed in. I learned shortly afterwards that his name was Tom. He was from Missouri, the doubting Show Me state and was in pre-law, minoring in history. In time, I ascertained that he was an agnostic with atheistic leanings. Tom gravitated to the fourth row from the front door and sat in the third seat back.

"Good morning, my name is Dr. Joseph Lucci," I greeted the class as I pointed to my name that I had printed on the whiteboard. "You now know my name, and I would like to learn all of yours. But first let us honor our country and say the Pledge of Allegiance."

You would think that I had asked them to swallow hot coals or stand on nails.

"Whaaa?" one moaned.

"I haven't done that since first grade," said one of the females.

"Man, that's lame," came a voice from the back of the room.

The discontent was glaringly obvious.

"Well, I'll start it off and anyone is welcome to join in or not," was my firm retort.

"I refuse and I'm offended," defiantly stated Simon, a small, thin black American, with long, black wiry hair tied in the back, who sat in the first row, second seat. Simon was from Chicago's Southside and was taking general studies, as he had not picked a major yet.

He had a Christian background, but through the influence of his brother, who had done time in prison, he was converting to Islam. As a gesture of diversity and tolerance, the prison system was now permitting radical Imams to be chaplains and counselors.

He had just about jumped up from his seat, and was standing stiff with his hands straight down at his sides, in a military style.

"It's Simon, I believe, and no one is forcing you to participate," I said addressing him firmly.

"Don't call me Simon; call me Ali Saful Islam."

"Is it okay if I just call you Ali?"

"That would be permissible," he replied, again answering in a clipped military tone while still standing rigid.

"Does your name have a meaning?" I gently solicited.

"Absolutely," he replied soundly and proudly. "It means Greatest Sword of Islam," and he promptly sat down.

Great, I have a micro-terrorist in training, I thought to myself, and without further hesitation I turned to face the flag, placed my right hand over my heart, and started to recite the Pledge.

For a few seconds mine was the only voice in the room. Then a weak second voice, which was female, accompanied me; it belonged to Maria.

Maria sat in the third row, second seat, almost directly in front of the lab table. She had nearly jet-black hair, soft brown eyes, and olive-colored skin with an angelic face. She reminded me of Natalie Wood who played Maria in *West Side Story*. I discovered she was a Roman Catholic of Hispanic origin. Her family had well-established roots in Texas; one of her distant relatives actually fought alongside Davy Crockett and Jim Bowie at the Alamo. She was in the BSN nursing program.

Finally, some other voices mumbled along as they stood up. I think most of them couldn't even remember the words; it probably had been years since last they uttered it. Besides, Maria had more than likely shamed most of them into saying it.

That first Pledge of Allegiance was tortuous for me and for them as well, I'm sure. However, it got easier with each recitation before each class started. I was not backing down. This was their first lesson; they had just poked their head out of the rabbit hole that lead to the Matrix they lived in, little did they realize.

CHAPTER FOURTEEN

BLUE PILL OR RED PILL

"**W**hy have you chosen to sign up for this class," I asked to no one student in particular.

"Just curious," responded Thad. He sat in the second row, fourth seat. Over time I found that Thad was fairly nationalist, a pro-USA libertarian type. He was from a Christian family in Colorado; but when his minister failed to sufficiently answer his questions about why a loving God would permit the death of innocent people, especially children, he converted to Buddhism. Thad was majoring in journalism, with a minor in astronomy of all things. "Figured I might be able to write a series of articles for the *Veritas Beacon*, regarding what I learn in this class. Anything that smacks of the Matrix is always in vogue with the students."

Huh, I reflected, *possibly a series of positive articles in our school paper*.

"I wanted an easy course to cruise through, and picking up three credits was a bonus," Philip immediately chimed in with an arrogant tone. He was in the back row and was leaning in his chair so it was resting against the rear wall. He was of Chinese ancestry from San Francisco. Philip was somewhat of a prodigy being a triple major in physics, math, and biochemistry. He was also fluent in both Cantonese and Mandarin dialects. His father was from Beijing where they speak Mandarin, which is the official state language of China. His mother was from Guangzhou where

Cantonese is spoken. He was a hard core, but honest, evolutionary atheist.

Maggie sat in the first seat in the second row, right in front of my desk. I got her number in short order. She was strikingly beautiful, and she knew it. Maggie had a full mane of thick, long, wavy blonde hair that had dyed dark streaks of color running through it. Her eyes were a dark green framed with heavy eyeliner and mascara. An old college buddy of mine would have described her as "zaftig." She certainly would have made it into the Mae West/Dolly Parton club hands down. And she always wore revealing form-fitting apparel.

As soon as I saw her, that first day in class, I immediately thought back to the old Hall and Oats song from the early '80s, "*She's a man-eater.*" Every move was planned and executed like a big cat on the prowl. She kept the guys salivating.

Maggie was from Southern California. Where else? Totally amoral and an agnostic, she wasn't sure if there was a God, and could care less anyway; but she was anything but stupid. Majoring in women's studies, she was totally honest though with her response. "I signed up for the course because I've always thought that Keanu Reeves was the bomb. He could put his slippers under my bed anytime."

With that it was time to move on.

"Like Morpheus in the *Matrix*, I'm going to give you a choice of the red pill or the blue pill. You take the blue pill, and you can leave the class no questions asked and return to your world of the Matrix, where your destiny is already planned for you. You will continue on with your mundane existence never knowing that the Matrix, not you, really controls everything you think and do."

I stopped momentarily to take a breath as I studied the faces of the students. Some had banal expressions, some curious, some bored, and some really intrigued.

"If you decide to stay in this class and take the red pill, the lies of the Matrix will be torn down brick by brick. The truth will slowly be revealed to you. Some of you may not like viewing the naked truth, others of you will embrace it—I cannot foretell the future for any of you. This journey will at times be very uncomfortable—veracity can be very painful. It will cut you open and bare the real you down to your core. Which pill will it be?"

CHAPTER FIFTEEN

CUSSIN' JAR

No one left the class. Everyone remained seated, almost motionless, kinda staring at me - waiting for the next shoe to drop?

"Also this class will absolutely, positively require you to think and analyze, not just memorize," I emphasized as my eyes scanned for signs of resistance.

It came quickly.

First from Matt. "Why can't you just hand out copies of your notes or give us the course textbook digitally so we can study it off our devices?"

Matt sat in the fifth row, fourth seat against the windows. He was from Florida. His parents, divorced Jews, were real estate developers there. Many of the upscale townhome retirement communities in Boca Raton and Bradenton were their babies. He was majoring in finance and marketing, with plans to go into real estate for himself. Matt was atheistic in his opinions and had a real wheeler-dealer personality, with a smile akin to a used car salesman. He was also a big sci-fi nut.

"Matt," I replied, "one of the objects of this course is to teach you to scrutinize, probe, critique, inquire—in general to actually *use* your brain."

"I'm sure Matt is not the only one with this attitude. Part of the Matrix philosophy that you are all entangled in, is to convince you to *not* use your brains—just memorize and regurgitate. After graduation you are to perform your job or career like a trained monkey. The Matrix doesn't want you to think too deeply, as you may conceive of an answer different from what they want imbedded in your cerebrum."

"Remember the Star Wars movies," I asked, still looking at Matt.

"Yeah, way cool," and he gave a double thumbs up to me.

"Obi-Wan Kenobi used a Jedi mind trick, that he said worked easily on weak minds. '*These are not the droids you're looking for,*' I believe were his words."

Maggie interjects, "Those droids were just too cute."

Philip, still leaning back on his chair legs against the rear wall, rolled his eyes.

"Guys, nothing personal, but most of you *are* those weak minds. Trust me I was one of those who had swallowed the blue pill hook, line, and sinker for quite some time. You must realize that all of you, myself included, are all *brainwashed,*" as I started to walk along the space between my desk/lab table and the first rank of seats. Brother Francis was right to grant me ample leeway to "perambulate" back and forth as he described.

Jude piped up immediately; "I am not brainwashed!" he interjected as he half stood up from his desk, his face turning a reddish-blue as he pointed his finger at me. Seems he took my accusation personally.

Jude sat in the fifth row, last seat almost butted up against the windows where I more than once would catch him looking outside daydreaming. He was majoring in political science. His plans, I deduced through many class sessions, was to become involved in Washington politics in the worst way. I got the impression that who or what he got involved with didn't matter; actually the more sordid the better.

Jude was from a middle class family on Long Island, whom he despised as being too common for what he aspired to; however, he was fine taking their very hard-earned money that was putting him through college. His parents had a thing for the Beatles and named him after the song of the same title. Jude was about as pagan as they come.

Nate turned around and advised, "Jude, chill out, man. We've just gotten started, and have a long way to go. You're going to give yourself a heart attack."

Nate sat in the fourth row, fifth seat, diagonally in front of Jude. Nate was from a financially well-off mercantile family in Boston. He was expected to take over the family business. Independent and proud, he wished to prove to his family and himself that he had the "right stuff." He was putting himself through college, majoring in business and computer science. During vacations and holidays he worked at his family's business, and they paid him an average worker's salary—he asked for no special deals. Honest and a straight arrow, he was knowledgeable in Catholicism but was not a practicing Catholic.

After the exchange, things settled down. I continued.

"I believe Jude has expressed feelings similar to which others may have as well. What I am trying to say is that everyone has a worldview that defines who he or she is. We are all biased or brainwashed in our worldviews, and there is no such thing as a neutral opinion or position."

"Outside forces—good, bad, and ugly—influence us to the way we think and act. These forces come primarily in the form of educational, religious, and media influences. Our parents are the initial and prime wellspring; however, even they are and were influenced by these same powers. Let me give you an example. This is when America lost its innocence. Please punch up on your tablets the YouTube video of the *Zapruder Film*," and I spelled it out.

Jim shouted first, "I got it."

"Ok, but find the one that gives you the frame by frame in HD," I recommended.

Jim was from Ohio and sat in the second row, third seat, directly in front of Thad. Jim had a short-tempered fiery and funny personality. He had lots of energy. Over time, I sensed he was searching for the truth. He knew something was wrong with the system but couldn't put his finger on it. It is why he signed up for my course—he was looking for answers. He was majoring in Ecology. Jim, about six feet tall and lanky, reminded me of Patrick Henry—firebrand of the Revolution, in manner, temperament, and size. He was a devout but confused Catholic.

"Yeah, we discussed all of the Kennedy assassination stuff in junior high," he wisecracked immediately. "This Oswald guy, the lousy coward, shot JFK in the back."

"Ditto on that," echoed Tom.

"Philip, you have a background in physics. Would you mind helping the class out?" I knew that challenging his ego would get him to answer.

"If I were to punch Jim in the face, which direction would his head go?"

"Backwards," Philip replied.

"And if I shot him in the forehead with a high-powered round?"

"His head would snap back," Philip answered in a bored fashion to the obviously dumb question.

Meanwhile most of the students had already been carefully surveying the Zapruder footage.

"Holy s**t," Tom blurted out loud, "Did you see that?"

"What the . . . ?" Jim bellowed.

"OK, before we discuss the video," I injected quickly before Jim could finish the obscenity. "Let's establish some ground rules. When we are with one or two friends, all of us are a bit loose with our lingo at times. However, when you are in a professional arena with people in a job or career setting, or classroom environs, it will be incumbent on you to watch your vernacular. Can you imagine a

CNN or ABC journalist using profanity giving a news report on a train crash or other dramatic event?"

Thad, the journalism major, immediately barged in, "Doc's right!"

"Here's the deal, anyone caught cussing in class has to put a dollar in a cussing jar," I articulated in as serious a timbre as I could muster. "I'll bring the jar into our next class session on Wednesday."

"Who's going to decide what is a cuss word?" asked Jude with a snobbish attitude in his voice.

"You are, all of you. Majority rules if it is a cuss word or not. If your own classmates deem it to be so, you need to put your buck in the cussin' jar. If there is an even number of students that day, if needed, and only then, I will be the tie-breaking vote. Got it!?"

Jude just sat arms crossed, lip poked out, like he had been weaned on a pickle.

There were no other objections. We went on with the Zapruder example. The questions and comments from the students came fast and furious.

Matt complained, "Why have we never seen this before?"

Followed by Tom and Pete's anger at having been misled all those years.

"For those of you who want more info, you may wish to check out the interviews of all the doctors and nurses who were present that day in the trauma bay at Parkland Memorial Hospital."

"Furthermore," I added, "to a man—and woman or doctor and nurse, each of them, stated they saw the ballistic entry at the right forehead and exit wound from the right occipital portion of the skull. They are all individually and separately interviewed in the film and use their fingers and hands gesturing in the same almost uniform fashion for entrance and exit."

"Finally before you leave, I challenge you to find me just one example of one totally unbiased person living or dead, if you can. Don't stay up too late. See you on Wednesday."

CHAPTER SIXTEEN

LUNCH BREAK

Father was already at the Holy Grounds coffee shop when I arrived about 11:00 AM. We had agreed to an early lunch. He was sipping on what appeared to be a savory iced tea.

As I sat down across from him, he asked in jovial fashion, "Well, me lad, how did your first day go?"

"Actually, pretty well for not having taught in decades," I replied motioning for the waiter to bring me an iced tea.

"How much did you reveal to them?"

Before I could answer, the waiter came to deliver my iced tea and take our order. Father ordered his favorite, corned beef on rye. I was in a burger mood and ordered one of their famous hamburgers made from beef raised by our agricultural students and monks on the property.

"I'll take one of the half pounders cooked as rare as the law allows, with the works on it." Looking at the waiter and then glancing at Father Ed I added, "thank God for the government protecting us from our decisions."

The waiter, a young naïve student, just gave me a blank stare and went off to fill the orders.

"Joe, that is why I brought you here to teach. The youth today have absolutely no concept of freedom and the rugged individualism that made this country the powerhouse that it once was. We now have a nanny state, where big brother protects us from every bump and scrape in life. Everything from cradle to grave is provided for by the state. Ben Franklin warned us: 'Those who surrender freedom for security will not have, nor do they deserve, either one.'" With that, Father Ed took another sip through the straw of his iced tea.

To that I piggybacked with, "Yeah, people now want guaranteed food, clothing, shelter, healthcare, cell phones, you name it. We already have a place like that where everything is totally guaranteed and secure, it's called a prison. Franklin was right," I exclaimed chugging down my iced tea, being thirsty from the one-hour class.

"Were you able to discuss with the students that all this security is a façade, an illusion, like your Matrix that the government dangles in front of the people?"

"No, Wednesday we start our trip down the rabbit hole. They will start to learn that in exchange for all these false promises, the government has a goal, and it's about power and control—over them!"

"By the way, Joe, will you and Emily be able to make it financially with you teaching only one class this year?"

"No, I'll still have to work a few shifts per month in the Emergency Department."

Our food had now arrived, and Father and I blessed ourselves with the sign of the cross, and together said grace over it.

CHAPTER SEVENTEEN

BIAS

I walked into class on Wednesday carrying the cussin' jar and placed it on the lab table squarely in the front for all to see. It was a big, wide-mouth plastic jar that formerly held almost five pounds of animal cookies. As the students rambled in, practically all of them noticed the jar immediately. However, no one said anything. As I predicted, they all took the same seats they had during the first session.

We all stood to say the Pledge of Allegiance, with the lone holdout being Simon/Ali who sat quietly in his seat and didn't budge.

"Okay, has anyone discovered a person, alive or dead, who is not biased in any way, shape, or form?" Scanning the class, I didn't see a single hand up. No hands.

Before I had a chance to go on, Jude spouted out, "Who is going to keep tabs on the money in the cussin' jar?"

I don't know why, but I half expected something like this to come up, and I was ready.

"Jude, I will make you in charge of the jar." He did a double take, not believing what he just heard.

Matt, adding to the conversation, turned around to Jude and stated, "And I'll double check your accounting."

Super, I thought, *the used car salesman checking on the K Street lobbyist*.

Thank, God, Nate came to the rescue. His eyes fixed on Jude and then Matt, Nate asserted, "Every company needs an auditor, and you're looking at him."

It was his way of letting both of them know he didn't trust either of them and would be watching their every move regarding the money in the cussin' jar.

"I think the pecuniary issues regarding the fiscal management of the cussin' jar has been acceptably arrived at by all parties involved." I tempered the mood with a slight British accent to my voice.

Nate gave me a big smile, as chortles and giggles were heard throughout the room. Jude and Matt looked at each other sort of dumbfounded.

"Okay, let us proceed with great vigor, to quote a famous British statesman," I said still using my British accent.

"Since I have not seen any hands up, I assume that none of you were successful in finding anyone without bias." I continued, "Everyone, repeat everyone is biased about virtually everything in life. It depends on which bias one decides to be biased about. And all our biases are based on other people's biases that we adopt as we go along in life."

Everyone just stared at me with a "What did he just say?" expression on their faces.

"Pick a topic, any topic," I directed to the class.

Juan raised his hand. He was sitting in the fifth and last row, third seat back against the windows. He wanted to become a teacher and was majoring in Education and psychology. Juan was of Hispanic descent and his family immigrated to the USA, and had been citizens living in Arizona for decades. He was a bit on the quiet side but gave strong opinions when he felt right about an issue. His family was Catholic, but he went to church only to please his parents.

"Doc, how about marriage? Some believe marriage to be between a man and a woman, others believe in gay marriage. You're saying both positions are biased?"

"Yes, absolutely," I emphatically responded.

"Regardless of which position you support, you take and adhere to that belief, because of the influences around you, be they your parents, friends, professors, the media, pastors. Whichever voices you listen to the most will be the bias you claim to be the correct one."

Andy now chimed in. "Whoa, whoa, are you saying some biases are right and others wrong, or what?"

Andy sat in the third row, fourth seat next to his brother, Pete, who sat in the fourth seat in the fourth row. Their family owned a fishing business in Alabama outside of Mobile Bay. Andy was taking marine engineering with a minor in architecture. Pete was a geology major minoring in marine science. These guys loved the sea and were salt-of-the-earth good people. They believed there was a God, but didn't know Him personally, as their parents were borderline Christians and only went to church on Christmas and Easter.

"Andy, you are getting close to the answer. Bias in and of itself just *is*. Now depending on the topic, one bias could be right and another bias wrong. It depends on the position and by whom or what has brainwashed or biased you."

"Let me be clear, the term *brainwashed* has negative connotations. I'm using the term to force you to think that everyone is biased or brainwashed whatever the topic. Get it?"

"Using Juan's topic of the definition of marriage, whatever your position on it is—pro-gay, anti-gay, pro-heterosexual or anti-heterosexual marriage—you believe what you believe due to those forces I mentioned."

Jude vigorously raised his hand. I acknowledged him, and he stood up.

"There is *no* right and wrong, and therefore anyone can define marriage any way he or she wants to," he stated abruptly and then sat down with a scowl on his face, which implied he knew it all.

"So Jude," I started, "based on what you just said, I have your permission to define marriage as only between a man and a woman, correct?"

Jude gets wide-eyed, "Yes . . . I mean, no. Gay marriage is right."

"So your bias, Jude, is for gay marriage as right and heterosexual marriage as wrong?"

"Yes, well, two normal . . . I mean heterosexual people can also marry. Man, you are confusing me."

"Okay, gang let's slow down, take a big breath, and see if we can approach this from another angle," I said, hoping to organize everyone's thought processes.

"How does one even determine what is right or wrong?"

"That's easy," Matt said as he raised his hand at the same time. "I determine what is right and wrong for me and my life. There is no God to tell *me* what to do," he proclaimed. Several students nodded in agreement.

"Fine," I replied, "then can I decide what is right and wrong for me and *my* life?"

"Oh, yeah," Matt smugly answered. "Anyone can make up his own rules for what is right and wrong. We all learned this in situation ethics and relative morality courses."

"Hands," I ask the class, "how many of you believe you should be able to determine what is right and wrong for yourselves?"

With the exception of Nate and Maria, everyone's hands went up. *Wow,* I thought, *do we have a problem in this country.* Jim looked around and finally put his hand down. I took note of it.

I throw out another question. "Therefore, do you all believe there is no such thing as absolute truth?"

Matt is on a roll. "That's correct, Doc. No one has a corner on the market on the truth," he said flashing his cocky used car salesman smile.

"I assume most of you agree with Matt's assertion?" I asked. Heads nodded in agreement, with the same exceptions being Nate and Maria. I took heed of Jim again. He stroked his chin, furrowed his eyebrows, as he seemed unsure of his position.

"I would like all of you to remember this moment. The majority of you have agreed that there is no such thing as absolute truth. We will discuss and elucidate on this in more detail as the course proceeds."

"How many of you have studied Nixon and Watergate?" Instantly, hands shot up all over, except for Santiago's.

"Que es Watering Gate?" Santiago inquired, posing his question to no one in particular.

There were some smirks and covered laughs from several of the students. I raised my index finger in a stern gesture of warning.

Santiago was supposedly a distant cousin of Juan and sat directly in front of him in the fifth row. He came to the U.S. illegally on one of the youth trains from Mexico during the Obama administration. Obama had opened the Southern borders to all comers, during his last two years in office. These illegal aliens were then allowed to have many of their "relatives" immigrate (chain migration) in later years "legally" and apply for all manner of government assistance. The Republicans didn't object, thinking the U.S. would get some cheap labor out of the deal.

The Dems knew statistically that 70 percent or more would vote Democratic for all the freebies. The Dems were right, and now the Democratic Party has control over both houses of Congress and the presidency.

Santiago's tuition was being paid for by the government—the taxpayer. He resented the U.S. and looked upon us as a bunch of fools. Santiago was majoring in the social sciences and psychology. Eventually, he wanted to become a community organizer in the inner cities.

I ignored his off-the-cuff question concerning 'Watering Gate'.

"Take your tablets and bring up the movie *All the President's Men*. I believe it's the tenth part where Robert Redford approaches his contact Deep Throat."

With that, Maggie breaks in. "I know how—"

"Maggie, we can dispense with your personal accomplishments," I immediately halted her before she uttered another word, and I spoke forcefully, my eyes narrowed, pupils pinpoint, and I'm sure one of my eyebrows was elevated.

Some low-level laughs and chuckling came from a few of the fellows, but my eyes quickly darted up from Maggie and toward them. Silence, as if on cue.

"I think we'll leave the Nixon Scandal until our next session, class dismissed."

CHAPTER EIGHTEEN

BRAINWASHED

I walked into the classroom on Friday, and to my pleasant surprise Brother Francis had made good on his promise. Arrayed along the window ledges was a bounty of beautiful flowers and plants; some already in bloom and others ready to burst forth their colorful blossoms.

Once again Simon/Ali resisted honoring the country of his birth by reciting the Pledge, after which I commenced the class.

"Juan, I believe we left off with you at our last session. We were talking about bias and right and wrong. The consensus being that each individual has the right to determine what is right or wrong for him or herself."

"Yes, that is what was agreed upon by the majority," he attested.

"By the way, have you been ill recently, Juan, you appear a bit peaked" I deduced.

"No, I've been fine."

Matt addressed him, "Man, I asked your cousin Santi (he preferred the shortened name) if you were ill or something."

Santi then confirmed what Matt asked him. "Yeah, Juan, I told Matt that 'usted no ha estado sintiendo hombre bien.'"

"Why didn't you say something to *me*, Santi," Juan pleaded with his cousin.

Both Andy and Pete gave their medical opinions of Juan's ill state of health.

By now Juan had taken his tablet and turned on the mirror app, and was carefully studying his face.

A few of the other students made mention of it and suggested that Juan perhaps should go to Student Health Services to get checked out.

Juan raised his hand and requested, "Doc, I *have* been feeling a bit queasy this morning, maybe I should go get checked out."

At that point, I called on Jim, "Should you tell him or should I?"

Jim indicated he would and said, "Juan 'ole buddy, you were the object lesson. Doc had us all in on it and wanted to show us how quickly someone could be brainwashed or biased, even as to their own state of health. You're really fine, like you first said."

"All you guys and the Doc were in on this?" complained Juan.

With that, Claudia emblazoned the conversation. "That was just cruel to play on poor little Juan. He's sensitive and gullible."

Claudia was known as the Ice Princess for two reasons. One, she looked like a younger version of the Duchess of Cambridge, Kate Middleton, tall and stately with long wavy brown hair. Second, she had an aloof attitude; she thought she was better than others, a sophisticate.

Claudia was always well dressed in the latest designer fashions. She shopped only boutiques, Lord and Taylor, and Nordstrom's. To say she was a clotheshorse would be putting it mildly. I don't think I saw her in the same outfit twice that year. Her family hailed from New York City. Her father was never at home, always working mega deals with Warren Buffett types. Likewise her mother was either traveling or at some spa having herself pampered. Claudia was the rich little "orphan." She was majoring in communications and literature, and wanted to be a TV anchorette for one of the big media outlets in New York; at least until she married some network mogul. She was a big liberal; and God, if she even believed He existed, never entered her mind.

Claudia didn't even realize her very comments were belittling of Juan.

"Juan, I must say you were a good sport," I told him, trying to put a positive spin on the object lesson. "Besides knowing that you are really okay, what would you say you learned about bias?"

"Man, I really get it. Bias is simply the way one looks at things. And those around you have a major influence on how you look at stuff. And now I bet you're going to explain how right and wrong fit into this bias."

"Juan, you nailed it. That 'stuff' as you called it, is called a worldview. Your bias and the way you look at right and wrong affects your worldview. And there is no such thing as a *neutral* worldview." I really hammered home the word neutral.

I looked around the class and saw everyone nodding. They got it—so far. Good.

Philip raised his hand and asked, "But don't the facts determine what is right and what is wrong?"

"Gee, I thought most of you agreed that each individual could determine right and wrong for themselves, obviously apart from the facts," I feigned bemusement; then stopped to see the reaction from the class. Silence, they realize they'd been had.

But not all.

Simon/Ali's arm shot straight up; I thought he was giving me a Hitler salute. "Only Allah, praise be his name, knows right from wrong."

"Well, Simon, I'm sorry, Ali, we may have to discuss that point further at some time."

I notice Claudia, who sat three seats directly behind him rocking her head back and forth and rolling her eyes as she mouthed the word *twerp*. And Philip, leaning back against the wall as usual, twirled his index finger next to the side of his head, making the universal sign of a loony. Since Ali sat in front of Claudia and Philip, he couldn't see what they were doing; and discretion being the better part of valor, I determined not to say anything.

"Has anyone heard of the Tylenol scare from back in the late '70s?" No hands went up. "Okay, punch that up on your tablets and see what you get."

Pete appears to be the first to find the info. "Wow! Some nut job in Chicago—hey, your turf Ali—offed several people by injecting potassium cyanide into Tylenol capsules and placed the bottles back on the shelves for purchase. Poor slobs didn't know what hit them. Bad news."

"Pete, what do you mean by *bad news*?" I asked with a very slight sarcasm in my voice.

Pete answered nonchalantly, "Well, that was wrong of the dude to just kill those people for no reason."

"And if the 'dude' as you say had a reason, would it have been okay then?" I pose.

At that point Andy, Pete's brother who sat next to him, backhanded Pete hard on the arm. "You jerk, Doc just set you up."

"What did I do wrong?" Pete hollers back at his brother.

"Wrong, is exactly the point," Andy howled back. "The Tylenol "dude" murdered innocent people."

"Good, it looks like some of you are starting to come around to the idea that some things are right and some are wrong. How do we as a society decide right and wrong?"

"The law!" Tom emphatically and vigorously called out. Tom was our pre-law/history major.

"Excellent," I acknowledge Tom's good, quick thinking.

"But the law, if not properly established, can become evil. Next session be prepared, we will discuss how this ties in with Hitler, the French Revolution, and the Age of Enlightenment."

Tom, still reveling and patting himself on the back, proclaimed to the class, "Damn, I'm good." To which the class rejoined almost in unison, "Cussin' jar!"

CHAPTER NINETEEN

NANA'S

Father Ed and I met again for a late lunch on Friday. He had a board meeting or some such administrative duty that morning and knew it would drone on for hours. I had some paperwork to take care of anyway. He would text me on my cell when the meeting was over.

My phone buzzed around 1:30 PM just as I was completing the work at my classroom desk. *Good timing*, I thought. I was to meet him at his car in the administrators' parking lot.

I got to his car about a minute before him. The door was unlocked so I sat inside. He arrived momentarily and hopped in the driver's side.

"Well, me lad, I'm going to treat you to lunch at a real Irish restaurant and pub."

"So where are we peddling your little Democrat car to?" I chided him. He drove one of those small hybrid cars that gets a million miles to the gallon, or some such insanity, but can get crushed by the impact of a housefly due to their lightweight aluminum structure.

"We are going to Nana's Irish Pub in Middletown. They have the best colcannon and soda bread this side of the Shenandoah River," and gave me a big grin as he started up the car.

"Is the engine running now?" I asked with marked irony to my question.

"Aye, at least it doesn't take a gallon of gas to start like your tank," he shot back quickly.

I felt the need to get in the last word in, on this tit for tat. "I see your personal parking space has your name painted on it. However, your little Democrat car has peed on it." I smiled triumphantly.

"At least it can, me lad. I recall yours had urinary, or was it fuel pump retention, and needed replacement recently, Emily told me."

Touché, he won that exchange. I'll need to talk to that woman when I get home tonight.

Middletown, Virginia, is just a little north of Front Royal off I-81, and it didn't take us long to get there. It was a pleasant drive down from the peaks of the Blue Ridge where Immaculate Conception College abided peacefully in its high meadow.

As soon as we entered the front door of the establishment, Philomena, the owner, gave Father Ed a big hello and wave from behind the cash register at the bar in the back. Father then introduced me to Philomena; she had one of the waitresses escort us to Father's usual table.

The pub used to be a bank and still had a very large, faded green steel walk-in door safe against a back wall. The side walls also had the original brick and the floors were the original wood planks, which squeaked when you walked on them.

Father ordered his colcannon which came with Irish soda bread, topped off with his usual pint of Guinness Stout. I ordered a plate of champ, as I love mashed potatoes with spring onions. I had ice water with lemon to drink. I was thirsty again from all the talking in class.

We ate with little small talk. I was just reveling in the atmosphere of the pub, while traditional Irish music played in the background.

After taking a gulp of his Guinness to dispatch the last fork of his colcannon, Father inquired, "Joe are you aware of what has been happening at the southern border these past few days?" as he proceeds to answer his own question. "My sources tell me that Islamic terrorist cells are planning some sort of attack, possibly in border towns, perhaps in larger cities instead. No reports yet from the mainstream media. They always seem to be a dollar short and a day late."

"Unfortunately, I was either at the hospital or teaching the past few days and haven't been following any of my e-mails or blogs," I admitted, still consuming the last of the champ.

"The chickens have come home to roost. During the presidency of Mr. Pen and a Phone, the porous southern border was absolutely unregulated," Father explained as he took another gulp of his Guinness. He continued, "Many Islamic terrorists crossed the Rio Grande during that period; they mixed and blended in with the swarms of illegal Hispanic immigrants."

"Not to mention the one hundred thousand 'legal' Muslim immigrant terrorists he imported per year from the Middle East, Africa, and Asian countries. Excuse me, 'refugees,' he called them," I added.

"These cells are now ready to coordinate attacks on us. It will also give the government and the Illuminati the excuse they're looking for to make biometric chips mandatory." Father then suggested we retire to the outside back patio for dessert and coffee.

"What I don't get is how these terrorist cells have been able to establish legal training camps right here in the U.S.," I posited in an aggravated tone.

"My friends in the agencies say they cannot stop people from congregating where they want to legally live," Father said as he waved to our waitress and pointed to the patio. She nodded in a way that she knew Father's routine.

"Yeah, except if they're Christian, and especially if they own weapons," I grumbled while trying to squirm my way following Father out to the rear patio. "Then they're tagged as Religious Extremists by our government."

"In deference to my buddies, they have to do the government's bidding. Our drones and security teams can at least keep an eye to see if these radicals stay in their compounds."

We found a table outside and Father lit up one of his Camacho Ecuador cigars. I understood why we needed to go to the bier garden.

Our waitress handed us menus again, so we could order dessert and coffee. Father already knew what he wanted and told her he'd have his usual.

I quickly reviewed the selection and ordered the chocolate brandy bread pudding and coffee.

As she left, Father asks, "Everything going smoothly in class?"

"A few road bumps here and there. I have my work cut out for me. Basically I'm at square one. The kids don't even know, or don't believe in, right and wrong—or absolute truth."

"Sounds as if you are at the infancy stage of development in teaching them. Just start with pabulum."

"Trust me, I am. I had them review the *Zapruder* film, and they were shocked."

The waitress returned promptly with my regular coffee and some creamers. In front of Father she placed a very generous glass mug of Irish coffee.

"Wow, I can really smell the whisky in that," I commented.

"Yes, laddie boy, it has an extra shot of Irish whisky in it."

"Bailey's?"

"Heaven's no! Bushmills, it's aged for twenty-one years. They keep a bottle just for me behind the bar."

"Here, Father, your Irish bread pudding," our waitress declared as she set it before him; then she almost dropped my chocolate brandy bread pudding in my lap. Lightning fast, my hands stabilized the dessert plate.

"That was close," I said after she left. I continued, "Then I attempted to discuss the Watergate break in. That didn't go too well, to say the least. I was trying to get across to them Deep Throat's advice to always 'follow the money' and that the money always leads to the goal of all tyrants, which is power and control." I took a big bite of the chocolate brandy bread pudding as I let the chocolate and liqueur linger on my taste buds a while.

"Joe, you'll have ample time to drive home those two points; you do have two semesters. When the Soviet Union was at its peak in the mid-'80s, the wall of power and control it had over its people and the satellite countries was called the Iron Curtain," he explained as he took a sip of his Irish coffee. "Now, *you* are calling it the Matrix."

"In China," I added, "it was called the Bamboo Curtain; we've swapped *iron* and *bamboo* for a Digitalized Curtain behind which Big Brother is controlling people—using computers, cameras, drones and satellites," I added, treasuring another bit of Nana's chocolate brandy pudding.

Father and I talked for a while longer, bemoaning the fact that too many in our culture were walking around in a happy fog of diversion created by the Matrix called Bread and Circuses. The Romans used this tactic to control and appease the plebian masses, offering them free food, and staging huge free spectacles in the Colosseum.

"*Panem et circenses*, is the Latin form," Father enlightened me, and then he took a draw on his cigar, as if he was luxuriating in some ethereal fragrance. "The 'bread' today is the welfare for the poor and crippling credit for the middle class."

I then followed through, "The 'circuses' being *Dancing with the Fools, Wild Housewives of Wherever*, and endless sports on sixteen channels. And in contrast, our 'plebian masses' are *required* to pay hundreds of dollars to attend gladiatorial-like sporting events."

Father paid the check, and I insisted on tipping the waitress. He then drove me back to the campus in his little Democrat car. We rode in silence, reflecting on the state of our nation.

CHAPTER TWENTY

ON THE DOLE

A few days later, I was driving up I-81 pushing the envelope on the speed limit a bit in order to get to my 9 AM class on time. I was lost in thought, pondering the discourse Father Ed and I had the other day at lunch in Nana's Irish Pub. The fact that I had a very rough day in the Emergency Department (ED) the day before didn't help.

If the taxpayer only knew, I thought to myself. *All these doctor shows on TV and they are all a bunch of bunk.* I've spoken with attorneys, firemen, and police officers, and they all echo the same sentiment. Most of what Hollywood portrays on these shows is not reflective of what occurs in the everyday reality in their career fields.

I remember how I read about studies that have shown that around 70 percent of what comes into the Emergency Department isn't a real emergency. Seventy-five percent of all ambulance calls are non-emergent. I had challenged my friends, whose only exposure to the ED is what they see on TV, to dial 911 and demand an ambulance for their stubbed toe or insect bite; one will be dispatched for them. "Yeah, but that'll cost me a mint to be transported for such a ridiculous complaint," was their reply. "Not for those on the 'freebie program,'" I had responded. "Someone absorbs the cost of the free medical McDonalds for the entitlement crowd. You're the fool the government taps to pay for it all."

My mind wandered to the story of the EMS crew that came in and told us of the time they were performing CPR in someone's home. The family roundly criticized them for not handling the compressions the same way some TV show did. And the EKG monitor never goes from a normal sinus rhythm to instantly flat line with that beeeeeep sound. That's strictly for TV and the movies.

My thoughts drifted to how the medical system has, in essence, collapsed. When Lyndon Johnson passed Medicaid and Medicare in 1965, it sounded good on the surface. We would be helping the poor was the mantra. I recalled one of our blethers when Father Ed was still teaching at Georgetown.

"That is not the role of the federal government," he reminded me drinking some nasty black brew that had to have been percolating for hours. I was having some tea, after just about spitting up the coffee back into my cup.

"Well, you know how it is Father, the libs will say if the federal government doesn't help, these people will die out in the cold or the heat, or starve."

"I get such a charge at the way Rush Limbaugh mimics them. 'We must help the chilrun.' The libs try to box you in by implying that there is only a yes or no scenario to choose from: the federal government or privation," I spouted, adding some milk and lemon to my tea. "Dr. Michael Savage is right, 'liberalism *is* a mental disorder.'"

"Joe, it's not the role of the federal government, it's the province of the states. Our Constitution is clear on this. If one state wants to provide cradle to grave health care and their citizens agree, so be it. Another may want to pass it off to the counties or the townships, that's their option."

"Our founders deliberately itemized what the responsibilities and obligations of the federal government were. Mark Levin has written extensively on the Tenth Amendment. Anything not specifically listed, was automatically relegated to the authority of the states," Father said before he swallowed more of the offensive beverage.

I agreed saying, "Our founders realized *everything* in the hands of the feds would lead to graft and corruption. The feds can print unlimited supplies of money, the states can't; which is why we are in the mess we're in to the tune of over $22 trillion in debt."

Father recalled President Johnson's comment on Air Force One, as he confided to two like-minded governors regarding his intentions for the Great Society: "'I'll have those n****rs voting Democratic for the next two hundred years,' Johnson had said."

"After four or five generations since Johnson's 'War on Poverty' began in the '60s, it has destroyed the black family. The 70 percent out-of-wedlock birth rate has spilled over to the white, Hispanic, and even the Asian communities as well. I have observed this first hand in the ED, getting progressively worse."

After having another sip of tea, I drew it out further, "The ED has become a microcosm of the lower echelons of our society by and large."

As I continued on I-81, I remembered telling Father Ed how the patients who were on the dole would come in with a demanding attitude, "When am I going to been seen? How long is this going to take? I want something to eat." And I would like to ask them, "And when did you make your appointment for the *Emergency Department?*"

I continued with my bellyaching. "We used to call them frequent flyers, but ever since the government required computerized charting, we call them scrollers. Their visits are so numerous that we must scroll the screens to review their records. They have the same complaints. It's déjà vu ad nauseam. They don't take their meds and never follow up with their primary care providers. Why should they? They are not held accountable – in any way! When they get sick again, for the umpteenth time, like clockwork they gravitate back to mommy and daddy—the ED, to kiss the boo-boo and re-admit them for the same illnesses, and again the working slob picks up the tab. Less than 5 percent of our patients are people we have never seen before."

Father Ed took a generous sip of his noxious brew and commented, "In order to control the masses, in exchange for their votes, the government must make those masses dependent, turning them into immature and defenseless children. If you take a wild lion cub and bring it into captivity—feed it, shelter it, protect it from every potential outside harm—once it's a full grown cat, what happens if you attempt to release it into the wild?"

"It *will* die," I answered forcefully, "Which is what I see in the ED. Poor doesn't have to equate with ignorant or stupid. My own ancestors sailed from Italy with barely the clothes on their back, but created businesses, worked hard, and thrived."

"Same with the Irish," Father immediately responded.

"The government," I said, almost burning my palate with the refill of hot tea the waitress had just poured, "has destroyed much of American society. These people barely know where to wipe. I've often instructed the nurses to ignore the fact they are dealing with cronological adults and just concentrate on their words, and the manner in which they speak. You realize you are listening to a spoiled child."

The waitress came over again to ask us if we would like to order anything else. It was her way of saying that we weren't spending much while taking up a lot of time at one of her tables.

I asked her to bring the check.

Father finished off his mug, and I noticed a small pile of gross coffee grounds at the bottom. He looked straight at me and remarked, "Do they have welfare programs in North Korea?"

"Of course not!"

"Once tyrants have absolute control over a society, they don't need the people's votes any longer. When you follow the money, it leads to power and control; and absolute power corrupts absolutely.

Absolute power leads to absolute control of the life and death of the citizens you were sworn to protect," he fumed, practically spitting out each word like it was venom.

I sensed he was having a bit of a PTSD moment from his time in Vietnam and North Korea.

The waitress brought the check. I quickly picked it up and placed it back in her hand with a couple of twenties and thanked her profusely. She gave Father and me a beautiful smile and walked off.

As we are walking out of the Georgetown coffee shop, I remembered, Father turned to me and stressed, "In North Korea they don't need your vote anymore. You are given a choice: work, gulag, or a bullet in your head. Useless eaters are terminated with prejudice."

"Is our now secular society headed in that direction?" I questioned.

"Only God in His infinite wisdom knows the answer to *that*, laddie boy."

My mind snapped back with the ringing of my cell phone. As I fumbled to retrieve it, I understood why the average consumer was willing to sacrifice his freedoms for Blue Tooth convenience. Emily was checking on my progress in getting to the ICC campus. "Hi honey, yes I'm almost there, another five minutes. Thanks for calling me; I'll call you back after class is over."

I gunned "the tank" up a particularly steep incline approaching the campus. Upon reaching ICC, I turned in and drove through the grand distressed brick wall on each side of the road announcing the entrance. Where the old wooden sign had previously stood was now elegant and graceful landscaping. A large, brushed brass plaque with raised, contrasting black lettering stating Immaculate Conception College was on the left wall. A matching plaque on the right wall contained the name of the abbey. As I passed through and drove around the circle, I saw our massive flagpole down the road and observed *two* flags attached to the halyard line.

I quickly found a parking spot and eased the tank into it. My eyes were still focused on the flags, but I couldn't seem to identify the second one. I got out and ran as fast as my old legs would go until I was in the quadrangle looking up.

The students were walking to and fro from class or on break, seemingly oblivious to the pennants. I stopped one of the students. "What gives," I asked pointing up to the flags. "I see the American Flag, but what's that banner below it?"

"That's just the World Ecology Flag," he responded nonchalantly.

"What's the significance of *that*?" I asked adamantly.

"Oh, it's to acknowledge Mother Gaia, who birthed the earth and our very existence."

"Are you *serious*?" I asked.

"The Department of Education approved the statute several months ago. All schools are now supposed to have the World Ecology Flag."

I stomped off to class in St. Al's Science Building, muttering to myself, "I'm running out of time."

CHAPTER TWENTY-ONE

JUDGMENT AT NUREMBERG

A s I entered the room, several of the students were already seated in their usual places. A few others are hanging out, talking with each other. I placed the cussin' jar in the middle of the lab table and organized my notes, as the rest of the students filed in.

We got right to it, with Tom, our pre-law/history major, entering the room last as usual, somewhat out of breath. We said the Pledge, as Ali sat in a rigid straight-back posture, silent at his desk.

"Has anyone seen the old classic movie *Judgment at Nuremberg?*" scanning the class for a response. The students sort of looked at each other and stared back at me with a "what's he talking about" expression.

"Tom?" I directed my question to him specifically.

Still slightly winded, he replied, "Wasn't that a trial at the end of World War II against the Nazis for crimes committed against humanity?"

"Very good, you are absolutely correct. To be more specific the movie revolves around four Nazi judges who used their positions to conduct sterilization and ethnic cleansing for the Third Reich."

"On your tablets bring up the IMDb website. There is a short trailer for *Judgment at Nuremberg,* as well as a script summary. Were these Nazi judges guilty of international crimes—"

"Or were they simply carrying out their government's own laws?" Tom finished my sentence.

"So, Tom, tell me," I instructed, "I assume what these judges did was *legal*, since they were only carrying out laws that had been passed by the Reichstag, their Congress."

"Yes, of course, but—"

"You seem to be hesitating, Tom. The Nazis murdered six million Jews and six million non-Jews, *legally*—correct?"

With that, Ali waved his arm vigorously. I acknowledged him, before he dislocated his shoulder.

"The Holocaust is a *lie*, made up by *Jews*," he declared as his face looked like a molten ball of anger.

The class was completely silent, gaping and staring alternately between Ali and me. Matt however, appeared as though he were going to explode. I discreetly motioned with my hand to try to calm him down.

Before Ali had a chance to continue with his diatribe, I asked him in a calm voice, "And what about the six million *non*-Jews?"

"Huh?" he answered with a deadpanned expression on his face.

"Ali, just for you, I would like you to YouTube *Eisenhower and Patton Visit the Nazi Death Camps*, which is a documentary of the Holocaust. At the end of class let me know what you learn."

Then without breaking my stride, I said, "Philip, I believe you commented a while back that 'the facts determine what is right and wrong.' Well these *are* the facts in this case; do they tell us what is right and what is wrong?"

Philip, who was always leaning his chair against the back wall, has all four legs of the desk planted solidly on the floor and his body is inclined slightly forward. He was looking at me trying to make something come out of his mouth, to no avail.

Nate, our business and computer science major, marshaled up some wisdom he probably remembered from his catechism or confirmation classes as a child. "Just because something is legal, doesn't necessarily make it moral or ethical."

Tom then blurted out, "Yeah, but it was *still* legal, what the Nazi judges did."

"Tom, you could have played the role of the defense attorney, Hans Rolfe, in the movie, since that was his position throughout the trial."

"What does the synopsis on IMDb say the prosecuting judge Haywood's conclusion was?" I asked, projecting the question to the entire class.

Thad, our journalism/astronomy major, raised his hand deliberately, but slowly. I point my finger recognizing him.

"These Nazis were intellectually smart men but had systematically denied justice to enemies of the Third Reich. They made decisions that were evil and bad, as generally accepted by the international community of nations."

Tom, still persisting, exclaimed, "Yeah, but that was a million years ago, back in 1947. Today, we are more accepting and less judgmental of different lifestyles, and tolerant of diversity."

Addressing the entire class, I said, "Tom is correct in that we as a society are more tolerant of diverse behaviors and lifestyles, *but* does that make it right?"

"During the French Revolution, amid the age of enlightenment, Robespierre and his cabal decided to eliminate all vestiges of religion from France. The entire society, including its new laws, was to be totally secular and *only* Robespierre and his cronies, the intellectual elite, were self-deputized to devise those laws," I exclaimed. I let that sink in, as I watched for any reaction from the students.

Andy asked, "The average citizen had *no* say in the making of laws?"

"Correct."

Pete exclaimed, "One teacher of mine told us that during that French Revolution they turned Notre Dame Cathedral into a warehouse and stable."

"Correct again."

"And they had parades and a Festival of Reason led by scantily clad women into Notre Dame Cathedral," Maggie said with a sensual smile on her face and a suggestive shake of her neck and shoulders. I let it pass.

"Right again."

"And they *tore down* statues of the Virgin Mary and replaced them with statues of Lady Liberty, in order to *rid* themselves of religion and establish a properly *enlightened* secular constitution," added Jude with a tone of arrogance and enjoyment regarding what the revelers did.

"That's right Jude, but at what price?" I asked.

Maria, who up to now hadn't contributed much, decided to speak up. I notice she had been wearing a gold cross around her neck since the first day of class. It was very similar to the one Laura Ingraham wears, albeit slightly larger. It was thicker and decidedly heavier from the way it tugged on her necklace. The links were stronger. What made it unique was that the crucified body of Christ was recessed into the cross itself. The corpus appeared to be of brushed silver. Never in my life had I beheld a cross with a recessed crucifix before. Clearly, it was a very expensive, but not an ostentatious piece of jewelry.

Christian and Catholic women usually wore only crosses because crucifixes tended to tear their blouses and sweaters and got tangled up in their clothes. I discreetly inquired about it once. She told me it was a special family heirloom given to her by her grandmother. When something in class upset her, she would always clasp it gently with reverence, evoking to whisper a quick prayer.

Maria's hand went up, and I conceded the floor to her. As she spoke, the sunlight coming through our windows reflected off it, which forced me to change my focus to her cross. "The price the French people paid was with their blood during the Reign of Terror. The head of Robespierre was one of the last to roll from the guillotine," she stated with unwavering force that left a chill in the classroom.

The silence in the classroom was deafening. Obviously, the lesson was over.

Ali immediately bolted from the room. I did not try and stop him.

CHAPTER TWENTY-TWO

A WORKOUT

My thoughts focused back on the present. The more delicate fossils needed to be wrapped very gingerly, first with tissue, then with the bubble wrap. For me it had been sheer joy watching as the students faces would light up, and the cogwheels of their minds spun with new understanding as I explained each fossil from a viewpoint they had neither expected nor been exposed to before.

Suddenly, I almost dropped one, and my thoughts turned to the time when I dropped a twenty-pound dumbbell and it almost landed on my toes.

***

As I walked to the St. Louis IX Sports Complex with my gym bag over my shoulder, I reflected on why Ali had so abruptly left the room at the end of class. Did he discover some unassailable facts regarding the concentration camps that struck a chord against the belief system that the Imams were indoctrinating him into?

The sports complex, named after the warrior Saint Louis IX, was one of the new structures that was added to the abbey complex by the investors. The style was modern. The brick facade had a washed out gray hue, which kept with the same color scheme as the original buildings. Only the entrance was reminiscent of the medieval motif.

The complex had an Olympic-size pool, racquetball courts, a small café/lounge with a large screen TV, and the requisite pool table. The basketball court, where our team the Crusaders play, had six nets with backstops. There was one at each end for the home games. The four other hoops were across from each other on the sides of the court. Their backstops were attached to an electric cable and could be folded upward and out of the way when any game or function was held. The long rows of benches likewise retracted in accordion fashion against all four walls when not in use.

We were an NCAA Division 3 team. I understood that the first few years were challenging, to say the least. The year before I started teaching we won a couple of games, I was told. The student support for our fledging teams was incredible. The booster club was extremely active. Close to one in ten students were involved with the boosters in some way.

I changed in the men's locker room and entered the multipurpose room. I looked over toward the rack of free weights resting on the Resilite mats. The last time I had worked out, I hadn't dried my hands on my towel, and that was when a lousy twenty-pound dumbbell slipped from my grip, clanged against the rack and fell to the mat, almost hitting my toes. I was able to shift my feet out of the way just in time, but some jocks who were working out snickered nonetheless. They were probably thinking, "Dumb prof ought a stick to his books."

I hopped on the elliptical machine and grabbed the TV remote. I turned on One America News (OAN), adjusted the settings, and began my routine. After several minutes, I noticed that Pete and his brother, Andy, entered the room. Pete went directly to the bench press and began to load three forty-five-pounders on each side of the bar.

Andy had gone over to the cable system and was adjusting the pin. He was about to lie down on the bench to work his hamstrings, when Pete asked Andy to spot for him. As a good brother, Andy placed himself behind Pete's bench to monitor his bench presses.

Three hundred plus pounds, and this was Pete's warm up? The guy was big, around six two; he looked like a WWE champion. Pete was a solid brawny guy with a head of jet-black hair, and three to four days worth of facial hair. Andy must have taken after some other distant relative, as he was tall, with a frame like a runner, and he was prematurely balding.

A number of other students and professors were also working out; some trying to get back in shape, like myself, and others just trying to keep Father Time at bay. The students, with few exceptions, were all on one sports team or another. Most were wearing ear buds, listening to their favorite iTunes while concentrating on their workouts.

Andy and Pete noticed me, and we gave each other conciliatory nods of acknowledgement, as they each continued their individual monotonous routines and repetitious sets.

Eventually I arrived at my last sets - the dumbbell curls. I made a concerted effort to make sure my hands were bone dry before grabbing the weights. When I finished, I immediately grasped for my towel, as the sweat was pouring off me, and quickly walked to the water cooler to quench my thirst.

Arising from the spigot, feeling like a satiated camel, I saw Andy and Pete leaning against the wall nearby as if waiting for me. They had correctly perceived I was finished, in more ways than one, and began to walk over to me.

"Hey Doc, looks like you're done with your workout," Andy observed. "Pete and I would like to kinda go over today's lesson." Pete was lightly nodding his head in agreement.

"Okay guys, how about we go upstairs to the café/lounge on the mezzanine where we can talk and get rehydrated?"

They both smiled and said "sure thing," and we all proceeded upstairs to the café area. There we found a grouping of four comfortable overstuffed sofa-style lounge chairs with a coffee table in the center next to a pool table where some guys were shooting a game.

Immediately, I plopped myself on the biggest chair and Andy took the one opposite me. Pete pulled one of the recliners to the side, replacing it with a standard metal chair, which he reversed and sat close to my right with his arms resting on the chair's top crest rail. I beckoned for the waiter. "I'll take your coldest lemon vitamin water, please. What do you guys want? It's on me."

"I'll take a green tea slushy," requested Andy.

"And I'll take a quart of soy milk," Pete promptly asked, to the waiter's surprise.

"Pete!!" Andy interjected forcefully. "The Doc's paying for this!"

"It's okay, it's okay," I rallied back while trying to look at both Andy and the waiter simultaneously. "Whatever he wants."

"Sir, it only comes in a pint."

"That's fine, bring him two," I ordered.

The waiter left, slightly shaking his head.

Pete then makes a poor attempt to defend himself. "I'm just trying to keep my protein level up," he said, looking at Andy like a poor pleading puppy.

We made some small talk for a while. We talked about their family's fishing business in Mobile, Alabama, and how they came to apply at ICC.

"So what do you guys like doing in your off time?" I asked.

Pete responded quickly. "Anytime I have off, I'm sport fishing," he said with absolute glee on his face. "Andy goes to Baton Rouge to *party*."

I catch Andy shoot a barely perceivable censuring glance at his brother.

The waiter returned with our drinks. He placed the drinks and two straws for Pete's bottles of soy milk on the low coffee table and then asked if we would like a sandwich with our drinks. "We have the best pork barbeque in town - really! The pork comes from our own farm-grown pigs, by our agricultural students and monks - it's excellent."

"No thanks, just put the bill on my tab and add 25 percent for yourself."

The waiter's eyes lit up. "Thank you, sir."

"Would you mind," I asked of him, "turning down the volume on the TV?" He nodded and went back to the bar area where he found the remote to lower the volume. I gave him a slight smile and small wave to say thank you.

"Well fellas, what's on your mind?"

CHAPTER TWENTY-THREE

WHAT IS TRUTH?

Pete jumped right in. "Man, that first discussion about right and wrong, the Tylenol deaths, then the Nazi judges, and finally the French Revolution with that big honcho guy Pierre something, making his own laws, getting his head chopped off," he said as he struggled to remove the cap on his soy milk, which popped off spraying some droplets across the table toward his brother. "That Age of Enlightenment needed some enlightening, far as I can see."

"So Pete, what do you think was missing in all these historical moments," I asked, handing him a napkin to wipe up his milk spots.

"I think I understand about the power-and-control thing somewhat, but why do men have to be this way?" he asked, ignoring the straw and taking several hearty gulps from his bottle of soy milk.

"Can't we all just get along?" Andy whined mockingly.

"Why?" I respond sarcastically, looking at both Pete and Andy.

I caught them both off guard. They looked at each other, hoping the other would offer a clever riposte.

"Look, you guys as well as most of the class, agreed that each of us determines what is right *or* wrong for ourselves as individuals. Most people these days believe that. Just look at those dumb bunny bumper stickers with all the religious symbols. But they are just that—a bumper sticker!"

They both were stunned and I didn't give them a chance to reply.

"The problem is most people have a bumper sticker brain. Everyone *can't* be right. There can be only *one* right answer to two plus two. So are you going to tolerate or placate those who believe two plus two equals five or three or seven or whatever? Last I heard that was called chaos!" I exhorted, slamming my bottle on the coffee table so hard it spurt the vitamin water out the top.

"But people do have a right to their opinions," Andy came back.

"True," I answered, looking at him and glancing over toward Pete, "but you know what they say about opinions?"

"What's that?" Pete asked leaning a bit forward on his chair.

"They're like A-holes. Everybody's got one," I said calmly as I cleaned up my mess.

Both brothers, as if they were electronically synced together, looked at me with eyebrows raised, eyeballs bugged out, and their mouths agape. "Fair and balanced is good for TV ratings with animated polemics, but is poor standard for determining *moral* principles," I divulged as I relaxed a bit on my sofa seat. "It's fine to have an opinion and debate on which tastes better - chocolate or vanilla, or should we raise or lower the tax on something, or should we build a bridge or roadway or not, but basic morality should *not* be negotiable." I argued taking another sip of my vitamin water. "We must have a firm foundation to draw our thinking from; otherwise, our arguments are based on shifting sands."

"Yeah, Doc, America needs to get back to its time-honored traditional morals, values, and principles," Andy declared firmly, with his right index finger pointed skyward, inadvertently mimicking a politician.

"Really, Andy? Which morals, which values, which principles?" I questioned, boring my eyes directly at and almost through him, as I sensed Pete was leaning even further forward on his chair toward me. "I hate that namby-pamby platitude. Many conservatives, politicians, even atheists use that phrase, when what the expression really implies is *Judeo-Christian* morals, values and ethics; otherwise the phrase is meaningless."

I stopped for a few seconds, letting that sink in for a moment, scrutinizing both brothers for a response. Again, they were both speechless.

"Let's say I'm from a remote Indian tribe in the Southwestern United States, and when a newborn baby dies, we boil and eat it," I said matter-of-factly, carefully observing their response.

They were both speechless. Finally, Andy countered with, "But . . . but that's not right," he whined.

"Excuse me," I barked. "How dare you judge me, you bigoted, self-righteous, right-winged, closed-minded, intolerant, Bible-thumping piece of human excrement!"

Both brothers were in a catatonic stupor now.

I gave a hearty laugh and told them, "You can both relax and chill out. I needed to get this point across *crystal clear*, regarding *whose* morals, values and principles."

"Boy did you ever, Doc," Pete answered, his voice wavering a bit.

Pete, who is now leaning forward on his backward chair, with his arms stretched out, got very exuberant, "I get it, I get it . . . I think."

Andy, still in a fog, said, "Get what?"

"What Doc is saying is that there can be only one answer, one correct position for all this right and wrong, Nazis, the guillotine, whatever; otherwise, we do have chaos. I think he's saying Christianity may offer that answer."

"All religion is man-made B.S.," Andy rebuked.

"I believe you mean to quote Karl Marx: '*die Religion . . . ist das Opium des Volkes.*'"

"Come again, Doc," Pete asked.

"'Religion is the opium of the people,' is the English translation. Marx was one of the co-founders of Communism."

Pete was on a roll, "So are you saying, Doc, that there *is* such a thing as absolute truth?"

I take another swig of my vitamin water. "Pete, many, many years ago a powerful leader asked that same question of a very important personage. *Quid est veritas?* What is truth?"

Andy offered in a bit of a snarky tone, "Did the dude give him an answer?"

Pete, still hyped up, turned slightly to his brother, "I bet he gave him a real good answer; and I bet it had something to do with being a Christian." His balance shifted and he fell forward on his chair, crashing onto the coffee table. What was left of our drinks went flying in all directions.

I jumped up and helped Pete to his feet. He was a bit stunned and embarrassed by his actions, but not hurt. The guys at the pool table stopped to check out the commotion.

"Pete, you're a rock. Pete, you are *the* rock, as you are the first in the class to grasp somewhat of what I will be teaching. Lesson over."

With that I stood and said good-bye. I patted Pete on the back and shook Andy's hand. Both said they would stay to clean up the debris.

CHAPTER TWENTY-FOUR

MOTHER GAIA

A violent storm raged outside the classroom. The branches of the poplar tree were making an eerie scratching sound against the windows like dulled wiper blades. We said the pledge, with most of the class having focused on the windows instead of the flag; the cussin' jar was on the lab table.

I posed a question to the class, raising my voice above the tempest that was going on outside. "So was Hitler right or wrong to have killed so many people?"

Tom declared, "This was wartime, he did what he thought was right to preserve the German heritage."

Jude added, "Yeah, he was trying to maintain the purity of the German race."

Matt, whose parents are divorced, Reformed Jews, remarked harshly, "Why don't both of you just say what you mean: the Aryan heritage, the Aryan race!"

Santiago admitted, "He was El Jefe; he could do want he want man."

Maggie added her thoughts: "That mustache was stupid; made him look like a lunatic Charlie Chaplin."

Philip, who always leaned back against the wall, almost fell out of his chair upon hearing Maggie's criticism.

The class hissed their judgments back and forth around the room, both pro and con.

I raised my hand for silence. "Well, that got resolved easily enough—not! Let me give you another challenge."

"If an indigenous tribe practices cannibalism as part of their ancestral rites, should cannibalism then be legal and acceptable in American society?" As I surveyed the class, I signaled to Andy and Pete with a slight shake of my head not to answer.

Tom, our history major and "resident barrister", again jumped on it first. "They have every legal First Amendment right to observe their religious customs," he stated with a professorial tone to his voice.

Claudia became indignant. She turned her nose up and stated in a haughty manner, "That's just reprehensible, uncivilized, and uncouth behavior."

Nate added, "That's just gross, man."

Jim followed up, "No, it shouldn't be allowed. It's wrong; it's . . . it's evil."

Thad, our journalism/astronomy major, attempted to be serious and reflective. He raised his hand and asked, "Don't the victims have a say as to whether or not they want to be eaten?"

To Thad's astonishment, a roar of laughter resounded throughout the room.

Santiago turned around and addressed Philip at the back of the room. "Hey hombre, don't you Chinks eat monkey brains? What do they taste like, man?"

Philip didn't take the berating lightly. He snapped straight up from his chair. "Wetback and fool that you are, they taste like chicken," he said with a laugh as he sat back down.

A round of catcalls erupted throughout the class.

I raised my hand once more for silence. I deliberately did not address the name-calling and gave Maria, who sat in front of me and had been clutching at her cross, a wink and a nod.

With her demure Mona Lisa smile, she dropped her eyes, knowing I was up to something.

"Would someone want to explain to me what that World Ecology Flag in the main quadrangle represents?" I inquired, scanning the room for a hand.

Jim, our ecology major, shot his hand up first. "It shows support for our Earth."

"I support our earth Jim, but I don't need a flag to do it." I leisurely started placing some small bottles of different elements in a line along the front of the lab table, pushing the cussin' jar aside.

"Well, we have been abusing Mother Earth, and we need to protect her from man's abuse," Jim replied.

"Okay, Jim, I agree that some thoughtless men and/or evil entrepreneurs, whose only motive is greed, have promoted bad legislation and practices." I continued to place the vials on the table. "So this flag is suppose to remind us of our abuse of, how do you say it - Mother Gaia?"

By now Jim was getting a bit frustrated with me, and his emotional side started to get the better of him.

"Doc, look, Mother Earth is all we got; she gave us *life*! We need to do all we can to nurture and protect her at *any* and *all* costs."

I saw a number of the students nodding in agreement.

"So, if I got this straight, Mother Earth or Mother Gaia was doing fine until we came along to mess things up—correct?" I scanned the class and noticed many students smiling, and one or two giving me a thumbs-up.

"Would someone be kind enough to tell me how Mother Earth came to 'birth' us?" I asked as I searched the class for a hand.

Philip raised his hand, still leaning against the back wall.

I acknowledge him. "With your background in biochemistry Philip, please elucidate for me."

"Doc, with all the science courses you must have taken, you've had to have learned this stuff."

"Philip, why don't you give all of us a quick, down-and-dirty refresher."

"Well, it all started about 4.5 billion years ago, when the earth was just a blob of chemical elements called a primordial soup. These inert chemicals combined somehow to create organic molecules, which somehow over millions of years, formed the first unicellular reproductive organisms."

I raised my hand asking him to stop there.

"I think it's starting to come back to me. And *somehow*, by undirected unknown chance processes, it has progressed from goo to you. Am I correct?" I queried, looking at Philip and then at the entire class.

Philip, not knowing where I was going with this, confirmed, "Yes, that is generally the accepted theory for the process," having a quizzical expression on his face.

"So all the raw elements from the periodic table that are in the human body are worth what—about a five-spot, would you say Philip?"

"Yes, I guess that's about right," he responded, as he shrugged his shoulders.

I tossed a five dollar bill on the lab table, as I stated matter-of-factly, "Hmm, raw elements to a reproducing organism, all by random processes—a blind accident. Amazing!"

Philip immediately interjected, "Remember, Doc, mutation and natural selection were at work to create this."

"Really!?" I rejoined sarcastically as I glanced down at Maria with a slight smile and wink again. I held each small cruet of elements, in turn I read each label aloud to no one in particular. "Carbon, sulfur, magnesium, potassium, sodium—all this together, we're just a chemical accident, virtually worthless protoplasm. Maybe Hitler was right. Bet we don't even taste like chicken." The class laughed.

"Philip, please explain to me and the class how mutation and natural selection work on *raw* elements to *select* for a reproducing life form?"

"Huh?" His front desk legs came down with a hard thud that startled virtually everyone in the room, as it sounded like a minor explosion. Philip sat straight up with a dazed expression, like he got hit between the eyes.

The entire class focused on Philip, never having seen him in such a trance-like state. They were confused as to what had just happened and why.

CHAPTER TWENTY-FIVE

BLIND CHANCE

"While we wait for Philip to come out of his coma, I'll let you in on what Philip knows. In order for natural selection and mutation to supposedly work, you need a living, reproducing cell to begin with. Dumb inorganic elements can't *select* for anything."

Jim implanted his perspective immediately and vigorously. "What about the Miller experiments from the early '50s that created amino acids—the building blocks for life?" he said, looking at me and then at Philip, hoping Philip will recuperate in time to support his claim.

"You're right, Jim. Amino acids *are* the building blocks for life. However, just *one* living, reproducing cell is akin to an entire functioning city. So, you're going to need more than *only* bricks."

"Ah, it appears Philip is back among the living. Philip, please enlighten us as to Miller's *amino acids*," I petitioned with sarcasm again in my voice.

Philip may have been an atheist, but at least he was an honest atheist.

"Any biochemist worth his salt knows that the Miller-Urey experiments were a flop on a number of levels."

Jim appeared angry and bewildered. "We learned, back in junior high, high school, and even my basic biology course here at ICC about Miller - he made amino acids using lightning or electric sparks or something." Many others in the class were making affirming sounds in support of Jim.

Philip continued. "First, all life contains *only* polarized, left-handed amino acids. If you introduce even *one* right-handed amino acid into a protein, it's useless, like breaking a chain. Miller produced a toxic mix of *both* left- and right-handed amino acids."

"Doc, should I go on with the rest of the story? It only gets worse, as you know."

"Go ahead, Philip, give them the full Monty," I encouraged, deliberately knocking over the first vial as a symbolic gesture of failure.

"Second, Miller assumed a primitive earth would have a reducing atmosphere."

"Better explain what that is to the class, Philip."

"A reducing atmosphere is one that contains poisonous methane, ammonia, hydrogen, and water vapor."

"C'mon Philip, tell them why Miller didn't use our normal oxidizing atmosphere which contains water vapor, carbon dioxide, nitrogen, and oxygen."

"Doc, this is painful man. Okay, Okay. Miller didn't use oxygen in his experiment because oxygen would eventually destroy anything he would, or could create."

With that I tipped over the next bottle of elements.

The class was abuzz and animated. They highly respected Philip's intellectual prowess, being a triple major. I could see that the lesson was very upsetting to some of them.

"Tell them about the ammonia, Philip."

"The methane-ammonia hypothesis is in big trouble because ammonia, on a supposedly primitive earth, would have quickly disappeared."

I interrupted Philip, partially to shorten the agony. "Give the class the final blow regarding sugars."

"If Miller produced any sugars - again, it would have been a toxic 50-50 mixture. Sugars, like those found in proteins and nucleic acids, must be only right-handed. Introduce even one left-handed sugar, and kaboom—biologically speaking."

I slowly pushed over the next bottle onto my lab table.

"Now, tell the class what happens when free amino acids and free sugars are placed together."

Philip swallowed hard. "They cancel each other out."

"Aaand . . ." I encouraged Philip to continue as I gave him the third-degree stare. He knew what he must say.

"Therefore, you can't form DNA, or any other proteins and enzymes. There, I've said it—are you happy?" He was very dispirited.

"And have biochemists made any progress, Philip, in the laboratory, in the last seventy-plus years, toward building a reproducing life-form from *scratch*, i.e. from raw elements?" I asked. "And I assume the Biochemists are using their collective intellects and not blind random chance."

Philip hung his head and quietly said "No." You could hear a pin drop.

"Not even one grain of a mustard seed?" I said not so much to rub it in, but as to clue the students in to how manifestly complex life is—even the lowly mustard seed.

After Philip's last revelation, I proceeded to dramatically flick the remaining vials over with my finger. Philip just sat there demoralized, feeling he had somehow let the atheists down. I then directed my attention toward Pete who was majoring in geology and minoring in marine science - although I addressed the entire class. "Oh, and by the way, with all the digging through all the strata of time, all that geologists have ever found is our modern oxidizing atmosphere—never a reducing atmosphere."

Maggie broke the silence. "So if life didn't come about by blind chance processes, how *did* it happen?" Maggie surprised me. She really had been listening and evaluating the discussion.

Before I had a chance to reply, Jude spouted off, "What does all this have to do with the Matrix?"

"Excellent question, Jude. If all of life, including humanity, is here by blind random processes - which appears to be skating on thin ice at this point - then, as the majority of the class agreed, each individual makes his own decisions of what is right or wrong for him or herself. And since each person is a god unto himself, it's all about gaining power and control over the weak on every level. A big dog eat puny dog world," I said as I approached Santi's desk.

***

Juan and Santi had approached me a few days earlier informing me that Santi was on psych meds—strong SSRIs. Since I was a physician, would I have any suggestions for Santi regarding these medications. When he crossed into the USA illegally, during the Obama years, he brought his two younger sisters with him. A coyote, people smuggler, aided them in this effort. However, in the confusion that took place at one of the Border Patrol camps, he and his sisters were separated. The coyote told him that if Santi ever wanted to see his sisters again, he would have to pay a huge sum of money. Santi didn't have a peso to his name, having paid the coyote all he and his sisters had just to get across to the United States. The coyote told Santi that was too bad and that he was going to sell them in Baton Rouge to a pimp. I asked Juan if Santi had reported the sex trafficking operation to the authorities. Juan said that Santi was just too scared and confused at the time. He had no idea where his sisters were even now, which has caused him much stress. I gave Santi a referral to an organization that would try to help him locate his sisters. He thanked me.

***

I bent over and whispered a request to Santi. He nodded and said "No hay problema."

I stood up and walked back to the front of the room and leaned against my lab table.

113

"So Santi, do you agree now that everyone can do whatever he feels is right in his own eyes?"

He proceeded to tell of his harrowing escapade with his sisters, alternating between tears, rage, and exasperation with a begging and pleading tone.

Then he turned specifically toward Jude with tears welling up. "So hombre, you still think there's no such thing as right or wrong? That coyote did what was right for himself and stole my hermanas to be sold like ganado. I was going to kill myself until I listened to today's la leccion. Are we here by blind oportunidad? There has to be *some* supremo being, *some* Dios who made all this. There just *must* be, or we are all perdido—lost!" He then slumped into his chair silently bawling his eyes out.

The class was like a morgue, dead silence. Everyone was just staring alternately between Jude and Santi. I noticed Andy become very pale and anxious, squirming uncomfortably in his seat.

I stood up and exclaimed, "It looks like you have a lot to think about tonight, class."

Suddenly, a flash of lightning and a heavy booming crack of thunder brought the group back to life.

CHAPTER TWENTY-SIX

THE HOAGIE

Father Ed wanted me to meet him the following day for lunch, for one of his blethers at the Holy Grounds Coffee Shop. The day was a pure delight, the air having been cleansed after the horrific storm with just a touch of Indian summer to it.

As I approached, I saw him standing straight as a rail with his signature high-and-tight Marine haircut—his hair still a medium gray—and wearing his long black cassock with clerical collar. *He must be one of the last Catholic priests to wear a cassock,* I thought. Father Ed was an anachronism, a dinosaur to most of the young monks and seminarians; however, they and the students respected him. After all, he had earned it.

"Okay, Joe, ready to chow down?" His military demeanor oozed through.

As we entered the coffee shop, he stopped and said something to one of the waitresses. She smiled politely, escorted us outside to the patio, and seated us at a small metal bistro set near the far wall, away from the building. Looking back, one could see the opaque stained glass windows of the coffee shop.

The wall was about three feet high and constructed with stones which were quarried from the Blue Ridge Mountains. The wall replicated the stone walls found along the Blue Ridge Parkway, especially at scenic overlooks. The vistas beyond the wall of the valley below, and the mountains in the distance were breathtaking.

Like many overlooks, there was a precipitous drop-off immediately on the far side of the wall, which cascaded somewhere down into the valley. Looking straight down, one could only see a tangle of shrubs, brush, trees, and other undergrowth that created an elegant green canopy, but which hid dangerous and deadly consequences for the reckless or foolish individual.

We both ordered the soup de jour, which was New England clam chowder, and a hoagie. Mine was turkey and ham, and Father had the chicken salad with cranberries and cashews. We both selected lemonade to drink.

"We need to talk, Joe," Father Ed confided. "Something is happening on campus and you're smack in the middle of it."

The waitress brought our drinks and served Father first.

"See that petite dark-haired young lady," Father said, nodding in the waitress's direction as she left. "Her name is Cindy, and she's married to a wonderful young man named Fred, who is majoring in marine engineering. She is busting her hump trying to raise two kids while putting Fred through school. She waitresses here part-time and works as a hairstylist to boot."

"Those two have some serious goals," I acknowledged.

"Yes, but it's getting tougher and tougher for the average American with some chutzpah to achieve the American dream. This nation is turning into a third-world country," he complained, taking a sip of his lemonade. "One of every three Americans is on some entitlement program and fully 25 percent of Mexico's population lives in the U.S. illegally, or otherwise, as Ann Coulter reported several years ago. The government is deliberately dumbing down the country through Common Core and by desperately trying to eliminate homeschooling." Father looked out on the mountains reflecting on his own statement.

"I thought that they somehow voted that down?" I queried.

"Joe, they just made some minor alterations and changed the name—that's all. Local communities, at one time controlled the education of this nation, and then the states took it over. Now the federal government is in control. Do you know why?"

"That's easy; it's a power and control thing. Hey, if I were a monarch, I probably would want the kids only to learn what I wanted taught." Cindy arrived with our food.

"Remember what I told you Hitler said? 'He who owns the kids owns the future.' Our Founding Fathers never wanted this. Show me in the Constitution where the federal government is supposed to run the education system, as well as a zillion other things? Or have we forgotten about the Tenth Amendment?" asked Father as he took a healthy bite of his hoagie.

I looked at my measly turkey and ham, and then at his scrumptious chicken salad hoagie. *Dang, I should have ordered the chicken salad,* I thought to myself. I decided to start on the clam chowder.

Still munching on his chicken sandwich, Father continued, "Yeah, dumb them down, brainwash them the way you want them to think, and guess how they are going to vote?" Some of the chicken salad oozed out of the corner of his mouth. He quickly grabbed his napkin to dab at it.

Father, speaking through his napkin added, "And the few, who break through like Fred, still do not receive what we used to call a well-rounded liberal education in philosophy, theology, world history, economics, government, the arts, etcetera. A person like Fred will know a lot about one or two areas and essentially be ignorant in other fields."

"I totally agree, Father. Instead, their heads will be filled with social justice and global warming ecology courses—the usual Marxist tripe," I concurred as I forced myself to take a bite of my blah turkey and ham. "And you know what the usual liberal response to the federal government controlling education is?" I asked. "It's under the general welfare clause, for government to take care of everything!" I put the sandwich down and went back to my soup.

"Yes, Joe, James Madison, within a few short years after the Constitution was ratified, needed to address this. Some representatives of the New England states wanted Congress to pass a bill to subsidize the cod fishermen, of course with monies from U.S. citizens." The frustration was all over his face.

"Guess those fishermen had a bad season or something," I exclaimed, trying to lighten up Father's mood while still staring at my mundane sandwich. "Yeah, I believe we call it a 'stimulus' now."

"What Madison, the father of our Constitution, stated, should be required memorization by every student, nay, every American. However, it'll be a cold day in hell before the libs place Madison's statement into a history textbook."

Father had stopped eating his chicken salad hoagie, and I kept eyeing it. "How did Madison put it?" I asked.

"Okay, it's been a while since I last negotiated Madison's quote, but here goes."

"'If Congress can employ money indefinitely to the general welfare, and are the sole and supreme judges of the general welfare, they may take the care of religion into their own hands; they may appoint teachers in every state, county and parish and pay them out of their public treasury; they may take into their own hands the education of children, establishing in like manner schools throughout the union; they may assume provision of the poor; they may undertake the regulation of all roads other than post roads; in short every thing, from the highest object of state legislation down to the most minute object of police, would be thrown under the power of Congress... Were the power of Congress to be established in the latitude contended for, it would subvert the very foundations, and transmute the very nature of the limited government established by the people of America.'"

With that soliloquy, Father took a couple of long chugs of his lemonade.

"Wow! The only thing Madison left out was health care," I exclaimed, trying to make a funny. "For all practical purposes, the entire Constitution has been shredded—for *quite* some time," I observed.

Father Ed was on a roll. His chowder was getting cold, however.

"Madison was spot on, even his comment on religion. And look what has happened to the police in our country. The local constabulary is now under the dictates of the feds. It started several years back with Ferguson, Baltimore, and Philly; the DOJ, in effect, required the cops to back off. Now, virtually all your inner cities are burning, figuratively and literally, with wanton unrestrained crime, controlled by gangs like MS13, Crips, and Bloods."

Father finally tasted his soup and then had a quizzical look, obviously wondering why it was cold.

"Government-backed-and-supported agitators were bused in," I supplemented, "fueling already tense situations. Instead of letting the courts sort it out, the paid agitators wanted street justice by rampaging and looting." I stopped momentarily to attempt another small bite of my pathetic meal. "How is looting and burning a store for its condoms and chips being supportive of some guy these hoodlums didn't even personally know?"

Father had stopped eating altogether, having lost his appetite. "Now, the law-abiding citizens and businessmen, whose stores had been plundered and torched, are asking the *same* authority—the government - who *fomented* the problem, to *solve* the problem; which the government was more than happy to oblige."

Still longing for some of Father's half eaten chicken salad, I added, "And the John Warner Defense Act of 2006 quietly repealed the *Posse Comitatus Act*, which restrained the federal government from using military troops in our streets, a la Jade Helm 'exercises,' as domestic law enforcement has been thrown into the dust bin of history, while armed drones rule the skies. Father, that reminds me, do you recall a YouTube video I sent you several years ago titled '*Prototype Quadrotor with Machine Gun*'?"

"Joe, that unit was almost four feet in diameter. Since then, my sources tell me they are now about three and a half feet in diameter and can hold up to two hundred rounds of ammo. Arnold Schwarzenegger's Hunter-Killer flying terminators have been reality for some time now."

My stomach was really talking to me by that point. "What was it that you wanted to tell me? Something that I'm in the middle of here at ICC?"

Father blinked in an absentminded way and shook his head. "Guess I got off on a tangent. I need to warn you that Professor Dietrich of the social justice department has got his sights lined up on you. You've stirred up a hornet's nest."

"Social justice department?" I asked, looking at Father and then at his mostly untouched chicken salad hoagie. "Are you going to eat that?"

CHAPTER TWENTY-SEVEN

SOCIAL JUSTICE

Appearing very antsy, Father Ed got up from his seat causing the metal feet of the chair to make a racquet against the paving stones. He walked over and leaned his lower back against the short stone wall as he took out one of his cigars, perhaps to help him relax. Still contemplative, he began, "Joe, unfortunately I needed to make some concessions to get ICC off the ground. One of those was a requirement, by some godforsaken bureaucratic government agency, that we have a social justice department," he said lighting his Camacho Ecuador with an old banged-up Zippo lighter that he had carried with him since either Korea or Nam.

He turned away from me, faced the mountains, and continued. "I judged wrong, thinking one small governmental intrusion into ICC wouldn't affect us much." He hung his head while supporting his body with his outstretched arms leaning on the wall, his cigar in hand.

Still seated, I replied, "The one rotten apple that spoils the bunch, huh?"

He suddenly whipped around, his face hard as stone, pointing his finger at me as smoke trailed from his cigar. "Professor Dietrich represents all that is vile and reprehensible in Washington," he boomed like God Himself. "Bunch of Pecksniffian pharisaic poltroons."

"Hey, Father, you have been watching too many re-runs of Bill O'Reilly's Word of the Day segment," I said trying to get Father to calm down somewhat.

His face and demeanor allayed a bit. "I didn't always agree with him, but he is a good man and really did try to 'look out for the folks,' as he liked to say. I believe his and my father's ancestors were from the same county on that enchanting emerald Isle," as a small momentary pensive smile appears on his face.

"Washington has 'encouraged' all the colleges to enact a department of social justice," Father continued. "Dietrich was handpicked by some lackey in DC to head up the department. He also has some minions running around campus—the Hitler Jugend I call them—doing his spying for him."

"Yeah, I thought I've seen some 'students' all dressed the same in a crisp paramilitary style," I said remembering the khaki pants with black military web belts, sky blue open collared button-down shirts with epaulettes, and black Corfam boots.

"Those are his minions. They attend a variety of classes and report back to Dietrich regarding any social justice violations."

"And just *what* is considered a social justice violation?" I inquired with a sarcastic tone.

Father leaned over, placing both hands on the bistro table, and, half chewing his cigar at the side of his mouth, attempted to define the problem. "That's the trouble. The whole thing is a phantasm, a bowl of Jell-O; it keeps changing. We can't get the government to give us a hard-and-fast definition—and it seems they *want* it that way."

"I get it. That way they can accuse and prosecute anyone who is intolerant, unfair, judgmental, or offensive in their eyes. In other words, anyone who follows Judeo-Christian morality, in short - biblical principles," I blurted. I was starting to get heated up.

Father stood and walked to the wall, leaning back against it. "Dietrich knows what you have been teaching and has his eye on you."

"I don't have any of the 'Hitler Youth' in my class," I exclaimed, half asserting, half questioning as I stood up to defend my position.

"Joe," Father chortled, coughing on his own cigar smoke. "Everyone on this small campus now knows what you are teaching. You don't need any overt or covert spies in your room. Besides there have already been a couple of articles in the *Veritas Beacon*."

I had totally forgotten Thad's article series about my Matrix course. "Do you want me to back off?"

"Absolutely not! Besides your conscience wouldn't let you," Father said, half laughing as he released a big plume of smoke. "I'm just giving you a heads up on Dietrich and company."

I was getting ticked in more ways than one. "Yeah, and the government numpties, to use your expression, are cultivating—no *championing*—Sharia Law. Hell, Minneapolis and Dearborn—excuse me, Dearbornistan—as well as a slew of other cities, are now rife with Muslim ghettos. Like England and France, the police give them a wide berth."

"Hey, Joe, calm down, you'll blow a gasket." Father laughed.

With that I heard a creaky iron gate open. The front end of the patio had a low wrought-iron picket-style fence with a gate that extended from the entrance wall of the coffee shop to the stone wall overlook. Father immediately recognized the young man coming through that iron gate. "Hey, Fred, come on over; I'd like to introduce you to a close friend of mine who teaches here."

Father leaned over toward me and quietly informed me that Fred was our waitress, Cindy's, husband he had mentioned earlier.

Fred appeared to be in his late twenties or early thirties. He was clean shaven with charcoal black hair and a touch of premature gray starting to show. He was average build and well groomed, very GQ, wearing a sporty causal-style jacket and pants.

"Fred, I'd like to introduce you to Dr. Joseph Lucci, who is a new professor this year on our staff."

We cordially shook hands. Fred had a good firm grip but not a crusher trying to prove something.

"Fred, Joe is teaching a new course called the Matrix Exposed," Father stated proudly with a big smile.

Fred looked at me and said, "Oh, *you* are the guy that's causing all the disturbance on campus!"

CHAPTER TWENTY-EIGHT

LOVE AND RESPECT

Father invited Fred to sit with us, and he pulled up a chair.

"I've got some time; my class got out early. Cindy is not off for another thirty minutes or so."

Fred turned around and spoke to Cindy who was standing near us. "Honey, would you mind bringing me something to drink?"

"What would you like?" she asked, letting her down-home southern drawl come through.

"I'll have what they're having," Fred said, looking at both of our almost empty glasses.

"It's gonna cos you," Cindy stated firmly, with her sweet Southern accent.

"Whaa?"

Cindy bent over and gave him a soft kiss. "There, that wasn't too expensive, was it? Engineers, linear thinkers," she said shaking her head and walked away.

After a slight pause, Father broke the silence. "So, Fred tell us how your studies are going."

"Just logging the hours. I told Cindy that I have a photographic memory. The only problem is that there's no film in the camera."

"I thought you engineering boys would have gone digital by now?" I said, trying to break the ice with Fred.

The three of us momentarily stared at one another and immediately cracked up laughing.

We small-talked for a while about his kids. Fred was extremely concerned as to where the country was headed, and what kind of a future his children would have to face.

"How did you decide on engineering?" I asked.

"Well, it's somewhat of a long story," Fred replied as he started playing with one of his cufflinks.

"Hey, you've got thirty minutes to kill," Father noted. "Might as well tell your story; we're in the mood for a good positive narrative."

"You mean *ma* thirty minutes," Cindy interjected firmly and decisively, setting Fred's lemonade down. She had also brought fresh refills for Father Ed and myself. We all looked at Cindy with strained plastic smiles on our faces, as we each thanked her for our lemonades. Her exhaustion showed, as she walked back into the coffee shop.

Fred was now toying with his glass of lemonade. "I started my schooling at Virginia Tech, and didn't know what I wanted to major in until I ran into this fellow who was specializing in marine engineering. We became close friends, and I began to spill my personal problems out to him regarding my marriage."

Fred gave Father a look of trepidation.

"Go ahead Fred, you're among friends." Father gave him a comforting smile and a nod of reassurance.

"This was a few years ago, and I thought our marriage was on the rocks. We were always bickering and fighting. There was just no peace in our house. No peace in our souls." Fred picked up his glass; his hand slightly trembled as he took a drink. "Cindy and I thought we were 'spiritual.' It's just a boneheaded excuse. In reality we dabbled in all kinds of mysticism - crystals, the Force, Hindu Avatar, channeling – but we were just trying to present an air of superiority to those around us. It was just to prove we had some amorphous link to a higher power."

The problem we had, and those who claim to be 'spiritual,' is that when pressed for an explanation, we each set our own rules, and we each played by them. We were self-centered and selfish in reality. Cindy and I obviously didn't believe in any kind of superior being or god. We didn't *want* to be answerable to anyone but ourselves. My friend challenged me to show him scientific evidence that a superior intelligence *didn't* exist."

Father and I looked at each other knowingly, having had the same discussion many times.

"I took him up on it, figuring this would be a piece of cake. Here my friend was a marine design engineer, and he believed in pie-in-the sky children's fables. 'He probably thinks the earth is flat and his boats will fall off the edge,' I thought."

"Oh, I tried to belittle him with the usual clichéd arguments such as: 'I only believe in things my five senses can detect,' I said, looking down my nose at him, 'and I don't sense *your* God in our three dimensional universe,' I said, almost barking at him. "

"You mean like gravity, Fred," I replied with a chuckle.

He smiled back and looked at me and Father Ed, who was also chuckling.

"Now I know why you are causing all the fracas here at ICC. Cindy had told me that one of the professors was riling up the students in his class, but she couldn't remember exactly who or what the situation was."

I interrupted Fred's flow, "Yeah, seems I was the last to find this out. Father has just brought me up to speed."

Fred continued, "I was such a dunderhead," as he is knocking his fist against the side of his head. "I actually began to gloat over him with my 'five senses' assertion when he interjected with the gravity illustration just as you did. My buddy could see the partial confusion in my eyes. And as I was about to make some foolish comeback, he abruptly cut me off, 'Fred not the *effects* of gravity, but gravity itself.'"

"I was ready to crawl into a hole. But my friend had patience, and thank God I had enough respect for him at that moment to just shut up and listen."

"Did he take you through the Miller-Urey fiasco?" I asked.

"Not directly. He gave me a book to read that literally blew my socks off. I was always led to believe that the scientific community was in complete unison regarding Miller and biogenesis, radiometric decay rates, transitional fossils, stratigraphy formation, anthropological hominid development—you name it."

"Are you going to keep us hanging? What was the name of the book?" Father asked, while he puffed impatiently on his cigar.

"*That Their Words May be Used Against Them* by Henry M. Morris. These were quotes by peer-reviewed experts in their respective fields: the heavy-hitter PhD authors and researchers who are or were atheists, but at least honest ones. I had no idea there was so much internal conflict among scientists."

"The government-approved textbooks don't allude to *any* of the conflict," Fred continued. "Of course, no oppositional viewpoint is permitted." The three of us nodded together in agreement. "So what happened then?" Father coaxed, still anxious for Fred to get on with how he and Cindy reconciled their differences.

"I don't like being deliberately lied to, and neither does Cindy," Fred said, taking several gulps of his lemonade to quench his dry mouth. "Boy, did Hitler know how to play the game," as Fred proceeded to quote the man. "'If you tell a big enough lie and tell it frequently enough, it will be believed.' Trouble is, the fool also believed his own lies. And our government is trying to force many of the same falsehoods down our throats, as we all sit around singing 'Kumbaya'." Fred then turned and pointed to the world ecology flag, the top of which we could barely see in the distance through the trees.

"And then with you and Cindy?" Father pressed.

Fred took a few more swallows of his lemonade and continued. "Cindy and I set ourselves on a PMA daily reading regime and we found out—"

"PMA?" Father interrupted.

"Positive Mental Attitude," Fred shot back.

"Why didn't you just say so?"

It seemed that the Professor Dietrich thing probably had affected Father Ed more than he was letting on.

Fred continued. "And I found out that a woman's primary drive of acceptance is love, and Cindy learned with men, it's respect. I needed to show her more love, and she needed to show me more respect." Fred had already finished off his drink and was looking around for Cindy for a refill. "Look at it this way fellas," Fred persisted, "take the worst druggie lowlife. He's more than willing to blow someone away who 'dissed' him. Respect is paramount even with those slimeballs. Then take the cheapest floozy who gets caught by the police aiding and abetting her boyfriend in some half-baked attempted robbery; when asked why she did it, what is her response? 'I *love* him.'"

"So where did you learn about the primary drives of love for women and respect for men that you and Cindy started to abide by? And this, you claim, is what started you both on the road toward healing your marriage?" Father challenged, literally chewing on his cigar now.

"Father?!" Fred exclaimed, looking at him with a strange questioning expression on his face. "The Bible of course. Ephesians 5:33."

CHAPTER TWENTY-NINE

ROCKY ROAD

Cindy showed up and was impatient to leave. I told her to put the entire bill on my tab and to add 25 percent for herself. Her demeanor softened and she thanked me.

While we were waiting for her to close out her till, I asked Fred, "How would you like to give a talk to my class?"

"Sure. When?" He asked enthusiastically.

"Well, we meet tomorrow at 9 AM for an hour. How does that work with your schedule?"

Fred checked the planner on his tablet. "Slight conflict. I wouldn't be able to arrive until around ten."

"Hmm, tell you what," I offered, "how about you meet us at the north end of the quadrangle at about 10:15. There's a great little grassy area with benches just off the walkway. We could meet there. You'll have a good group of my students that would love to hear a young man like yourself, rather than some old fart like me."

"Super, I know the location. I've seen some of the other professors with their classes lecturing there. See you mañana."

Just as we finished making arrangements, Cindy showed back up with lemonade in hand, having anticipated her husband's need for a drink to go. They said their goodbyes, as she and Fred walk away hand-in-hand like two lovebirds.

Father excused himself. "I have another useless admin meeting to go to," he said with a heavy sigh, as he walked off through the iron gate toward the administration building, leaving me alone with his chewed-up half-burnt cigar smoldering in the ashtray on the bistro table.

***

I arrived back home at a reasonable hour after going to Kroger with the honey-do list that Emily had texted earlier to me. As I came through our kitchen door, the wonderful aroma of fresh pasta teased my olfactory senses. "Smells awesome," I announced as I came into the kitchen and gave Emily a big hug and kiss.

"It's just the pan of lasagna I made last week. I'm reheating it now."

I quickly checked my email and then it was time to eat. We sat down and said grace. I looked around the table, "Any bread?" I asked.

"Yes, honey, it's warming in the oven. You New York Italians and your bread. Oh, and I purchased a nice Shiraz from Sam's Club last time we were there, remember?"

"Yeah, the Black Dog Shiraz we like from the Chateau Morrisette winery we visited a few years ago."

"Sam's had it on sale, and I bought a few bottles for us."

I reached for the bottle and started to open it.

***

After dinner I loosened a notch on my belt. "That was your best lasagna yet," I said taking another sip of the robust, full-bodied wine.

"You say that every time I make it, Mr. Rockefeller."

"Mr. Rockefeller? What's that about?" I asked with a puzzled look on my face.

"Well, I just received, on my email, your 'tab' for the month at ICC," she said handing me a copy of my campus expenses she had printed off. "This is the amount that will be deducted from your paycheck this month." She looked at me with her arms folded and a mild scowl on her face, which broke into an amusing smile.

"Well, the students are broke, and Father is on a fixed income, and the student waiters and waitresses need the money," I stammered, trying to plead my case.

"I know," she says sweetly. "One of the reasons why I love you is because you are generous with those who need it." She leaned over and gave me a kiss. "Mmm, that Shiraz on your lips tastes good."

"By the way, what did you have for lunch when you met with Father?"

"Oh, part of a chicken salad sub."

"Part?" Emily looked at me strangely.

I changed the subject. "What do you have planned for dessert?" I asked, licking my lips trying to savor the last bouquet of the Shiraz.

"How about a root beer float with rocky road?" Emily offered as she got up from the table and started to pick up the empty dishes.

"I'll help you clear the table," I offered. "How about we take the root beer floats and relax in the living room?"

As Emily was preparing the floats, I asked her how her day went.

"Oh, I almost forgot. The power company came onto our property sometime while I was out running errands today and installed that smart meter." I sensed a slightly disturbed tone in her voice.

"I thought you made it clear to them that our old meter was functioning *just fine,*" I stated emphatically.

"They have been pestering us for months," Emily pleaded, as she finished putting a straw into each of our floats. "I've tried to keep this from you Honey."

We carried our root beer floats into the living room. I plopped down into my lazy boy recliner and Emily into her comfortably wide overstuffed chair with ottoman. "I have responded to numerous emails and flyers," Emily comments. "Each time I've emphasized that we don't want one. And today they sneak onto our property to install it."

"Honey," I reply, "I've seen the ads: 'Monitor your energy usage, control your costs, conserve energy, save our planet.' I oughta go outside and rip out the whole damn thing."

"Then we wouldn't have any electric power for sure," Emily answered, thinking I'm really going to do it.

I'm still irked. "What difference does it make? What a bunch of fools we are. I believe that over thirty states now have these devices. The government first softens you up by making you think you are in control, and that the meter will help you save on your utility bills." I paused just long enough to scoop up some of the rocky road. "'We will install them free of charge for you,' they say. What B.S.! The sheeple don't realize that the meter works both ways. It sends *and* receives a satellite signal much like our smart phones. If the powers-that-be don't particularly like your politics, if you're ruffling too many feathers, off goes your washer and dryer—or your whole house!" I got so worked up I spilled a little rocky road on my shirt and quickly spooned it up. "So now it's gone from an option, to forcefully imposing their will on us," I stated, swabbing the smudge with my napkin while cussing under my breath for being so sloppy.

CHAPTER THIRTY

SECRET SECTS

"**W**hat's the matter with people?" Emily implored, flailing her hands like an Italian.

I must be rubbing off on her, I thought.

"Don't they get it?"

"No!" I replied emphatically. "They are robotons—busy with work, social activities, watching the TV 'reality' shows, or blowing several hundred dollars, that they don't have any way, going to some sporting event. The lamestream media doesn't report on many critical and crucial topics. They can't. Look who owns and controls them." I get up from my lazy boy to wash the stain off my shirt. "Speaking about the Rockefellers," I continued. "David Rockefeller, around thirty years ago or so, at some big hoity-toity dinner, thanked the press and media CEOs and owners for working so well with them. Hell, some of those big shots were at the latest Bilderberg meeting." As I returned to my lazy boy, I brushed at my now wet, discolored stain on my shirt.

"Don't worry; I can get that stain out," Emily said, commiserating with my frustration regarding both the people and my stain.

"I'm going to find that quote of his, doggone it." I turned on my tablet and fudged around a bit. "Ah, here it is. Listen to this pompous ass."

"We are grateful to the *Washington Post,* the *New York Times, Time* magazine and other great publications whose directors have attended our meetings and respected their promises of discretion for almost forty years.

It would have been impossible for us to have developed our plan for the world if we had been subjected to the lights of publicity during those years. But the world is now more sophisticated and prepared to march toward a world government.

The supranational sovereignty of an intellectual elite and world bankers is surely preferable to the national auto-determination practiced in past centuries." (David Rockefeller, Baden-Baden, Germany 1991)

"Notice what Rockefeller said with respect to when most of this 'legal' organized crime and corruption was organized—almost forty years prior to his 1991 statement. The Bilderberg group was formed in 1954."

"And the pièce de résistance . . . give me a second while I bring *this* up. You're going to *love* this," I said as I proceeded to Google the statement. "Good, here it is. I'll read you some selected portions of a speech given by JFK before the American Newspaper Publishers Association at the Waldorf-Astoria Hotel in NYC on April 27, 1961."

"The very word "secrecy" is repugnant in a free and open society; and we are as a people inherently and historically opposed to secret societies, to secret oaths, and secret proceedings. . . .

And there is very grave danger that an announced need for increased security will be seized upon by those anxious to expand its meaning to the very limits of official censorship and concealment. . . .

For we are opposed around the world by a monolithic and ruthless conspiracy that relies on covert means for expanding its sphere of influence. . .

It is a system which has conscripted vast human and material resources into the building of a tightly knit, highly efficient machine that combines military, diplomatic, intelligence, economic, scientific and political operations. . . . .

Its preparations are concealed, not published. Its mistakes are buried not headlined. Its dissenters are silenced, not praised. No expenditure is questioned, no rumor is printed, no secret is revealed."

"So tell me, Babe, was Kennedy writing his own epitaph? A year and a half later he was assassinated. Nothing to see here, move on," sarcasm dripping off my words.

"But why, Joe?" Emily asked, squirming very uncomfortably.

"Because he wouldn't dance to their tune. Those international elitists and Illuminati that run the banks and mega-corporations want to own everything—including the U.S. He fought them and lost. It's been downhill ever since. Ironically, the poor and some of the middle class will suffer the most. Unfortunately, so many are blitzed out of their minds on drugs—legal and otherwise—zombied out on a raft of pain killers, psych meds, sleep meds, anti-anxiety meds. The only thing many of them care about is when their next check will cash. And again, Big Brother likes them in that easily controlled dependent state."

"But it isn't right that the government forces itself upon us," Emily whined.

CHAPTER THIRTY-ONE

WRONG OR RIGHT

"Right and wrong is basically what it's all about, the truth subverted. One of my students, Pete, is just starting to grasp that concept," I explained to Emily as I took a big sip of my float. "He's beginning to understand that if there is no right or wrong, then might makes right and only Darwin's survival of the fittest prevails."

Emily shifted to a more upright position in her chair as she reflectively stated, "That's when it becomes all about money, which leads to the power and control thing you always talk about - What David Rockefeller said and what Kennedy was fighting against."

"You got it, Babe. A good percentage of people know things are getting worse but can't put their finger on it. This is not rocket science." I took another sip of my float, but it was too thick. *I'll just wait for the ice cream to melt, rather than taking the chance of spilling more on me,* I thought to myself. "Take any indices you want, and you can see it getting worse by the year. Crime, rape, civil unrest, homosexuality, abortion, loss of faith, fewer youth attending church, government corruption, international corporations in bed with the major banking firms screwing everyone."

"Why?" pleaded Emily, practically wringing her hands.

"Simple. As we move away from God, society becomes more pagan and corrupt like ancient Rome. Oh excuse me, there is no God. Darwin has 'proved' that."

"People claim that there were evil individuals and societies in the Bible," Emily asserted.

"Correct. Pagan societies, pagan peoples, and even the Israelites themselves when they rejected God in the Old Testament. Remember the Rabbi Jonathan Cahn DVDs we watched? He has abundantly testified to ancient Israel's aberrant behaviors. And we are following suit."

"Some of my Catholic girlfriends claim that one doesn't have to be a Christian to be moral."

"Oh, boy; yeah, but whose morals and whose ethics?" I challenged.

"Huh?" Emily asked, looking at me quizzically.

"For a pagan to be 'moral' as you say, they need to 'steal' from Judeo-Christian morals and ethics, otherwise whose morals are they abiding by—pagan Rome or maybe a remote Indian tribe that boils stillborns or cannibals whose tribal rituals include eating people," as I suck violently on my straw; the ice cream clogging it up.

Emily was getting very animated. "I remember you telling me about how Jesuit Fordham University canceled a talk to be given by Ann Coulter and then turned around and invited Peter Singer, the bioethics professor from Princeton who believes in infanticide and bestiality! My God, and this guy is a bio*ethics* professor!?"

"Honey, Notre Dame University asked former President Obama to be their commencement speaker and awarded him with an honorary degree, even though the guy voted to legalize late-term abortion. This is known as dilation and extraction. You know the scissors deal where the base of the infant's skull is punctured with the surgical shears and then the brain is suctioned out. Forceps are finally used to crush the cranium, making it easier for the now dead fetus to be withdrawn."

"No more, no more," holding her hands against her ears. "What is happening with Christians; with *everybody* in the U.S.? Have we gone mad?"

"Babe, we have become the Israelites of the Old Testament who have forsaken God. Don't forget Obama 'asked' Notre Dame to cover all its religious symbols, prior to his speaking engagement."

"But why?" Her hands were clenched in anger.

"If Darwin and evolution are true, there is no God, no right or wrong. And if evolution is true, we came from nothing, and therefore when we die, we go to nothing. So, truth and morality become relative. Each person decides right or wrong for himself. This is what I'm slowing trying to get my class to realize."

Emily's eyes lit up. "Ahhh, but with Christianity there are guidelines, like the Ten Commandments. We believe when we die there will be a reward or retribution," she stated matter-of-factly as she settled down in her huge lounge chair.

"So tell me, Honey," I said, leaning forward to get her complete attention. "What has the school system, including the Catholic schools, universities, and even seminaries, been teaching now for decades?"

"Darwinism! And therefore *everything* must be tolerated, except Christianity, of course," she heartily concluded.

"Correct. And if evolution's true, how dare you criticize my actions - if I want to berate a nurse, throw rocks and bottles at fire and EMS personnel, rip you off, lie, cheat, or whatever. This attitude that there is no right or wrong mentality - with *no* shame, permeates our culture; whether it's a purse-snatching thug, the lying mainstream media, a corrupt politician, or embezzling CEO of a multi-national corporation," I elucidated while still trying to get my straw to work. "I'll do whatever I can get away with," I mocked in an arrogant voice. "That's why they actually have formal college courses in situation ethics and relative morality. The assumption being that you probably believe in evolution *before* even registering for the class."

Emily, still somewhat confused, asked, "How come so many people say, then, that they believe in God?"

"Honey, the Devil believes in God! Why would he waste his time following just any 'crazy man' around the desert for forty days *if* he didn't think that person was really God? Someone telling me they believe in God doesn't impress me one single iota. At least the Devil really believed that 'crazy man' in the desert could change stones into bread. Whereas, half these people who claim to believe in God don't believe that same 'crazy man' could change water into wine." I leaned in a little, "And you wonder why everyone, including, priests, ministers, nuns, and rabbis are becoming more pagan, or should I say more *evolutionized* with each passing generation?"

I took a moment to finalize my thought. "The kicker is, that the left makes us feel guilty, that we're the hate-mongers if we don't agree with their positions on abortion, homosexuality, etcetera. What drivel! What sane individual would despise his brother if he's a homosexual or loathe his daughter if she's had an abortion? Okay, they might disagree with their lifestyle and choices, but they would and should still love them," I concluded finally giving up on my float.

I looked at my wife who just seemed to be sitting there kinda stunned and somewhat bewildered. "Honey, I think it's time we go to bed."

As I was dropping off to sleep, I realized I hadn't even mentioned to her what Father Ed had told me about Professor Dietrich.

CHAPTER THIRTY-TWO

UGLY ALIEN

We concluded the Pledge with Ali still resisting. I proceeded to make an announcement to the class. "For those who are able, we will be meeting a young engineer at the north end of the quadrangle after class, around 10:15, for a brief talk. It's entirely optional."

Andy asked, "Is he a young dude, always wearing cool threads?"

"Yes."

"He's into marine engineering, married with a couple of kids?"

"Yes again, Andy."

Andy then addressed the class. "I know this fellow. We've taken a few engineering courses together. You've got to meet this dude. He is sharp, always pressed, and has a way with words."

Claudia seemed particularly interested in what Andy was saying. He continued, "Nothing personal, Doc, but this guy is with it."

"Okay then," I confirmed, "It's settled. After class, around 10:15, north end of the quadrangle, the grassy spot by the trees."

Everyone nodded, acknowledging they knew where it is. Whether they would come was another matter.

***

I pulled a coin out of my pocket. "Here, catch," I said as I tossed the coin out to the class. Andy caught it.

"Andy, being an engineer you have a very logical mind. Let me propose a scenario. You are an astronaut on a rocket and are about to engage the propulsion system into hyper-drive after exiting the earth's gravitational field."

Matt, our Star Wars aficionado commented. "Way cool, I want to be on board, too!"

"Okay, Matt, you too."

"Where are we going?" He asked.

"'To boldly go where no man has gone before,'" I replied.

"That's Star Trek," he groused. "At least we can launch into hyperspace with warp drive."

I don't even need to look to know that Philip, leaning back on his chair, was rolling his eyes.

"By now both you guys are millions of light years out in space. You land on a solid planet. Your sensors tell you that the 'air' is the toxic gas hydrogen sulfide. You put your space suits on and exit your spacecraft. The World Space Agency wants you to collect rock samples, and while doing so you find a coin."

Matt hops over Pete and grabs the coin from Andy, as if he's really its first discoverer on this distant planet.

"What conclusion can you come to by examining the coin?"

"It has some weird writing and symbols on it. I can't read it," Matt complained.

"What does that tell you, Andy?" I questioned.

"That some intelligent life force dropped the coin and—"

"Yeah, some ugly alien that eats people came to that planet and lost it. It probably has magical powers." Matt broke in before Andy could continue.

The class, by now, had had its fill of Matt's vivid imagination. Claudia stepped up to the plate. "Matt stifle yourself! You need to attend to this germane application," she chided, as the rest of the class mumbled in affirmation.

I proceeded to question Andy, while Matt cooled his jets. "Andy, so what you found was not raw iron ore or copper or bauxite. You used two words: *intelligence* and *coin*. How do you know it was an intelligent life force that dropped it?"

"Well . . . uh . . . unusual specificity."

"Explain." I asked him.

"I'm trying to think of another example."

"Let me help you. Would you consider Mount Rushmore in that same class?"

"Yeah, that's it. Wind, water, erosion couldn't have carved out Mount Rushmore anymore than the elements could have made that coin. Someone with ingenuity and intelligence, and with knowledge of metallurgy, had to design, forge, and manufacture that coin. Same with Mount Rushmore."

"Andy, when one sees a painting, what does it preclude?"

"That's a dumb question, Doc. The painting had to have a painter, someone with the creativity and intelligence to paint the thing. Rembrandt was brilliant. He didn't just throw paint on a canvas," he said half chuckling to himself and those around him.

"How about the NASCAR engine for Bobby Allison?" I asked.

"Woo wee, number 12!" shouts Pete, "He's a hometown hero," he blurted out, waving his hands in the air. "Man, that engine wasn't just designed, it was blueprinted!"

"You guys specifically used words like *design* and *intelligence*, among others. I want you and the class to hold those two words hostage in your brains for a while."

Jude intervened abruptly. "I know where you are going with this," he stated in a very condescending and snarky tone.

Before he could advance his position, I countered Jude firmly. "Well, I'm glad that you are a step ahead of the class. You can present your information at the end." Letting him know obliquely that he's not in control of this class—I am.

Jude sat pouting with his arms crossed.

"Some of you, as you were entering the class, received some objects. I asked that you keep them concealed, which I would like you to continue to do. But raise your hand if you received something from me."

Several hands went up.

"Good. Without revealing your hidden article, please try to describe what you have to the class. Pete, you can go first."

"Yeah, I have a curly spring like thing."

"I assume it was designed and machined to a specific gauge and tolerance?"

"No doubt," Pete responded affirmatively.

"What would you make with it?"

"How the hell, oops . . . would I know."

Matt, who was coming around, looked across at Pete and with a biting remark stated, "That'll cost you, big guy."

Pete, the honest fellow that he was, promptly walked straight to the front, took a dollar from his pocket, and put it in the cussin' jar.

Nate had put his hand up. I recognized him.

"I've got some kind of piece of metal, which is twisted and bent at one end."

"Again, I assume that it was designed to withstand a certain degree of pressure and torque. Any ideas, Nate?"

"Beats me," he conceded as he shrugged both shoulders and put his hands palms up.

Santi was waving his hand. "Go ahead, Santi."

"I've got a very especialized creación: a clasp or hook of some sort."

"Any clue?" I asked him.

"No sé," he admitted, shaking his head.

"I've got some kind of wooden board," Santi's cousin Juan claimed. "It's cut, trimmed, and crafted to handle a certain amount of weight and pressure!?"

"What's it for?" I asked of Juan.

"I haven't the foggiest idea, or even what I *could* do with it."

Maggie's had her hand up. "Okay, Maggie, what do you have?"

"Some kind of rod or little pole," she described slightly moving her head to the side and raising her eyebrows to indicate she had no clue what it was or was for.

"Let us recall the Miller experiment. Philip advised us that there was no way, starting with raw elements, from blind chance, to create DNA and enzymes, which are proteins."

"Let's look at Darwin's own statement: 'If it could be demonstrated that any complex organ existed, which could not have possibly have been formed by numerous, successive, slight modifications, my theory would absolutely break down.'"

"He's saying that each step of evolutionary development must give an organ system like the digestive system, circulatory system, respiratory system, etcetera - a little more of an advantage."

Jim, our ecology major, wanted in on the discussion. "Darwin has made a boo-boo," he stated.

"How so?" I enquired, directing my gaze at him.

Jim stood up to address the entire class. "Organ systems can only exist in something that is already alive and already functioning. And we haven't even discovered how raw elements can form a lousy protein."

"Jim, you are magnificent!"

"I am?" he replied, still standing, his face turning red.

"You have come to a conclusion that most educated people have never arrived at."

"I have?" he asked quizzically.

"What was the title of his book?"

"*On the Origin of Species by—*"

"Stop!" I commanded him.

"Repeat the first part of the title again for the class."

"*On the Origin of Species,*" he repeated slowly.

The entire class was quietly focused on Jim. Jim was seriously reflecting on the title. His expression suddenly changed, and he began to laugh, almost doubled over. The students all looked at one another, wanting to get in on the joke.

Still chuckling, Jim brought himself upright. "The title itself is bogus!"

CHAPTER THIRTY-THREE

BOREL'S LAW

"**D**arwin never discussed how life itself *originated*," Jim explained. "He rambles on about plants and animals, mostly about variations in fancy pigeons, but he never explains how they got from raw elements to even basic life itself, let alone how they reached the species level."

He then smacked himself on the forehead with the heel of his hand. "I could have had a V-8."

The class was in an uproar.

Jude waved his hand furiously. I acknowledge him.

"Time is the key. Given enough *time*, nature will find a way."

Matt turned around. "Hey, Jude, wasn't that a line from one of the Jurassic Park movies?" Several students chuckled.

I was about to continue when Nate raised his hand. He had a serious expression on his face. Nate, our business and computer science wizard, spoke when something of importance needed to be said. He addressed me, but spoke to the entire class. "Doc, I've been surfing around and doing some calculations on my tablet ever since we began this discussion of trying to form a basic protein from raw elements."

"What have you discovered, Nate?" I asked, knowing his answer would put the kibosh on Jude's wild speculations.

"We all know there are twenty basic amino acids. It takes around three to five hundred amino acids to form even one average protein." He looked up from his tablet.

The class knew that Nate was no fool and was a straight shooter. "Go ahead, continue," I instructed, waving my hand in an affirmative way toward Nate.

"Darwin talks about the evolution/advancement of organ systems like the lungs, heart, and so on, that you mentioned, Doc." Nate appeared uneasy, as the entire class was as quiet as a cemetery, watching and listening to him.

"There can be upwards of four thousand *different* proteins in just *one* bacteria cell. And we have just a few more cells than a bacterium," he said, giving a weak smile, trying to lighten up his presentation as he felt real self-conscious at the moment.

Jude was watching him like a hawk.

"If we assume *only* two hundred amino acids bonding for some imaginary *specific* tiny protein, the number of possible protein combinations that could form is 10 to the 260th power. That's a one followed by 260 zeros."

Jude rudely interrupted. "Yeah, Nate, *but* given enough *time*," he said loudly enough to cause Nate to jump in his seat and turn to face Jude. "Time is the key factor, and we have 15 *billion* years of history." Jude was being so boisterous that some spittle inadvertently landed on Nate.

"Actually, I did my calculations based on 20 billion years, so I'm giving you an extra 5 billion, Jude," Nate calmly countered, as he wiped the spit from his shirt.

Jude was a bundle of emotion and practically screamed, "So what?"

Nate turned back around and continued, "Well, in 20 billion years, there's less than 10 to the 20th power of seconds in the entire known universe, and even if a new set of proteins were produced every second for 20 billion years, the chances of finding the one *exact* protein with the particular combination of 200 amino acids we need, is one chance in 10 to the 140th power—that's a one followed by 140 zeros."

"Nate, could you translate that last part into English for us non-statistic types," I asked.

"Sure. All statisticians adhere to Borel's Law, which states that once you reach a statistical probability of 10 to the 50th power, that's a 10 followed by—"

"And that means?" I interrupted Nate.

"No probability of an occurrence happening. Just plain zero, nada, zilch, goose egg." He quickly and quietly sat down.

Thirty sets of eyes, including mine, were all focused on Jude who was still standing beside his desk at the back of the room by the window. He was standing straight, arms stiff at his side with his fists clenched. His jaw tightened as the masseter muscles were clamped down rigid. One could have cut the tension in the room with a knife.

Maria then turned around to the class, her focus directed at Jude. "Listen to this article on C/NET from November 17, 2010. Researchers from the Stanford University School of Medicine have spent years engineering a new image model of our brain—"

"Who cares!" Jude still hyped up rudely interrupted.

Maria slowly stood. Her soft doe-brown eyes had fire in them, as she placed her hands on her hips. "The rest of the class, Jude, may be interested in Stanford's findings."

The standoff ended with Jude heatedly resuming his seat. Maria continued. "Stephen Smith a professor of molecular and cellular physiology, and a senior author of the paper stated, 'A single human brain has more switches than all the computers and routers and Internet connections on earth.' Maria took a deep breath. "All together—combined—not even equivalent to one human brain!"

Jim immediately bounded out of his chair railing against the Matrix and its control over the education system. "Why do we never hear about any of this strong convincing and challenging evidence? Ever!" He then plunked himself down again.

The students attempting to digest Maria's information seemed stunned, with a deafening silence which swept across the room.

CHAPTER THIRTY-FOUR

MR. AND MRS. MOUSETRAP

J im again broke the silence. "Hey, Nate, ole buddy, you made a slight error."

Jude who had subsequently seated himself perked up.

"I have? I double checked all my calculations."

"You said you based it on 20 billion years of time?"

"Correct." Nate answered with a very puzzled expression.

"According to Jude and most scientists, the universe is about 13 to 15 billion years old, and according to them, life on earth only began around 3.5 billion years ago. So your results were actually much more generous than they should have been." Jim smiled and half laughed to Nate, and the class as a whole.

Nate immediately started punching in numbers on his tablet. "That really should make it 10 to the—"

"Ten to the who cares which power," Jim said. "It's still one big fat zero, man." He cast a sideways glance at Jude, who was not a happy camper.

The class, responding to Jim's antics, stamped their feet and slapped their hands on their desks with laughter—all except Claudia, Maria, and Jude, of course. Nate was still concentrating, intent on re-working his calculations.

I still needed to cover our 'mechanical organism' to really ram home a few more points for my scoreboard. "So let's give Darwin a temporary dispensation. Assuming there is enough time, how does any organism know which parts to manufacture first, and then assemble it in a coordinated fashion to advance itself to the next evolutionary level, and *still* keep itself alive to reproduce? I want those of you with the objects I gave you to pass them around and share them with the others. Can someone tell us what the parts make up?"

After about twenty seconds, Philip answered. "They are parts of a mouse trap."

"Are you sure that they are not parts of a bear trap?" I asked.

"C'mon, Doc, they're too small," Philip responded.

"It was specifically designed for small mice only," Andy added.

"Are you telling me, Andy and Philip, that while blind chance is trying to assemble these five parts—remember, it took an entire class with brains to figure out—this mousetrap organism starves to death trying to design and organize itself?"

They both looked at each other quizzically.

"I'm baiting you. Pun intended," I added, smiling.

"Oh, yeah, why didn't we think of that?" Andy, our engineer, tilted his head and pressed two fingers against it.

Jude, not willing to give up on the time deal, comments, "There's got to be some way, over time, for it to assemble itself."

Philip turned to Jude. "A 'living' mousetrap organism will *starve to death* way before it's able to design, construct, and then in a proper sequential order, collate its parts. The enzyme and co-enzyme systems, hormones, feedback programs, and regulatory switch points—all protein based—are myriad."

I tried to advocate for Jude a bit. "Jude was not thinking as clearly as he could."

"I don't need anyone to defend me," Jude responded with rancor.

Jim piped up again. He's really humming on all cylinders. "And where is Mrs. Mousetrap? She has to *evolve* at the same time, same place, and with a perfectly complimentary reproductive system for mating with Mr. Mousetrap." He curled his fingers and put his hands to his eyes as though looking through binoculars for Mrs. Mousetrap.

The class is in hysterics. They were starting to get it—somewhat. I was about to bring up that intelligence = design = a designer = creator when Maggie giggled her way in to the fray.

"And what if Mr. Mousetrap's thingy *evolves* too big or Mrs. Mousetrap's thingy *evolves* too small or vice versa?" She was giggling to beat the band.

CHAPTER THIRTY-FIVE

MENTAL MASTURBATION

Thad, who had been taking all of this in, raised his hand. I desperately hoped he would bring some relevance and stability to the discussion, as I needed Maggie to stop her giggling.

"Doc, what about mutations? Aren't they supposed to advance evolution? How do they fit in?"

I cast my eye surreptitiously toward Jude. He sat upright and was now back in the game.

Philip commented. "Yeah, Doc, that *is* a challenge. Some mutations do offer an advantage."

"Good . . . you guys are thinking. Let's analyze this," I said, noting that Maggie's giggling had subsided.

"The classic mutation is sickle cell anemia," stated Andy.

"It's true that it can confer some protection against malaria," I confessed to the class.

Jude felt he has won a round and pumping his fist in the air delivered a loud "Yeah!"

Ali, who up to now had not contributed much, opened up. To Jude he said, "Listen man, I have sickle cell disease. It is called a *disease* for a reason, you jerk."

"Ali, I . . . we appreciate you giving us your personal insight on the subject. But could we dispense with the name calling, please."

"Sorry Doc, it's just when a sickle cell crisis hits it's . . . it's unbearably painful. My joints ache, I sweat, become short of breath;

I even had to have my spleen removed because the sickle cells plugged up my spleen. Now my immune system is weak, and I get sick more often."

"Tell the class why it's been given the name sickle cell."

"My doctor told me our red blood cells carry oxygen and are round, kinda like a donut without the hole. Round red blood cells are normal, but with sickle cell anemia, they are abnormal, shaped like a sickle, and don't carry oxygen well and can get stuck in blood vessels."

"So if I . . . we all understand what you just said, round is the normal cell and sickle is the abnormal cell, correct?" I ask, emphasizing the words *normal* and *abnormal*. "Now, evolution is supposed to be about advancement for the benefit of a species. Ali, according to evolutionary theory you are now more advanced with your abnormal sickle-shaped red blood cells." I stressed the word *abnormal* again.

"Doc, are you nuts? If I'm more advanced with my sickle cell *disease*, I'll take the *normal,* everyday, round ones anytime."

I assumed a serious tone. "Okay, no more semantics. This disease offers protection against malaria, but at what cost? The original red blood cell is normal and round. There was a *loss* of information that made it assume its sickle shape."

"Disease denotes something is wrong. Round to sickle shape equates with a *loss* of information, savvy?!"

Jude was very quiet, holding his head with both hands looking very distraught.

"Evolution, by definition, is supposed to equate with an ever upward and onward *gain* of information, not a *loss* of information."

Juan spoke. "There are wingless flies on windy islands that lost their wings so they don't blow away. It is an advantage."

Santi turned around to his cousin. "Hey, hombre. It's still a loss of information man."

Thad added, "I get it now. Same for the blind cave fish. Loss of sight, which is loss of information."

"Curious little finding a few years ago," I mentioned to the class, "There is a protein called HSP9O which *already* exists, and controls the gene expression for sight."

Jim interjected, "Betcha it's in the *off* position for those blind cave fish! Coulda had a V-8, man." He turned around and smacked Thad on *his* forehead and the class burst out laughing.

"That's right," hollered Nate, "that genetic off/on switch screams intelligence and engineered design; not some mystical environmental magical pressure of Mother Gaia."

Matt had decided to add his two cents. "One doesn't build wealth by losing money every day from his bank account."

"That's a real good analogy, Matt, good thinking."

Matt's chest puffed out. "Could I make another observation on this," he requested.

"Sure, have at it."

"If mutation is supposed to be a driving force for evolution, it's going backwards."

A low hum pulsated around the class. Even I was a bit surprised by Matt's astute analysis. Jude sat mum.

Maria put her hand up. "What do you wish to add, Maria?" I asked.

"Why even bother giving any degree of credibility to this worthless theory that doesn't hold water?" She asked as she stood to face the entire class. "Given the failed Miller model that Philip has presented, and brainy scientists who can't even create protein one from scratch raw elements, let alone a living, reproducing organism. As far as I'm concerned this has been a useless exercise in mental masturbation!" She abruptly sat down. The room was electric. The class was taken by surprise and left speechless by such words of truth coming from sweet innocent Maria.

CHAPTER THIRTY-SIX

E.T. PHONE HOME

*T*hese kids still have no idea of where the source of truth and the basis of correct thinking originates, I thought. I wanted to move on and start tying the discussion in with some of what Emily and I were discussing the other evening.

Philip had his hand up.

"Philip," I said, giving him a slight wave of my hand indicating for him to proceed.

"Doc, there is a school of thought among some scientists that agree evolution is incapable of occurring on earth, for many of the same reasons we have been discussing here." He looked around to see if anyone else in the class was aware of this.

Wanting him to clarify I said, "Go on."

"Well, some quarters of the scientific community believe that life came from outer space, and the earth was seeded by aliens bringing DNA or intact organisms, or possibly even fully formed humanoids."

Matt, our sci-fi guru, was beside himself. "Yeah, ancient aliens, man. That's the ticket. They came to the earth eons ago and seeded life here," interjecting, clapping his hands.

Jude was bulking up and ready to re-engage now. Speaking with assurance, as if it was already proven. "Absolutely, a superior race of beings came from some distant galaxy and planted life on earth."

"Really!?" I responded with a slightly doubtful tone.

I looked down at Maria and gave her one of my winks. She winked back. I believe she knew the tact I was going to take.

Matt was still babbling. "Yeah, real aliens. Cool. I really would like to meet one of my ancestors."

"Jude, question. Where and how did this superior race of beings originate?"

"Huh?" was Jude's response.

Meanwhile, Pete leaned over and smacked Matt a few times on the arm to get his attention. "Chill out, Matt, I think the Doc has something up his sleeve."

"Okay, it seems Philip and Matt, and of course you Jude, are changing course that *no* evolution was capable of occurring on earth, correct?"

"Yeah," Jude conceded. I saw he was a bit nervous, as his eyes shifted around the room looking for someone to supply supportive evidence for his position.

"So if there is no evolution, how did *this* race of superior beings come about?"

Jude was repeatedly wetting his lips, as his mouth was becoming dry, and he was fidgeting with his fingers.

"They were seeded by another even *more* superior race from some other planet."

"Even farther out in space, I suspect." I narrowed my eyebrows with doubt. "And who seeded *them*?" I asked as I leaned my elbows on the lab table twiddling my thumbs.

"I . . . uh . . ."

"Jude, we could play this game ad infinitum." I stood up placing my outstretched arms on the lab table. "The problem is, you eventually will have to fall back on the evolutionary model as the starting point for one of these distant societies, which supposedly began the seeding process planet to planet. And you and Philip agreed that evolution doesn't work, *right?*"

Matt was completely bummed out. He had his head in his hands and seemed to be staring at the top of his desk. "I get it now. The discovery of water on other worlds is just not enough. And I really did want to meet an alien; I really did." He was shaking his head while still holding it. "There is no life in outer space. There will be no contact. No aliens. No E.T. They don't exist." He looked like he was about to cry.

Santi, who actually felt bad for Matt, tried to use himself as a joke to pick up Matt's spirits. He turned in his seat toward him. "Oye, hombre, I'm an alien; I'll be your friend."

Matt, dejected and still looking down at his desk, said, "Santi, I didn't mean an *illegal* alien."

The class broke into uproarious laughter.

CHAPTER THIRTY-SEVEN

THE ROD

I t was premature of me to think that the class had ended on a positive note. I thought I was going to have a few minutes to collect my thoughts before taking the class over to the quadrangle to meet with Fred.

We all heard a loud thud. Jude had not taken the day's lesson lightly and had slammed his fist down hard onto his desk. I thought I heard a crack. Was it the desk or the bone of his right fifth metacarpal and digit?

"Jude, are you all right?"

He mumbled something incoherent and just ignored me and the class; he turned his gaze out the window, massaging his hand.

I figured it was best to just leave him be.

Then Maggie, the libertine and exhibitionist, started in. I noticed during the class that her left wrist had a professionally done bandage. Maggie was right handed.

She stood up and took out the small rod that I gave her when she entered the class. She had been the recipient of one part of the mousetrap puzzle; the hold down bar that attaches to the clasp that keeps the spring and hammer in place.

She turned to face the class and began to caress the three-inch rod seductively.

"I like poles," she purred, as she rubbed the tiny object up and down. Then, in an almost imperceivable motion, she quickly thrust out her tongue toward the little shaft. She partially opened her red lips and curled the tip of her tongue behind the back of her upper lip and slowly slid it across her top teeth while moving the little rod up and down between her breasts.

All the guys in the class were bug-eyed, fixated on her. Claudia's nose was so out of joint and up in the air, she could catch flies in it. Maria squeezed her gold cross so hard that it likely left an imprint in her hand for quite some time. I was dumbfounded, never having had to deal with anything the likes of this while teaching decades ago. I just stared in total disbelief.

Tom, who hadn't participated at all during the lesson, stood up.

Maggie didn't see him at first, as she had turned toward the front, facing me.

Tom began to mimic her actions and took his hands palms up, placed them at the sides of his chest moving them up and down, as if to imitate Maggie's large heaving bosom movements. "Hey Maggie, that would be all well and good, if those things were real," he chided, laughing at her expense.

Maggie turned to confront him, her green eyes ablaze and her ruby-colored nails extended like claws. She recoiled very slightly into a subtle crouch as though poised to pounce on her prey.

Tom's eyes grew big with fear. He cowered and took a step back.

Maggie's lips retracted revealing her pearly white teeth, gritting, almost fang like, while spitting out - "You bastard." She threw the little rod at him. It missed his head by bare inches and cracked the window. I heard the metal hold down bar tinkle down, lost among Brother Francis' plants on the window ledge.

"You never had any complaints when we were in bed together—*with* your twin sister," she spewed.

Somehow I managed to clear my head sufficiently to coalesce some words into a sentence. Then exerting some baritone authority, I announced, "That *will* be enough from the both of you! Class dismissed. Maggie, you stay!"

CHAPTER THIRTY-EIGHT

MAGGIE'S CONFESSION

The students exited the room by both the front and rear doors, some glancing back at Maggie, who was seated quietly in her desk at the very front of the room.

As the last student left, I asked him to leave the door open. I walked around from the back of the lab table and propped myself on the left front corner of my wooden desk.

Maggie was still silent, blankly staring at the back of my desk, obviously ignoring me as I was almost directly in her line of sight. The whites of her eyes were becoming slightly red and puffy and starting to glisten. She wanted to cry, but was holding it back.

With her eyes still fixed on my desk, she spoke slowly in a very low, almost inaudible voice. "I'm dying from the inside out."

"Maggie, why don't you tell me about the self inflicted cuts." Delivering my statement in as compassionate a tone as I could, I pointed at her left wrist.

She immediately looked up at me. "Who told you? How did you know?"

"No one, Maggie. I've been a physician for years and have seen this kind of thing many times."

"My whole life has been one big mess," she confessed as tears started to run down her cheeks.

"When did this all begin?" I asked, again in as amiable a voice as I could effect.

"Trust me, you don't want to know," she said, looking back down at my desk in an attempt to avoid a very painful part of her life.

"Try me," I said, mustering a tone that conveyed I really did want to listen to her.

"Whatever," she indifferently responded; still looking at the back of my desk, feeling that it won't make any difference one way or the other.

"Did you have a pleasant childhood?" I asked, trying to kick-start the conversation.

"Yes," she looked up at me, responding in a very positive tone to pleasant childhood memories.

"Any favorite times?" I continued, trying to get her to engage.

"Oh I remember very clearly, like it was yesterday, when I was about five or six years old, I had a small bit part in some forgettable Hollywood movie."

"Really!" I exclaimed, wanting Maggie to give me more info.

"My dad had a catering business, which fed the cast and crew on the sets. He often went on location with them. He also ran a transportation leasing company that supplied trucks and other vehicles for the movies. One period film took place in the early 1900s and they needed one of those open-carriage type Model T cars. You know the ones they needed to crank up in the front and the driver would wear a long coat with the funny hat and goggles?"

"Yes, I've seen a few of those types of movies. So your dad furnished the car?"

"Yes, and the scene called for the couple to have their daughter with them in the car. I happened to be on the set that day. My dad would take me with him sometimes. It was exciting to be on a real Hollywood movie set."

"I wound up playing the daughter in the scene. They dressed me all up in a fancy dress with a big brimmed hat with a giant bow on it. Everyone said I looked like the little girl in *Gone with the Wind*."

"That sounded like fun."

"I still have some of the photos that were taken on the set that day," her face beamed as she reflected on those happy times.

"But it didn't last for long." Maggie's face suddenly dropped with sorrow.

"My dad and mom were always fighting like cats and dogs. Mom had a very weak personality and my dad had an arrogant and abusive ego. He was very good looking when he was young, and had a roaming eye. He cheated on my mom with a lot of the young up-and-coming starlets."

"He would come home drunk many times and berate my mom, throwing his male macho conquests right in her face. He didn't even *try* to hide his affairs. My mom internalized it all, regressing into her own small world of anti-depression pills. Before my mom became totally withdrawn on her drugs, she took my sister and me to church sporadically. I even attended Sunday school off and on for a few years."

"What happened to change you?" I asked.

"I felt that the whole religion thing was a phony racquet. Where was God? Wasn't he supposed to help my mother? She was just getting worse and worse. Then the Sunday school teachers and even the minister couldn't answer my questions."

"Such as?" I queried.

"Who did Adam and Eve's children marry? They can't marry each other; that's incest. Why do people have to suffer with diseases, like Ali? How did Noah squeeze millions of species of animals onto the ark? Where do ape-men and dinosaurs fit into the Bible? It doesn't even mention them."

"What did your Sunday school teachers and the minister tell you?"

"Nothing! Just trust in Jesus or ask your science teacher at school. What a load of crap. I eventually wound up on psych meds like my mom, including lithium for a while. I always felt like a zombie." I could hear the frustration and anxiety in her voice.

"Then the California school system, by this time, was teaching gender neutral identity and pushing sex on us, as early as the first grade."

"Yes, I remember when that started. It's pretty much spread around the country now. Letting children choose whatever gender they would like to identify with and which bathroom to use." I shook my head.

"I thought to myself, why identify with only one sex and only have half the fun? By eleven years old I was having sex with both my male and female classmates." Maggie looked down at the floor, shaking her head, knowing that what she did was wrong.

"Then my mom OD'd on her psych meds and died. At that point, I was about ready to end it all myself. By fourteen or fifteen I was attending Rave parties, getting drunk, doing all kinds of illegal drugs, and having sex with whomever. Nothing mattered to me." Maggie's eyes were watering heavily now.

"Would you like a napkin or something? All I have are these rough brown paper towels."

"I'll take one. My makeup is a disaster by now, anyway."

I handed her a couple of the paper towels. Her eyeliner and mascara *were* a mess.

"How did you manage to do so well in school? I've seen your records."

"I was lucky to get a good brain. My dad was smart and an excellent businessman, although a bit of a wheeler-dealer. I just needed to hear something once from a teacher and I got it. I was bored to death in classes, and half the time I came in with a hangover or strung out on drugs, legal and illegal."

"And now? Why choose my class?"

"No particular reason, perhaps for kicks. The name and description sounded intriguing to me. But after the first few sessions

. . ." Maggie really started to break down and sob. I waited for her to regain her composure.

Still sniffling and dabbing her eyes, she continued, "For the first time in my life, you made me think that there was something else. Something . . . maybe, just maybe, beyond ourselves. That we are not just a jumble of chemicals. That we are not just born to live, die, and go to nothingness."

Maggie continued, "Otherwise, if nothing means anything, then the strong powers that be, the Matrix will dominate and control us, knowing we have no other superior power we can turn to. And I'm not the only one thinking this way in your class. At lunch, some of us have had some real philosophical discussions about what you're teaching us. The turning point for me was when Santi broke down about his sisters. At that point, I decided to literally absorb everything you are teaching us."

"What did you do to change?"

"I swore off all the booze, all the drugs, and . . . and all the sex, at least for the time being." She looked down again at the floor somewhat embarrassed.

"I'm really, really sorry I lost it today in class; and I take full responsibility for it. It's just today was rough for me. It was last year that Tom and I—"

"Maggie, you don't need to explain that to me," as I cut her off.

She looked up at me somewhat relieved as well as a bit surprised, and still sniffling a bit. "Somehow Doc, I have a feeling that you are going to help us get our heads straight by explaining about diseases, pain, and suffering; Adam and Eve and Noah; cavemen, dinosaurs, and . . . and life's purpose and meaning."

I slightly nodded my head, giving her a faint smile. "I guess you'll have to stay sober and straight . . . and celibate for a while longer, until you get all your answers."

Maggie gave a slight smile and laugh, but the tears and mucus half choked her up in the process.

"Maggie, I'm going to ask you something in all seriousness. Would you be willing to meet with Dr. Dorothy Mercurio? She's the head of the religious studies department. She is also a qualified Christian psychologist who has helped many students. By the way, NO psychotropic drugs to zombify you!"

Maggie looked thoughtfully at me for only an instant. "Yes, I would," she stated very definitively. "Doesn't her husband, Vince, teach Tai Chi?"

"Yes, that's correct."

"Some of my friends take Tai Chi with him."

"That's nice," I said perfunctorily. "I'll let her know that you will be contacting her."

I looked at my watch. "Wow! Fred should already be there by now," I announced with an anxious tone.

"Could I still go?" Maggie pleaded.

"Of course, Maggie; I really believe you're going to be fine," smiling at her and giving her a thumbs up.

"Would it be okay with Mrs. Lucci if I gave you a hug?"

"Yeah, she probably would be giving you one herself if she were here."

Maggie stood up, came over, and gave me a modest hug.

"We better get hustling over to the quadrangle." And as we were both leaving the classroom, I looked at Maggie. "Your makeup!" I exclaimed loudly.

She turned in the opposite direction toward the lady's room. "I better fix my face before I freak everybody out," she stated while running down the hall.

CHAPTER THIRTY-NINE

MISTER FRED

By the time I reached the north side of the quadrangle, Fred was already in rare form. Most of the students had decided to come, especially Claudia. She was sitting on the grass in front of Fred with her skirt hiked up, showing Fred some leg with conspicuous alluring bedroom eyes. He was ignoring her.

All were there with the exception of Simon/Ali, Jude, and Tom. I was pleasantly surprised that Matt showed up, even after the "sci-fi" mental trouncing he had sustained in class. Some were sitting on the grass, a few on benches; others leaned against the large shady trees. Andy and Pete had secured possession of a very massive boulder and were both sitting on the top. Probably it had been excavated during the construction of the Sports Center and placed there by the landscaping committee.

To everyone's shock and amazement Maggie appeared, and quietly and unpretentiously sat on one of the benches. But something was different about her.

"Fred, go on, don't let me interrupt you," I said as I sat down on the bench with him. I gave Claudia a bit of a frown, and she pulled her skirt down, but just a little.

Fred had been talking about irreducible complexity when Matt asked him about mutation and evolution, which caught Fred off guard, but just momentarily.

"Don't bacteria mutate and evolve when exposed to antibiotics?"

"Good question, young man," Fred responded.

"It's Matt, sir."

Not missing a beat, Fred looked at him. "Okay then, Matt Sir." The group laughed loudly.

"I told you he was quick," I said to the class.

"Guess I must be getting old, Doc. First time I've been addressed as sir."

"But to answer your question, Matt, let's look at it objectively. What is one bacterium that is wrecking havoc in hospitals?"

"MRSA, big time," Matt states.

"For those of you who are not familiar, MRSA stands for Methicillin Resistant Staph Aureus. This bacterium is resistant to the antibiotic methicillin," as I barge in.

"So, Matt, what is the genus for this bacteria?" Fred queried Matt again.

Matt was looking around unsure of how to answer.

Maria, our nursing major, replied. "The genus is *Staphylococcus*, Mister Fred."

"Now, I'm *Mister* Fred," he answered, rolling his eyes while the class laughed again. "You are correct. That's the long form of the name. Sometimes we shorten it to just staph."

"And the species name?" Fred asked, looking at Maria for the remainder of the answer.

"*Aureus*," she replied politely as usual.

Looking over toward Matt, Fred asked, "Okay, Mister Matt." There were some chuckles. "The genus and species is *Staphylococcus* or *Staph Aureus*. What has it evolved into?"

"Huh?" Matt's forehead furrowed and he looked quizzically at Fred.

"Well, Matt, you said that the bacteria, in response to antibiotics, Methicillin in this case, has mutated and evolved. What has it evolved to? Its genus and species have not changed. It hasn't mutated into a different species of bacteria, let alone some other higher organism. Variation and adaptability, yes, but evolution?" With that Fred held his hands palms up and lifted his eyebrows, waiting for a rebuttal from Matt.

Matt just sat there dumbfounded. Several other students were scratching their heads.

Maria turned to Matt. "We're back to a loss of information again."

Philip asked Maria, "What about plasmids in bacteria that exchange DNA information as a means to develop antibiotic resistance?"

Before Maria had a chance to respond, Philip caught himself. "Oops, my bad," leaving several students wondering what happened.

Fred looked at Maria, "Better explain what that Asian gentleman said."

"Plasmids *exchange* DNA information, which *already* exists. There is *no new* DNA information created. Evolution claims, as Doc said, to move upward and onward creating more and new different information. A horse has more info (DNA) for eyes, lungs, heart, etcetera than an amoeba. Where is this evidence that evolution creates new information?"

I glanced toward Maggie who was listening very intently. She was nodding her head, as were the others—they got it.

"Thank you, young lady," Fred addressed Maria. "You must be majoring in one of the life sciences?"

"Maria is a nursing student," I told Fred.

"And a very intelligent one, at that," Fred added, complementing her.

"Just to put the final nail in the coffin on the idea of mutating bacteria 'proving' evolution, I'll tell you this story," Fred stated, as I stood to stretch my legs.

"A number of years ago, they found the frozen bodies of some explorers who died around 1850. Their bodies were discovered north of Canada around the Arctic Circle. They were trying to find the Northwest Passage."

"How disgusting," Claudia chimed in, as I note a slight sallow color change.

"The point is," Fred continued, "that autopsies in 1988 showed some of the bacterial strains found in their gut were *already* resistant to powerful modern antibiotics such as cefoxitin and clindamycin."

The class was silent, not exactly sure what to say. Finally, Maria turned to the group and asked them, "When was even basic penicillin first used in any quantities?"

Jim was the one to finally speak. "Guess I'll need another V-8. These guys died almost a hundred years before penicillin was even discovered, and then used during World War II in large amounts. And these strains of bacteria in the gut of the explorers' dead, frozen, bloated bodies were *already* resistant to modern sophisticated antibiotics!"

I noticed Jim momentarily shift his eyes toward Claudia as he was stating this, aware of her delicate sensibilities. She was turning a putrid shade of green.

"Absolutely correct," Fred remarked looking at Jim and glancing at queasy Claudia. "Again, no true evolution, no new information has taken place—just variation or modification on what *already* existed."

Suddenly I realized what was different about Maggie. She had toned down the war paint.

CHAPTER FORTY

BOMBARDIER BEETLE

I walked on the grass to the edge of the rosé colored paving stones that covered the quadrangle. I could still hear Fred, as he was only about thirty feet from me. I could also see the marble statue of Mary somewhat down a ways on my left at the edge of the quadrangle. But something was going on, in the center, around the flagpole. Someone was setting up some speakers on extension poles with tripod bases. The small circular wall, which enclosed the garden at the base of the flagpole, was considered to be a free speech zone. On occasion there were placards or signs. One could frequently find students gathered there with someone standing on the wall, using it as their soapbox to present their discourse on whatever topic suited them. This led to lively and, at times, volatile exchanges. But this was definitely different; more of a professional style setup.

I walked along the edge of the quadrangle, passing the statue of Mary until I could see one of the student parking lots through the trees on my left. There was a large van with the logo of one of the big three local affiliate networks on it, complete with satellite dish and antennas. Something was up.

These guys were from Harrisonburg, about sixty miles down I-81 from Front Royal. The Harrisonburg market encompassed us on their northern periphery. Father called them the Atheist, Communist, and Numbnuts Broadcasting Corporations.

What are they doing here today? I thought. I noticed Fred was approaching me.

"Hey man, you guys finished up?" I asked Fred, as we continued to walk along the quadrangle's perimeter.

"Yeah, and you've got some very sharp cookies in your class. They are really thinking things through, Doc. I see that you already covered irreducible complexity with the mousetrap - they were all over that."

"Anything new I should know about that you already went over with them?" I asked.

"We covered the bombardier beetle, the woodpecker, and the giraffe," Fred explained. "They were laughing like hyenas over the bombardier beetle."

"I was wondering what was going on with you guys. I could hear the group breaking up all the way from here."

"Well, when challenged to describe how an insect with two 'tanks' filled with explosive gases and twin synchronous rotating machine guns could evolve slowly over eons of time without blowing itself up each step of the way, they just couldn't contain themselves."

"That student of yours, Jim, the V-8 guy." Fred began.

"Yes?" I asked, wondering what antics Jim had been up to.

"He kept looking around for Mrs. Bombardier beetle to see if she hadn't blown herself up yet, so they could mate."

"Yes, that's Jim alright," I said lightly shaking my head.

"Oh, and that leggy brunette who was sitting in front of me?"

"Yes, Claudia," I answered in a half apologetic tone.

"She asked me what my wife does."

"What did you tell her?"

"Oh, I coolly mentioned that she likes to file her nails down to a point. She must have bounced back a foot and then jumped up looking around, even up into the trees."

"What?" I stated somewhat confused.

"I guess she was half expecting Cindy to swing down like Tarzan—or should I say like Jane—and scratch her eyes out. She then took off like a shot."

Both of us laughed, picturing Claudia running in her high heels down the path like a mad woman.

Fred pointed to the TV truck in the parking lot. "What gives?"

"I was about to ask you the same question."

"Well, look who's getting out of the van," Fred remarked sarcastically.

CHAPTER FORTY-ONE

COVER GIRL

"It's the B-witched lady herself, Kathy Owens," Fred stated with marked cynicism in his voice.

"Yes, I recognize her," I noted. "She's the anchorette on the six o'clock news from Harrisonburg. She thinks she's hot stuff."

Fred sneered slightly and shook his head. "Liz Wheeler, she ain't. She doesn't have the personality, nor the knowledge, nor the class Wheeler has."

"I get the impression she has designs to move up the news ladder to Washington where the big bucks are. The Harrisonburg market is just too common and plebian for her tastes. We are the unwashed masses to her."

"The only thing Kathy and Liz have in common is that they are both blondes," added Fred. "Do you know she wears five or six-inch heels to make herself look taller? Kathy's only about five one."

"I didn't realize that," I admitted with a slight downturn of my lips, indicating I couldn't care less. "By the way, what did you call her—B-witched?"

"Oh," Fred chuckled, "Cindy and I use that term, especially when the kids are around. We don't want them to pick up any bad language and then use it with their friends."

"I see now," I laughed. "Substitute the W for the B, got it."

I pointed. "Check it out Fred - she's got *two* cameramen with her. Someone has orchestrated something for the free speech zone and has clued Kathy Owens in on it—for the big scoop!"

"Oh yeah," said Fred, "a Pulitzer would be a *big* feather in her hat, and launch her to journalistic stardom."

"And the megabucks that go along with it," I concluded.

We both noticed three very large charter buses pulling into the student parking lot at the back end, as if to stay out of camera range. They were fully packed with people.

"Those are definitely not ICC buses. Someone is attempting to rig this spectacle in their favor," Fred observed. "Look over there, Doc. Coming this way, from the Student Union building. It's Erik Meisner and a bunch of his SS wannabes."

"Erik is the lieutenant and muscle for—"

"Let me guess," I quickly interjected. "Professor Dietrich?"

"I knew I smelled a rat," Fred replied, really sneering now. "Dietrich and Owens . . . it figures - two really bad apples."

Erik appeared to be of above average height with an athletic build. He had sandy blonde hair trimmed in a semi-military or athletic style: close with a tapered cut on the sides and gelled on the top. I later discovered that he had piercing blue eyes. Erik, as well as his crew, all had on their "uniform": khaki pants, sky blue collared button-down shirts, and black Corfam boots.

"Fred, what's with the wooden nightstick dangling in the holster off his belt?"

"That's his calling card, Doc. The guy is a real throwback to the Nazi storm troopers. And I've seen him use it - even on his own men."

"They also call themselves the Blueshirts." Fred reflected, "I wonder if they are aware that Hitler had his Brownshirts and Mussolini his Blackshirts."

We both take note that Erik bossed around the cameramen and others on the TV crew. As her high heels clicked a mile a minute, like a secretary at an old metal typewriter, Kathy flew over and got right in Erik's face.

"Look Blue Boy, these are *my* men, and they take orders from *me*, and *me* only. You stick to being a tin soldier with the other little Blue Boys, got it!?" she screeched, pointing her index finger almost up Erik's nose.

Erik just stood there and took it. His face was red as a beet, his jaw was clenched, and I just about saw steam coming from his ears.

"Man, I've *never* seen Erik like this before," Fred stated half serious and half laughing at seeing the sight. "He doesn't even realize that Kathy is ridiculing him, by using the reference to Gainsborough's famous painting, *The Blue Boy*."

"Oh yeah," I replied laughing, "that's the one of the pansy-looking rich kid Gainsborough painted wearing the blue duds."

Erik backed off and sulked away, calling his men together for a strategy session regarding the free speech zone fanfare that was about to start.

Fred then pointed out. "Look, the man himself, coming out of the social sciences building. It's Professor Dietrich."

"That's Dietrich?" I reacted with incredulity. "The guy looks like a clown. Fred, you really need to get with him and teach him how to dress; obviously he never had a mother to do it."

Dietrich was about five six or five seven, probably in his late forties to early fifties, severely balding with quite a beer paunch on him. He had a few residual strands of gray hair on top. The hair on the sides was pulled back into a small pigtail.

"That's him," Fred answered, "Birkenstocks and all."

"Geez, Fred, you're right. I missed the Birkenstock sandals; and when was the last time he pressed his khakis?"

"They're always that way. Probably takes them out of the dryer damp and wrinkled, and just puts them on. It's his '60s style tie-dyed T-shirt which clashes with the faded sport jacket he out-grew twenty years ago that denies him 'Cover Girl' status."

"'Cover Girl'," I repeated Fred's derogatory satire, as I wiped tears of laughter from my eyes. "Oh my, God, is that lipstick he's wearing?" I was really about to lose it.

CHAPTER FORTY-TWO

THE WORLD ECOLOGY FLAG

"Yes, Dietrich was one of the many Washington bureaucrats to come out of the closet when the Obama Supreme Court legalized same-sex marriage several years ago."

"He's married to some guy? Is Dietrich the male or the female?" I asked Fred in amazement.

"He and his partner, spouse, or whatever, divorced a few years back." Fred replied.

"Who got custody of the children?" I looked at Fred with forged sarcastic curiosity, unable to keep a straight face, as I was still wiping the tears coming down my cheeks.

"Doc, you better see what's happening." Fred's demeanor turned serious.

The people were exiting the buses, and Erik and his troops were escorting them to the area about the flagpole in front of the twin tripod speakers. They timed it for the end of the morning class sessions and the beginning of the lunch hour breaks. Students and faculty began to mix in with the crowd of paid interlopers.

Most of my students had apparently hung around after Fred had finished speaking with them. They were curious as to what was going on. Again missing were Tom, Ali, and Jude. Claudia and Maggie were also absent.

The boys were all the way at the back, away from the crowd. They were a short distance, perhaps thirty feet from the statue of

Mary, aligned like the Rockettes, in a straight formation. Maria, the only woman now, stood on one side of the statue.

The crowd was ready and prepped. Kathy Owens was close to the front near the edge of the wall surrounding the flagpole. She gave a small hand signal to Dietrich and a nod to her cameramen. Fred and I, who were off to the side, moved a little closer to make sure we could hear her. One of the cameramen was up front with Kathy to capture Dietrich talking. The other was a short distance away scanning the crowd to capture their reaction as Dietrich spoke.

Dietrich advanced forward on Kathy's signal and attempted to mount the small two-foot wall and almost tripped. Luckily the camera was focused on Kathy at that moment.

"This is Kathy Owens, coming to you *live* on a beautiful fall day from the lovely campus of Immaculate Conception College in Front Royal. We are at their free-speech zone, centrally located by their massive flagpole."

Father Ed had shown up and was standing at the statue of Mary opposite Maria. He saw me and nodded.

Kathy continued, "We have a great turnout today of students and faculty to hear words of wisdom from one of the intellectual powerhouses in the academic community: Professor Marvin Dietrich." Her assistant handed a cordless microphone to Dietrich.

"Thank you, Kathy, and thank you all for being so kind as to turn out today. I have some information of importance to bestow on you," he announced, giving the crowd a big plastic smile and a wave of his hand.

I turned to Fred, "Humble, he ain't."

"And pretentious, he is," Fred shot back.

Meanwhile Kathy's assistant actually held up an applause sign for the rent-a-crowd people to clap. The cameraman adjusted for a tight close-up of a few of the hired help clapping.

Some of the real students and faculty looked at each other with mouths agape. "Is this some perverted afternoon game show?" I asked Fred with a scowl on my face.

"The first order of business . . . I . . . a . . . things I would like to talk to you about, is our wonderful World Ecology Flag. We are uniting our world together in the spirit of the Age of Enlightenment: Liberté, égalité, and fraternité."

"He sure knows how to butcher the French language," Fred commented. Dietrich's pronunciation *was* atrocious.

"We will still fly our American flag, as it is important to the people of the United States. But as we have become a One World . . . ah . . . um . . . unified world, we must give precedence to the whole, as we are just *one* of its parts."

Dietrich continued, "We must not appear imperialistic or nationalistic with expansionist designs any longer. We must lead the way in the unity of all nations - none greater or lesser than another."

The applause sign went up, accompanied by loud hooting, clapping, and the blaring of air horns from the rent-a-mob. Some of our own students were clapping. Oh boy, there is Jude in the center of the crowd, rooting and cheering along with them.

With his last statement, Dietrich looked over toward Erik, who sent two of his Blueshirt lackeys up on the wall. They tromped up to the flagpole, trampling all the flowers as they went. They unwrapped the halyard line from its cleat hitch and lowered the flags.

Kathy Owens, looking into her camera, addressed her TV audience. "This is a milestone nonpareil, as flags all around the country today are positioned in their *proper* order. It was decided for Virginia to document this historic occasion at a local college. The students are our future, and they bear witness to this landmark event," she announced as she gave a cheesy toothy smile to the camera.

The two Blueshirts reversed the flags, placing the Stars and Stripes beneath the World Ecology Flag, carelessly permitting our nation's symbol to drag along the ground. They proceeded to hoist them back up to the top of the pole.

"I want to vomit," I admitted to Fred. "Now those two blockheads of Erik's are saluting the accursed thing."

I glanced over toward Father. He had his stone face on, and one hand was gripping the base of the statue of Mary so hard I thought he would crush the marble.

"Classic socialist approach. Soften up the masses by getting them used to something first; then the hammer comes down, but in such a way they don't even realize they've been clobbered."

Fred nodded his head with pursed lips. "How many months did they have that damn thing up there to begin with?"

"I got a good close look at that Ecology Flag while they had it lowered. Did you see what I saw Fred?"

CHAPTER FORTY-THREE

A NEW RELIGION

"Yeah, I believe I picked up on most of it." Fred responded. I commented, "The flag itself is white, and it has that huge circle divided into three sections, each separated with a semicircle."

Fred followed through. "Blue for sky, green for sea, and brown for land. With white birds in the blue sky portion, white fish in the green sea section, and then white trees and grass in the brown area."

"Yeah, I saw that Fred, but did you see what was ringing that tripartite circle?"

"That I couldn't clearly make out. I just saw some very small black markings encompassing the circle spaced away from the outer edge of it. What were those symbols?"

"Fred, those tiny black characters were the symbols for each of the major world religions. You've seen them on bumper stickers."

"Oh, yeah."

"Well, the powers that be, want us all to get along or coexist or tolerate one another, but with one big caveat."

"What's that?" Fred asked inquisitively.

"We are to do so under the overarching umbrella of Mother Earth. It's as if the religions were all bowing and subservient to her authority—and rule. That's why they were presented as so small and insignificant around Mother Gaia."

"Got it. Yeah, the Illuminati look at all religions as equal— equally *useless* in the scheme of things, or detrimental and intrusive at worst. These cognoscenti are the high priests of this new religion. They alone possess the proficiency and competence to interpret and dispense the laws of this new religion. The temples where this crap is taught are the schools and universities. Mother Earth first and foremost, and man the parasite, last."

"Fred, you nailed it man."

"And Doc, what a slick con game to tax the people more. Hey, it's to protect and promote our Mother who gave us life." Fred snidely remarked.

"Fred, you could have written my course curriculum. I've already started to cover some of this confidence racquet indirectly with my students."

With my last comment to Fred, Dietrich's voice became shrill and crackling over the loudspeakers. "Under our new banner which now flies above us all, we will truly have freedom, equality, and fellowship among men, women or whichever chosen gender orientation. Freedom of sexual partners, freedom of recreational pharmaceuticals. Everyone will be equal in all financial matters and all endeavors. No favoritisms. Tolerance and equality are to be our watchwords. And unity with Mother Gaia, our touchstone."

The crowd went wild, cheering, clapping, and hollering with fist pumps in the air all around. There were also some signs and placards waving.

I observed that all the various signboards were made of the same thick white poster material, and the wooden stakes they were attached to were exactly the same. The writing on the signs was different, but their inscriptions were all made with the same black and red markers. All the printing or cursive was done using the same wide chisel tip pens.

"Hey, Fred, what do you make of the signs?" I asked, wanting to see if he picked up on the same clues I had.

"That bunch of clowns came off the buses with those posters. They even handed some to our own students to hold. Look at all the misspelling on some of the signs. College students, my ass!"

Dietrich continued with his sermonizing and grandstanding. "This is to be a worldwide revival of the Age of Enlightenment, a new French Revolution for the world. No longer a globe of petty bickering and rivalry among religions. We will all work together for the common good with Mother Earth, our beacon and North star."

Another round of howling and clamoring ensued. Kathy Owens' bubble-headed assistant was jumping up and down with her applause sign. She looked like a sixties Berkeley reject, wearing the huge round black coke bottle eyeglasses.

"Boy, is he ever full of himself," Fred commented, shaking his head.

"The bigger they are the harder they fall, as the old adage goes. And Dietrich is pretty big!" I mimed Dietrich's protuberant potbelly while puffing up my cheeks.

Fred laughed loudly, bending over putting his hands on his knees. There must have been a lull in Dietrich's speech at that moment and the crowd was relatively silent, making Fred's laughter stand out. Dietrich turned his head toward Fred and I. His eyes narrowed and squinted a bit, but he applied his broad fabricated smile to his face for the ever-present cameras.

Fred straightened up, realizing something was amiss as Dietrich addressed me in a controlled and deliberate voice. "Well, it seems we have one of our new professors with us this fine day." His counterfeit smile was still plastered on his face. He probably caught Fred and me in the act.

"Perhaps Dr. Lucci would like to join me on the stage . . . um . . . wall here, and add his thoughts to our discussion of liberty, tolerance, and fairness for all, in our new Age of Enlightenment?"

What sounded like a polite request was really a demand.

CHAPTER FORTY-FOUR

RENT-A-MOB

Dietrich took a breath and continued. "I'm sure our esteemed doctor feels as we all do, about equality and fairness for all." He beckoned the troops with a wave of his hand. Kathy Owens gave her applause sign girl an elbow to wake her up and do her thing.

The throng responded accordingly, clapping to encourage me to join Dietrich on the wall. This was his perfect opportunity to get me to agree with these supposed universal axioms. Who would or could possibly defy them, especially in front of the cameras?

I hopped up on the wall and gave the crowd a cursory wave and polite smile, and then turned to Dietrich. "Professor Dietrich," I said shaking his hand and looked him square in the eye. I gave a hint of a polite smile before quickly donning a serious expression.

"Well, Dr. Lucci, I'm sure you are in rapport with these time-honored maxims that we should all live by?" Dietrich held the mic so close to his mouth that his words came through somewhat distorted.

I turned my body to face the assemblage. Deliberately speaking in a low, mild voice, I got the response I was looking for. "We can't hear you," the mob at the rear shouted.

Giving Dietrich a closed mouth smile, I extended my hand, and he willingly gave me the mic. I gave a slight sideways glance to Kathy who had a cautious questionable look on her face.

"Yes!" I shouted and pumped my fist in the air. "Professor Dietrich is absolutely on target." I looked over to Kathy's gnome of an assistant, who got the message and raised the applause sign up to a round of cheers. The cameraman tightened his focus on me. Dietrich was beaming.

"Liberté, égalité, and fraternité," I used the correct French pronunciation, giving another fist pump, getting the crowd whipped up. Our little troll was dancing, raising the applause sign up and down to the accolades of the troops.

"Now that marijuana has been accepted by almost all the states, we need to move to legalize *all* drugs!" I gave another big fist pump and screamed, "Yeah!" so loudly the speakers reverberated with distortion. The masses were with me. Virtually everyone was screaming "yeah" and pumping their fists in the air.

I looked way back behind the crowd and saw my students standing there sort of dumbfounded. They were looking at each other with puzzled expressions. I could almost hear their thoughts: *has Lucci gone crazy?*

Pete leaned over to his brother, Andy, and whispered something, which Andy passed on down the line. Soon they were all smiling and laughing with one another.

Pete gave me a thumbs-up, which the cameramen and the mob in front of them didn't notice. I gave a brief fleeting smile and nodded back to him. Pete took heed of it. I looked over to Maria leaning slightly against the statue of Mary and gave her a wink. She couldn't wink back, as she was covering her mouth, trying to muffle her laughter. I saw her move slightly toward Father Ed to give him the skinny on what was about to occur.

"Crystal Meth—Yeah!" The horde was fist pumping and chanting "yeah" with me.

"Heroin—Yeah! Cocaine—Yeah!" The rent-a-mob was going berserk, all cheering and fist pumping like crazy. Jude was wild eyed and intoxicated with excitement.

My students at the back were really going at it, laughing and cracking up. Pete had obviously coordinated the sham. They were really putting on a show. The cameraman for the crowd had moved closer to my students, being as they were so much more animated than the borrow-a-bum ensemble.

There were two members from the rental crowd standing below me, in a vibrating frenzy. I leaned over with the microphone and asked them their names.

"Vincent, but yuz can call me Vinnie."

He looked like a squat compressed Arnold Schwarzenegger. "Where are you from Vinnie?" I asked bending over and extending the mic to him.

"Yo, Brucklun," he said proudly in his Brooklyn accent.

"Oh, New York," I responded.

He shook his head, as I extend the mic down to him again. "No, Brucklun." He emphatically replied.

"Isn't Brooklyn one of the boroughs of New . . . never mind." I glanced toward Kathy who wasn't smiling anymore.

"What are you majoring in here at ICC?"

Vinnie momentarily looked toward Kathy who shot daggers back at him. Vinnie then glanced over in Erik's direction for guidance. Erik just rolled his eyes. Some union buddy behind him whispered something to Vinnie.

"Yeah," Vinnie cleared his throat as I extended the mic down again. "I'm majoring in weight lifting." The speakers crackled and the crowed murmured, "What did he just say?"

"And your minor, Vinnie?" I asked still holding the mic in his face. Vinnie's gears were turning, and he erupted with "Latin!" A wave of guffaws and chuckling revolved around the group. Kathy's lips were so tight she could spit nickels.

I then directed my attention to the woman next to Vinnie. "And what is your name and where are you from young lady?"

I leaned over and stretched the mic toward her. "Um, mine is Annee with two Es. But is totally pronounced like the Broadway show *Annie*; and I'm totally from California, fer sur."

"San Fernando Valley?" I ask.

"Ehmagawd! Totally! How did you know?" Her thick accent blared over the loud speakers.

"Just a lucky guess, I suppose." I turned my head slightly to see Dietrich cover his face with his hand.

"And what are *you* majoring in?"

"Um, ballet, fer sur, and I'm minoring in . . . in diabetes, totally." She was gnawing on a large candy bar, which was not helping her Type 2 diabetes.

"Can you do a pirouette or grand jeté?" Observing this eighties style woman who was about five two and weighed in easily at over two hundred pounds.

"Um, fer sur, totally," she uttered, obviously uncertain as to what she just confessed she could do.

My students, at the back, were in hysterics. The multitude was now laughing with abandon.

CHAPTER FORTY-FIVE

LIBERTY, EQUALITY, FRATERNITY

As I straightened up, I held my hand up to quiet the crowd and then proceeded. "Keeping with the spirit of the Age of Enlightenment, I'm sure you wish to live and abide by the three rallying cries of the French Revolution. Are you committed to liberty?" I asked, pointing the mic at the herd.

"Yes!" they replied in unison.

"Are you committed to equality?" Again I pointed the mic at them.

"Yes!" was the response.

"And fraternity, which means brotherhood or union?"

Again, a resounding "Yes!" came from the crowd.

"These three rights are bestowed on you *by* our benevolent government. "

Once again with the mic pointed in the crowd's direction, they cried, "Yes!"

"We are to live in harmony with Mother Gaia—all equal, all the same, all together, all in union with one another?"

The mob once again responded, "Yes!"

"Are you absolutely sure?" Raising my voice for a more powerful response.

"Yes," they screamed back at me.

My guys at the back are making a spectacle, hollering, clamoring, and fist pumping the most. The rear cameraman moved even closer to capture this.

I asked for quiet again, as I leaned over. "So, Vinnie, you're all for this liberty, equality and fraternity stuff, right?"

"Yo, sure mang."

"And drug rights for all?" I asked him.

"Absolootly! I'll drink to dat!" He laughed, as he turned to his buddies who were yucking it up with him. "Yeah mang . . . sex, drugs, rock 'n' row . . . booze, ceegars, bongs, joynts, whaever. We shh av the right to doo it all." The speakers thundered his message.

He turned away from me and the mic, and toward the frenzied crowd, who were all shouting and yelling with Vinnie. He was doing double fist pumps by then and in sync with the swarm. Kathy's front cameraman zoomed in on Vinnie.

I waited for them to calm down a bit from their fevered pitch before using my hand to silence them. I then leaned over to Annee. "From all your gyrating around Annee, I surmise that you agree with all of this?"

She craned her neck up to speak into the microphone. "Oh, gnarly . . . like totally tubular." Her roly-poly stature was a big detriment.

Addressing her directly, I said, "Share and share alike . . . everyone equal. Union in brotherhood—and sisterhood too, of course."

Then I rotated the microphone back for her response. "It's like totally bitchin'," she said, giggling and cackling at the same time.

All of this was fed to the upfront camera and piped full pitch over the twin tripod loudspeakers for all to hear.

"So you're cool with equality and fraternity with Vinnie." I pointed my finger at Vinnie standing next to her.

"Vinnie, the bod, like totally." She batted her fake eyelashes at Vinnie who turned to the crowd and body posed, flexing his muscles to their cheers.

"That's really good to hear, Annee. So when Vinnie gets a myocardial infarction—a heart attack—from doing cocaine or liver failure from boozing too much or from doing steroids, you'll pay for his health care and disability, right?"

"Huh, gag me with a spoon. No way! He screwed hisself; let him pay for hisself." She turned toward Vinnie with bitterness, as if he had really put himself in that medical state.

Meanwhile, Kathy Owens, whose face was getting purple with rage, was attempting to attract Professor Dietrich's attention. She was mouthing at him to "get the mic."

"What happened to all the liberty, equality, and brotherhood, Annee?" I questioned in a sarcastic, teasing way.

Dietrich was unsuccessful at bending over trying to relieve me of the mic, as his expansive gut caused him to become unsteady on the wall.

"Like barf me out. Screw all that. He can spend his own bread." The loudspeakers trumpeted her words to everyone.

"Get the mic! Get the mic!" Kathy was screaming, forgetting she was still holding her own active microphone, being carried on real-time satellite transmission!

My students were falling over each other laughing, as their cameraman was also transmitting their antics as well.

Vinnie turned to Annee and got in her face. I managed to get the mic right between them to capture him saying, "Isen dork, I don wan yur stinkin doh anyway, you lil' toad."

Dietrich made one last heroic attempt to grab the mic and almost fell into the mob. Some of the union boys, who were right up against the wall, supported him back into position.

I heard one of them say, "Dey ain't payin me enuf for dis s**t!"

Annee screeched back into the mic at Vinnie, "Bag your face and eat my shorts, muscle head." The front cameraman caught it all, up close and personal.

Still bent over, I maneuvered the mic to myself, while looking at both Vinnie and Annee. "Being as Professor Dietrich is *more* equal financially than you both, and has that brotherhood of fraternité and fairness in his heart, I'm sure he'd sell his estate and Mercedes to pay the health-care costs and disability assistance for you both – due to your abuse and trashing of your own bodies." The loudspeakers projected my message clearly. "Because, I'm *not* paying one more dime for deadbeats!"

The mob was flustered now and becoming unruly, arguing one with another, and among groups, as to who should pay: Vinnie, Annee, Dietrich, both, all, or whoever.

I stood up pulling the mike away from Vinnie and Annee. I turned to Professor Dietrich who had just regained his balance. "Well, Professor Dietrich, I'm sure the troops are now ready to hear you articulate words of eloquence and elocution on the benefits and rewards of the French Revolution. Bon chance!"

I flipped the cordless microphone to him, which he almost dropped. *He catches like a girl,* I thought.

I hopped off the wall, leaving Dietrich with the surly mob. Kathy Owens was running to where her second cameraman was still actively recording my students who were having convulsions of hysteria.

Her high heels clicking fast, like an archaic typewriter, she screamed as she was rushing toward her cameraman, "You... [blast of an air horn]... jackass, turn off the camera, turn off the camera!"

By now I had almost reached my students, as well.

Pete, speaking to the boys said, "What a potty mouth she has. We should have brought the cussin' jar with us." This brought on another paroxysm of laughter.

As I ambled past Kathy, I commented with a smirk on my face, "So, how is it going today with Dietrich?"

She just snarled at me and spewed out her noxious reply, "Damn you, Lucci!"

"That'll cost her another buck," Pete nonchalantly stated, as another round of mirth and delirium bounced around the guys again.

CHAPTER FORTY-SIX

BROTHER FRANCIS

My mind was back in the classroom, still bubble-wrapping specimens, when I decided to take a small break and walk over to the windows. The day was magnificent, the Blue Ridge Mountains crystal clear in the distance after yesterday's rain; although, I can't locate where that singing bird is in the poplar tree.

I realized I was looking out of the pane of glass that had been replaced by Brother Francis; the one Maggie hit when she threw the holding rod from the mousetrap at Tom several months ago. I could barely detect the new replacement. As I looked down toward the window ledge, I see the tiny metal rod neatly placed up against the side of the window frame. I wonder why Brother Francis just didn't throw it away.

I chuckle, as my thoughts wander back to when I bumped into Brother Francis on one of the walkways about two weeks after the Owens-Dietrich calamity at the flagpole. I had been on my way to see Dr. Dorothy Mercurio at the time.

As we approached each other, I waved and he gave me his typical big generous smile. "I noticed that the broken window in my classroom was repaired, and I have a notion as to who the angel was that repaired it," I said, giving him a big smile in return.

"Well, I needed to come by and water the plants in the room anyway, when I saw the broken window pane. While I was replacing it, I found a small metal bar down between the pots, which perfectly fit the size of the hole in the window. What happened?"

"Trust me, you *don't* want to know." I replied, not wishing further inquiry into the matter.

I shifted gears quickly. "I'm really glad I bumped into you today. I've been meaning to get with you. I understand that you have a CDL license to drive the ICC buses."

"Yes, that's true. I've done it all from MMA fighting to dirt track racing—open-wheel midget to full-bodied stock cars and even the big rigs. And I've got the scars and tats to prove it," he said, rolling up the wide sleeves of his brown tunic to show me.

My eyes bugged out at all the tattoos on both his arms. "How in heaven's name did *you* become a monk?"

"My life was going down the fast lane, and in the wrong direction, if you catch my meaning. I had a really bad accident during one of the race events. They told me I'd never walk again." He gave a heavy sigh, reflecting on this life-changing moment of his.

"I didn't even know if God existed. But while strapped to that hospital bed, I had a lot of time to think. I made Him a promise that if He got me better and walking again, I would do something positive with my life—and here I am!" he exclaimed, giving me that big smile again. "I'm able to work out and even teach Mixed Martial Arts on the side to the students."

"That is an incredible story of yours, Brother Francis, truly inspiring and uplifting. You need to share it with others."

"By the way, where do you plan on going that you need an ICC bus?" he asked.

"Well, I'm planning on taking my class on a trip to a local fossil dig and then to some museums in a few weeks. I was wondering if you would be available to do the driving for us, as we probably will be away for about a week."

"I thought fossils were only at the Grand Canyon, Montana, and Utah?" Brother Francis asked, voicing some doubt.

"We have fossil beds right here in Virginia and Tennessee, a few hours down the road on I-81."

"Really, I never knew!" Brother Francis looked really surprised.

"There are fossil graveyards all over the world. There may even be one right under where you are standing."

Brother Francis looked down at the walkway. "No s**t! Oops." He quickly blessed himself, as his face immediately became the color of a turnip. "Sorry about that. I sometimes fall back into my old habits. But how do they know where to dig?"

"Wind, rain, and erosion cause the fossils to reveal themselves, and then paleontologists know where to dig." I answered, ignoring his slipup. "There also are a lot of rock formations along I-81, which reveal evidence for Noah's Flood, that we will stop to examine along the way."

"Noah's Flood? I thought that Genesis story was just a biblical metaphor or possibly only a local event that took place in the Middle East somewhere." Brother Francis looked at me like a cow staring at a new gate.

"If Noah's Flood was just a local run-of-the mill rainstorm, why bother spending years building the ark? All the animals could have been outta there in a nanosecond, and Noah and his family could easily have taken their time and walked over the hill to escape God's warning of the upcoming 'local' flood, still years down the road."

"Doc, are you saying that this really happened? That Noah and the Flood was a real global cataclysm?" he asked like a confused pagan.

"Where do you think all the dead animals and plants that became fossils came from, Brother Francis?"

"I . . . uh . . . I thought it took millions of years for something to fossilize," he stated, still totally confused.

"We have known for decades now that fossilization can occur in a matter of months to a couple of years, at most."

"Get outta town. Are you for real, Doc?"

"We have discovered fossilized spark plugs, hats, sacks of flour, a petrified ham, and even a severed part of a lower leg with its foot bones still inside a cowboy boot—all fossilized. Those objects didn't take millions of years to fossilize!" I said as I searched for an image on my tablet:

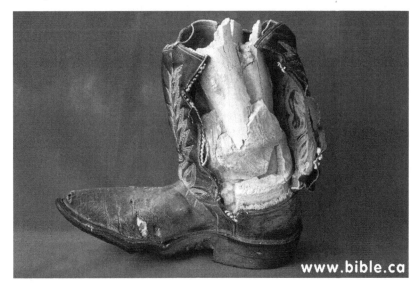

Photo of cowboy boot with foot bones inside. www.bible.ca
Photo credit: Dr. Don Patton

"Wow! This totally blows my mind. I had *no* idea."

"Do you know homeowners can now order wood floors for their houses and have the wood custom fossilized—basically transformed into stone—before installation?"

"No . . . incredible! Wow! If only they could turn coal into diamonds?"

I just stared at Brother Francis with a smirk on my face while nodding my head.

"Are you serious? Diamonds? It takes a lump of coal millions of years to transform into a diamond."

"No, not millions of years, just a lot of pressure, basically—and in a few days! And you can buy them for your mom or fiancée for half the cost or less. Even a gemologist can't tell the difference."

Brother Francis was silent. He was pensively contemplating and analyzing all that he just heard. He started to mumble, "Animals, plants, coal, fossils . . . so you're saying that Noah's Flood was worldwide. I've done some biblical calculations and that puts the Deluge roughly about forty-five hundred years ago, is that correct?"

"Yes." I said, giving his mind a chance to absorb all this new information.

"Where do the dinosaurs fit into this picture; they aren't in the Bible."

"I was waiting for you to ask me that question."

CHAPTER FORTY-SEVEN

ASK THE ANIMALS

"**W**hen was the Bible translated into modern English?" I asked Brother Francis, forcing him to reflect back on his theological studies.

"Probably by Tyndale, in the early sixteenth century. The most popular translation was, and still is, the King James Version, finished in 1611. The Catholic Douay-Rheims was completed about the same time frame . . . 1609, if my memory serves me correctly. And the word *dinosaur* doesn't appear in any of them, to my recollection."

"And does the word *Deoxyribonucleic Acid*—DNA—appear in any of those translations, Brother Francis?" I asked the rhetorical question while raising an eyebrow at him.

He looked at me askance and then nodded his head before replying. "DNA was not discovered yet, so the word was not in the Bible. Then neither were dinosaur bones yet discovered. Is that what you are driving at, Doc?"

"The first to coin the word *dinosaur*, which means 'terrible lizard,' was a British naturalist by the name of Sir Richard Owen in 1842. That's over two hundred years *after* the English Bible was printed."

"Richard Owen . . . hmm. Any relation to Kathy . . . oh, hers is Owens." He started to chuckle a bit. "What a circus that was a few weeks ago, huh Doc? The major news networks heavily edited out the carnage for their evening reports, but InfoWars and OAN replayed *all* the juicy tidbits."

"I'm sorry, are you okay on time, Brother Francis?"

"No problem, I've got the afternoon off. The first MMA class I teach at the sports complex doesn't start until 5:00 PM."

"Would you mind if I stopped by sometime? I would really like to get back into the martial arts again. I studied Isshin ryu for several years in my youth."

"Hey, no problem, Doc. Would love to have you workout with us." Francis was reflective for a moment. "Yeah, Isshin ryu—great combo style for street fighting."

He wiped his brow with his long tunic sleeve. "Let's move to a bench in the shade."

"My thoughts exactly," I expressed, since we were both standing in the sun and the walkway was heating up.

"So, Doc, are you saying that somewhere in the Bible dinosaurs are mentioned?"

"Multiple times. A number of diverse authors such as Job and Daniel have recorded them."

"Job? I did an extensive report years ago for one of my seminary classes on the book of Job regarding suffering and wisdom, and never came across any theme related to dinosaurs."

I took out my tablet and asked Brother Francis, "How many times have you been to a 7-Eleven?"

"Gosh, hundreds of times in my life . . . so far."

"Well then, draw for me on my tablet the logo, with the proper colors."

He picked up the stylus and hesitated. He then looked at me with befuddlement and said, "I can't."

"I thought you have been to 7-Eleven innumerable times? You're not lying to me, are you Brother Francis?"

He looked flustered and turned bright crimson.

"Brother Francis, I was just yanking your chain. It's a common legal tactic used to discredit crime witnesses. We place in our memory bank only what we deem important and necessary. You were simply not looking for dinosaurs in the book of Job when you wrote your paper."

"You're right, Doc; I was focused on Job's suffering and God's wisdom."

"Shall we take a peek into Job using my tablet?"

"I've got to see this! Job lived *after* Noah's Flood, perhaps around 2000 BC, or four thousand years ago, give or take." He shook his head. "Job and dinosaurs?"

"Remember, the Bible doesn't use the word *dinosaur*; the Israelites used words like *behemoth* and *tannin*. Keep in mind that God speaks to Job about a number of animals he created—all of which are real: lions, ravens, goats, deer, donkeys, etcetera. Read Job 40:15–19, please."

I handed my tablet to Brother Francis and he began to read out loud. "'Look at Behemoth which I made along with you and which feeds on grass like an ox. What strength he has in his loins, what power in the muscles of his belly! Its tail sways like a cedar; the sinews of its thighs are close-knit. Its bones are tubes of bronze, its limbs like rods of iron. It ranks first among the works of God.'"

He looked up at me and I asked, "Well?"

He looked again at the reading, and then referred to the commentary. "It says in the commentary that behemoth was probably an elephant or a hippopotamus."

"Brother Francis, is the commentary portion of the Bible inspired?"

"No," he replied.

"Does an elephant or a hippo have a tail like a massive cedar tree?"

"No, but why would the theologian writing the commentary make such an obvious error?"

"*You* fell for it; it wasn't obvious to you, was it? Kinda like the 7-Eleven, huh?"

"You're right, Doc!" Brother Francis stopped and thought more about it for a moment.

"You know, Doc, when I wrote that paper I remember God telling Job to 'ask the animals, and they will teach you'. If God is using animals He created as part of his lesson for Job, why would He all of a sudden speak to Job of an animal that was imaginary?"

"Good thinking, Brother Francis. Job would have been confused and discombobulated. Like, 'hey, Big Guy, run that behemoth thing by me again.'"

We both laughed.

"You know, Doc, I just realized something else. For all those atheists who believe the Bible to be just a book written by a bunch of ancient guys with long beards sitting in the desert making up stories . . ." He paused for a moment. "How could one of those old prophets write a lesson about suffering, wisdom, and common animals; then throw in an animal that had supposedly died out millions of years ago, when the prophet would never have known dinosaurs existed to begin with anyway . . . unless, he had really faced one." His expression was focused and intense. "As you said, dinosaur bones weren't discovered and named until the 1800s! Or should I say *re*-discovered!?"

"Why write for a 'primitive' audience about an imaginary creature that their readers would not even know what the author was talking about?" I completed Brother Francis' evaluation.

Brother Francis sat bent over, elbow on his knee, stroking the goatee on his chin. All of a sudden he jumped up and started hopping around like a deranged person, holding his head with both hands, almost screaming, "Oh, oh, oh . . . I got it, I got it!"

CHAPTER FORTY-EIGHT

MYTH AND FAIRYTALES

Brother Francis, still hopping around, rattled on. "Thad's articles on the Matrix and Dietrich, and the World Ecology Flag . . . and . . . and . . . the Bible . . . that's it . . . I get it!"

"Whoa, whoa, slow down, get what? I have no idea what you are talking about."

Brother Francis was pacing quickly back and forth; his sandals were making a slapping sound on the pathway. A couple of students walked by and stared at this mad monk, with strange looks on their faces. Brother Francis was oblivious to their glaring expressions.

He slowed his pacing a bit and tried to collect his thoughts for me. "Okay, follow me on this, Doc," he said breathing heavily.

I sat patiently, waiting for him to speak.

"Thad, as you know, has been writing a series of articles on your Matrix course. As I understand it, he is also presenting it in an exposé format, mirroring your class instruction."

"Okay," I said, wondering where he was going with his analysis.

Brother Francis stopped his pacing and looked at me on the bench. "I believe I speak for many souls, both student and faculty, here on campus who are not happy with this World Ecology flag thing superseding and lauding over our own flag. It is a travesty!"

I listened to him intently.

"However, many, possibly most of us, have bought into this evolution thing to one degree or another. Once you add Mother Gaia into the mix, we are at an impasse as to how to argue against it, since we have been agreeing with this devious monstrous idea for years. I take that back—for over a century! When exactly *did* Darwin write that satanic-inspired book?"

"It was published at the end of 1859," I responded.

"I now know clearly why Dietrich, with his Washington connections, was trying to make a fool of you. Boy, did you ever turn the tables on him and that . . . that . . . vixen of a newscaster, Owens. Dietrich wants to take you down in the worst way."

"Yeah, I can't imagine what he has planned next," I said shaking my head.

"There are many on campus silently rooting for you, Doc, thanks to Thad's articles."

"So what was in this latest article that has you all riled up?"

"I have to admit I just skimmed over the last couple of articles. But it's all starting to gel."

"How so?"

"The premise for this World Ecology Flag–New World Order sits on the concept of there not being a God and evolution being their 'proof.' The God of the Bible, our Designer, has given us the rules of life to follow. Kinda like a designer of one of my race cars. I didn't *have* to follow the owner's manual regarding oil changes and optimum RPM shift points. But if I didn't, I could blow a rod on my engine. The power brokers are doing their own thing—sound familiar?"

"I'm following you so far, Brother Francis."

"No God, means the government becomes a substitute lawgiver and enforcer, and then decrees what we need and who should receive it. The problem is that if you remove God as the Creator of our laws, as Thad so succinctly put it, you will wind up with the French Reign of Terror, which is the result of man-made laws without divine biblical guidance, which is just opinions; and you know what an opinion is."

Chuckling, I smiled at Brother Francis, "Yeah, I've already defined 'opinion' with a couple of my students." We both had a short laugh together.

"May I add," Francis stated, "that our Constitution is . . . well . . . *was* biblically based, contrary to what the revisionist historians would lead you to believe, which is why our Constitution has lasted for over two hundred years. All other country's constitutions were not biblically based; they have had multiple constitutions, and therefore multiple problems with their governments, and poor economies—relative to ours. Even the great Chinese economy has faltered badly. Thad points to its command economic model, which is just dictatorial, godless top-down communism. In addition, Thad stressed that the first French Constitution was established in 1789, same as ours. But they have been through five constitutions since. 'So much for the Age of Enlightenment—without God,' he wrote in one of his articles."

"I'm very impressed with your analysis, Brother Francis. Let me expand on your race car example—okay?"

"Please do!" He appeared anxious to see how I would flesh it out.

"Our operator's manual is the Bible. We don't have to follow it, but then we could blow a rod, following your analogy. If we only believe that the Bible is a nice book that occasionally teaches some good things, and is by and large a storybook, but not a real *history* book, many tend to reject the whole thing out of hand."

"Let me piggyback on my last statement, by asking you a question."

"Okay," Brother Francis said with a queried expression on his face.

I stood up and approached him. Looking at him with all seriousness I asked, "Can you name for me one book, any type of book—religion, philosophy, math, science, fiction or whatever—" I paused before continuing, "that you read the first few chapters and decided that the book was gibberish, stupid, or not making any sense, and yet you continued to read it?"

"Of course not! Why waste my time!" Brother Francis exclaimed, looking at me as if I were a screwball for asking such a dumb question.

"Take Genesis then, with Noah's Flood." I peered back at him with the same expression.

His eyes grew wide and his jaw slacked open—speechless.

"We Christians run around attempting to evangelize the pagans, the evolutionists, the atheists in our own society, telling them to believe the latter chapters, but not the first chapters. We tell them that the first chapters are only metaphor and allegory—brilliant!" I exclaimed in as sarcastic a tone as I could invoke. "And which book of the Bible is the most maligned, attacked, berated and criticized, Brother Francis?"

Looking down at his sandals, he quietly says, "Genesis." He was silent for a moment.

"And what of the world's largest catastrophic global geologic event in history documented in Genesis? Unfortunately it is presented as a story, or should I say fairytale."

"Noah and the Flood." He paused and then lamented, "Oh, my head hurts."

"It should," I replied. "We say *metaphor* and *allegory*, but they hear *fairytale* and *myth*. So tell me, Brother Francis, how many convicted converts are we making—especially with the youth? And I know you know the stats on this."

His hung his head. "Overall, the numbers are dismal. By the time they hit college, 70 percent of Christians, Catholics included, have given up on the faith. And specifically with Catholics, within fifteen years after confirmation, 84 percent have turned their back on the church, and less than one in five returns later."

"And why should they?" I asserted. "We are not answering their basic questions regarding how the universe or this planet came to be from a biblical viewpoint. If the universe truly started with a Big Bang, it also ends with a heat death."

I continued, "You . . . we are literally telling the kids 'don't believe Genesis—how everything started, just believe the last chapters Apocalypse/Revelation.' Minor inconsistency in our teaching, wouldn't you say, Brother Francis?"

"You're right, Doc. If Genesis is only metaphor and allegory, the kids figure 'what other parts are also myth and fairytales?'"

"Truth, therefore, Brother Francis, becomes relative—one's opinion; so why not lie, cheat, steal, covet. You only go around once in life, so make the best of it. These kids aren't stupid. We told them real history is only learned in school, and specifically that Genesis is *not* real history—the Bible is a nice storybook. Then they grow up and become corrupt politicians, avaricious bankers, Simon Legree-style owners of corporations, perverted rock and movie stars, lying media newscasters and journalists, vicious gangbangers . . . *and* we have a mess."

Francis looked dejected. A small tear formed in his right eye. "That was me," he entreated. "I was living only for today, like there was no tomorrow. Thank the good Lord He brought me back from the brink."

He asked in an almost pleading voice, "Doc, you say you have evidence for all this Genesis stuff?"

"I better! If we're wrong, then life arose by meaningless random chance processes; and government, chaos, and the guillotine *will* rule!" We both stared at each other, nodding our heads.

"Thad has obviously got you thinking. The trip to the fossil site and rock formations should convince you that Noah's Flood was the real deal; the museums will then tie it all together," I explained, smiling now at him, trying to end on a positive note.

"You give me the dates, and I'll make sure I clear it with the Prior," he stated with enthusiasm, now truly looking forward to this road trip.

We shook hands and I turned to leave. Suddenly he grabbed my shoulder and turned me around. "A thought just occurred to me. If Noah's Flood formed the fossil layers, and dinosaurs are in those fossil layers, which they are, then dinosaurs didn't die out millions of years ago!" he exclaimed, half questioning.

I just smiled at him. He didn't let go of my shoulder as another thought occurs to him. "Job lived after the Flood, and he saw dinosaurs—right?!"

Francis, in contemplation, stared right through me while still squeezing my shoulder with his martial arts grip. He then blinked and gazed at me with a totally puzzled look. "That means that Noah had to have some of the dinosaurs on the ark with him for them to come off the ark after the flood to reproduce for Job to see them. How did those behemoths fit on the ark?"

His grip was so firm now that my arm was becoming numb.

"Brother Francis! I'm surprised at you!"

He looked at me with a very strained confused expression.

"God would have sent Noah juveniles, not lumbering old stodgy giants that needed Viagra to propagate!"

We both started to laugh. "Boy am I stupid," he stated shaking his head. "I just can't wait for this trip."

"I'll see you on the bus then." I waved goodbye with my good arm, as I walked toward the social sciences building rubbing my sore shoulder.

CHAPTER FORTY-NINE

DR. MERCURIO

I crossed through the quadrangle and walked up the path to the social sciences building. Dr. Dorothy Mercurio's office was on the second floor. Dorothy put on a good front but had a heart of gold. She was a tough bird who wore her heart on her sleeve. Although somewhat rough around the edges, people knew where they stood with her. A no-nonsense woman of integrity, she reminded me somewhat of a female Father Ed, without the collar.

Dr. Mercurio was another anachronistic icon on the campus. An attractive woman, she was probably in her late forties or early fifties, and let her gray show. She favored a '50s style, mid-calf length print dress, usually with flowers on it. It certainly wasn't in fashion, but I really liked it—very ladylike. She blew it however, with the sneakers. I probably never saw her with "real" shoes.

Around campus, she was always walking at a fast gait and carrying stacks of files and/or books in her arms with her glasses on top of her head. It was how she got her exercise and kept in shape. She told me once it was to counteract her chain-smoking—only in her office, however.

I climbed up the flight of stairs to the second floor and walked down the hall to her office door on the right. A small simple, glued-on plastic sign, probably from one of the office supply stores, attested as to whose office it was. Dr. Dorothy Mercurio was on the top line. The bottom line stated: Chairwoman—Department of Religious Studies and Clinical Psychology.

I knocked gently, twice. A gravely blustery voice commanded, "Enter, it's open."

I took my last good breath and walked in. Her office was decorated in hoarder style and five-alarm firehouse fashion. To say it was cramped would be an understatement. Piles of books and files were stacked all over the place; even the one straight-backed wooden chair for visitors was piled high.

Dorothy's desk was no better. There was a very large glass ashtray stuffed with mountains of burnt cigarettes smoldering like a half extinct volcano. There was a newly lit cigarette hanging off the edge. She was working at her computer, hooked up to an old bubble-butt CRT monitor with a glass screen, that she insisted on using. She had a majestic view out her windows of the Blue Ridge Mountains in the distance. It was perfect for relaxing, but she was too focused on her work to notice.

"Damn thing, I hate these mechanical monsters."

"Dorothy, when are you going to update to a touch screen?" I asked while she motioned for me to sit down. "And why don't you ask for a proper sign to be put on your door?" I looked around for a place to sit.

"Just take that pile off the chair and place it on the floor for now," Dorothy directed. "And you know damn well, Lucci, I don't want a touch screen and have those regulatory bureaucratic jackasses watching me. As for the sign, if they can't read that one, they won't be able to read a fancy one, either."

We have had the same discussion before. It was a little ritual we went through.

"You know that the NSA can still monitor all your transmissions, Dorothy."

"Yeah, just like they were monitoring Hillary's e-mails," she exclaimed with blatant sarcasm. "Why didn't they just ask China or

Russia for copies; hell, she had a wide-open server, and in a toilet of all places! We had to wait for Wikileaks to expose her. A lot of good that did." Her gravelly voice was still dripping with sarcasm as she continued, "And God knows, she probably compromised our national security by opening herself up to blackmail! The whole damn mess is still tied up in congressional committees. So many influential people connected to Hillary and Bill's 'activities' are worried about their careers and money!" With that she pushed the keyboard away, grabbed for the cigarette in the ashtray, and sat back on her comfortable swivel chair, placing her forearms on the arms of her chair. "Okay, Lucci, what's up?" she asked as she moved her glasses to the top of her head.

"Just wanted to touch base with you to see how it is going with Maggie. I also understand that Santi is seeing you."

"Maggie is progressing wonderfully. I'm sure you have seen a change in her in class."

"Dorothy, you must have a magic wand. It's like a complete makeover with Maggie in just a matter of weeks. She's removed the black tiger streaks from her hair, which she has also trimmed, and she's discarded the green contacts. I didn't even know they were contacts until she came in one day with stylish black glasses. She has beautiful blue-gray eyes. But there's still something different about her that I can't pin down."

"Well, Lucci, she is dressing more conservatively."

"That's obvious. Conservative, but still stylish. No more wild woman. There's something else, though."

Realizing what I've missed, Dorothy smiled at me and said, "Stop thinking about it for a while . . . it'll hit you."

"So what's your secret, Dorothy?"

"They both need some sincere love by someone they know cares . . . not just a bunch of pills. And they need an adult mentor. With Maggie, I had her reading the Og Mandino series of books. She really liked *The Return of the Ragpicker* story. Currently, both are reading *Hung By the Tongue* by Francis P. Martin. Santi is reading it in Spanish, at the moment. He is, however, bound and determined to learn proper English. Oh, and he's off those SSRIs and doing just fine."

"Really! That is awesome."

"As you know, Maggie approached me on the day of the World Ecology flag dedication. That's why she wasn't there. She mentioned something important was about to take place by the flagpole, and we watched it live on her tablet. You realize that both Dietrich *and* Owens now want your head on a silver platter!" she said carelessly flicking some ashes on the floor.

"Well, it's still securely on my neck, and I plan on keeping it there. And I'm not going to make it easy for them. *Molon Labe* is my battle cry!"

"King Leonidas you ain't, Lucci. And you don't have the three hundred to back you up," she observed as she exhaled a large plume of tartar and nicotine smoke into the air.

I changed the subject back to Maggie. "Do you know, the day after the flagpole fiasco, Maggie waited until the class had arrived before entering the room? She then walked calmly up to the cussin' jar and put her dollar in and sat down." Dorothy was aware of what had happened between Maggie and Tom, and everyone seemed to know about my cussin' jar.

"Let me tell you, Lucci, that took a lot of guts and class. She'll be fine. If you can believe it, she and Maria are starting to become friends."

I leaned forward a bit in my chair. "I need to ask you about another one of my students that I'm concerned about."

"Which one is that?" She asked with genuine interest.

"Jude. That same day, I arrived early, and Jude and Matt were already in the room talking. Jude had a cast on his right hand and forearm from an . . . um . . . incident a couple of days earlier. As I was inquiring about how his injury was doing, I noticed he was wearing a large pentagram ring on his left hand with a horned goat on each side. Very ostentatious, the ring was black and the silver-gray symbols were raised. It had a large faux emerald stone in the center of the pentagram. He attempted to cover it when I commented that it was an unusual ring."

"Oh yes!" Dorothy sat up with the cigarette still dangling from her mouth. "That fellow is a ticking time bomb. I'm not sure how he even got into this institution to begin with. His MMPI is a disaster."

"Do you mean the Minnesota Multiphasic Personality Inventory?" I asked.

"Yes. I really would have liked to run the MCMI-III on him."

"I'm unfamiliar with that one." I responded.

"It just gives me more info on one's psychopathology. Jude is aggressive with an underlying depressive disorder. He's also anti-social with paranoid features. In short, watch your back, Lucci," she warned, blowing smoke from both her nostrils.

CHAPTER FIFTY

MARX'S FRIEND

"**W**here does God enter into the picture with Jude?" I asked Dr. Mercurio, canvassing for an intellectual psychiatric reply.

"He doesn't. That's the point. Jude doesn't want God in his life—that would make him accountable for his actions and make him feel guilty. Our modern society coddles people. Guilt! Sin! Oh, we can't have that!" She stood up and walked to her windows; then turning to me she said, "And you do know he is a homosexual."

"I had my suspicions," I said shifting in my seat still uneasy with her pronouncement.

"Lucci, you are looking at this with just the logic of scientific evidence. These people could care less about logic and evidence. Perish the thought. That's why many pseudo-intellectuals vote Democratic. The *Demon-cratic* Party gives them what they want—with its blessing. 'Vote for us, and we promise to support every perverted anti-biblical lifestyle.' Remember the Democratic National Convention of 2012?"

Dorothy gazed out her windows through the haze of accumulated cigarette smoke residue. "That's right, I almost forgot. Their official position, as part of their platform, was to reject God. YouTube kept a video of it—'*Democrats Boo God.*'"

Dorothy turned to look at me. "The Republicans aren't any better. They play to a conservative base. Some are truly legit. But just like a small handful of Dems who believe in the Almighty, the true conservatives must toe the line or they are marginalized. Without the party support there is little money for their campaigns. Remember, it was Senator Mitch McConnell's Republicans who continued the support for Planned Parenthood, and put the Iran Nuclear Deal over the top for Obummer. And now they have nukes. Surprise! Surprise! Surprise!" She shook her head back and forth with each word, while waving her cigarette around in circles in the air.

A bit frustrated, I pleaded, "What of the constituents who do believe and want America back on a biblical footing?"

Leaning back with her arms stretched behind her and the heels of her hands on the window ledge, smoke still floating upward from the cigarette in her mouth, she explained, "Like Vladimir Lenin's 'useful idiots,' they play them like a violin for their vote."

"What's their goal?" I asked, seeking to understand the psychology behind the politicians thought processes.

"Lucci, for a smart guy, sometimes you are really *dumb!*" She proceeded to take a long drag on her cigarette, while apparently waiting for me to respond.

I just stared at her and then out the window, trying to think of some fancy psychiatric pathology behind all this.

Dorothy shook her head back and forth, frustrated with me, while a cloud of smoke enveloped her head. "Lucci!" She practically screamed at me. "What did you and Ed develop?" She always called Father Ed just Ed. "The Matrix Exposed. What is it to *expose*? *Think*!!"

I rattled the cobwebs from my brain. "Oh, yeah . . . a . . . that's right. Money, which leads to power, and ultimately to absolute control."

"And why are they craving for the seven deadly sins, Lucci?" She was coaching me, although she looked like a fire breathing dragon at the moment.

"They don't want to believe in the God of the Bible." My mind readjusted its thinking away from the psycho-babble.

"Ding, ding, ding! You win the door prize." She feigned exhaustion and turned back to the window with her arms crossed. "And has there been a human on earth, beginning with Adam, who didn't want to do his or her *own* thing? Being answerable to no one but themselves? The '60s hippies think they started and invented that expression. The fools!"

"Dorothy, you're right. There's not a teenager alive who's not bucking his parents, or should I say his or her co-creator in some way."

She walked over to her desk and put out the butt in the ashtray, adding to the heap. Then she lit up another one and sat on the edge of the desk.

"Lucci, in some respects, what you are trying to accomplish is admirable, but unless these kids absorb and take it into their heart . . ." she stopped to take a deep reflective sigh, ". . . the logic, science, and mind thing alone won't matter." She looked upward and slowly exhaled the cloudy vapors into the ceiling fan.

I watched as the smoke twirled around the blades of the fan.

She continued. "Remember in John chapter 9, when Christ healed the man 'blind from birth' on the Sabbath?" She repeated it again. "'*Blind from birth.*' In a small hovel of a town."

"Yes, I do."

"And how did the Pharisees behave toward Him?"

"They chastised Him for healing the guy on the Sabbath."

"Now, Lucci, I really want you to analyze that incident from the prospective of your Matrix," she instructed as ashes from her cigarette fell onto her dress.

I thought back to medical school when the psych professors quizzed us. I always felt pressured, like they were also psychoanalyzing us in the process.

"The Pharisees totally ignored the fact that He had to be God; I mean, instantaneous healing of a man born blind? Kinda obvious.

Instead they were concerned about maintaining their power and control over the people, and Christ was a threat to their power base. He had to be eliminated."

"Very good Lucci, you win the kewpie doll. Sheesh. It's like pulling teeth with you!" She threw her hands up and almost knocked over her monitor.

Like a flash, I jumped out of my chair and caught it just before it hit the floor.

"You've got some fast hands there, Lucci, I'm impressed." After adjusting it in place, she patted the monitor like it was a dog. "Now stay!"

She shifted her weight slightly away from her computer. "This is not rocket science, Lucci. Likewise, the intelligentsia and glitterati must maintain their power and control at any and all costs, even if God in all His majesty appeared before them. This Mother Gaia/ecology thing is a godsend for them. Pun intended."

She continued. "I'm not sure that even you fully understand what is going on here." She pointed her fingers at me with the cigarette locked between them, as some of the ashes landed on my hand. She didn't notice and I didn't wince.

"Please elaborate for me," I asked, feeling she had something to offer I was unaware of.

Dorothy stood and started pacing around her office. "It's really very simple. Darwin destroyed God. From time immemorial, no one has wanted to be answerable to an authority figure or a Creator—there have always been 'hippies' and 'teenagers' throughout history. Atheists were basically castigated and rejected from society. Darwin gave them respectability and credence. Believability for the first time."

"Are you familiar with *Das Kapital*, Lucci?"

"Yes, that was the opus of Karl Marx, the co-founder of Communism." I was happy I knew something.

"Did you know that Marx dedicated his second edition to his *friend,* Charles Darwin?"

I stared blankly at her. That important connection I was unaware of.

CHAPTER FIFTY-ONE

ÜBERMENSCHEN

Not waiting for me to reply, Dorothy followed through. "Did you know that Marx wrote his co-conspirator, Engles, regarding Darwin's book *On the Origin of the Species* to let him know that this was the book that, in effect, would give their socialist atheist philosophy of Communism scientific support?"

"Even Hitler and his National Socialist Party—the Nazis—used Darwinism to support his genocide of millions. He believed he was doing society a favor by eliminating inferior stock," elucidating, as she waved her finger with the cigarette at me, while pacing the room. "And if you doubt me, check out the transcript of Hitler's Wannsee Conference, which set the agenda for the Final Solution of the Jewish Question. Reinhard Heydrich, who was the SS coordinator for that conference, personally stated that 'history will honor us for having the will and the vision to advance the human race to greater purity in a space of time so short Charles Darwin would be astonished'."

"Are you aware, Lucci, that even today in Communist China, when one converts to Christianity, they say to that individual, 'so you gave up Darwin'?"

"Okay, Dorothy, I'm somewhat familiar with the Nazis and the Communists, who are atheists, and use Darwin as their foundation and teaching tool to justify their actions. But how does this link to the Mother Earth crowd?"

"Gosh, you *are* dense, Lucci. I'm getting to it." She waved her hands around wildly again, while walking and puffing madly.

"I'm giving you an overarching timeline, culminating with the radical eco-movement, so you can be on the same page as moi." She gave me her irked expression while blowing more smoke into the ceiling fan.

"We all know, by the late 1800s and early 1900s, both the Protestants and Catholics had bought into this evolution crap. The radical Jesuit Pierre Teilhard de Chardin had to be reprimanded a number of times by ecclesiastical officials for his evolutionary writings. Unfortunately, he has received some praise by recent Popes."

I nodded my head in agreement. "Yeah, the church has bought into evolution hook, line, and sinker, thinking they could blend, meld, or somehow make Christianity dovetail with this philosophy. The church has given its blessing on it."

Dorothy walked past her monitor and patted it on the top again; then she deliberately blew smoke at it. Obviously, she was still frustrated with her "mechanical monster."

"Charles Darwin had a cousin named Francis Galton who actually coined the term *eugenics*, which means . . . better yet Lucci, why don't you bring up the Oxford Dictionary definition on your tablet." She sat back down in her comfortable chair. "You'll be able to bring it up quicker than I can with my monster."

"Yup, here it is." I cleared my throat. "'The science of improving a human population by controlled breeding to increase the occurrence of desirable heritable characteristics. Developed largely by Francis Galton as a method of improving the human race, it fell into disfavor only after the perversion of its doctrines by the Nazis.'" I then looked up from my tablet.

Dorothy suddenly sat up straight. "Perversion? Perversion? By *only* the Nazis! Holy hell! The whole concept is perverted. What the devil was Planned Parenthood doing with those body parts of aborted fetuses - playing mahjong? The whole damn organization is a bunch of butchering Angels of Death. You know who *he* was, don't you, Lucci?"

"Yes, Dr. Josef Mengele, the SS officer and medical doctor who performed horrific experiments, mostly on twins. Lethal injections, amputations, sewing exchanged body parts and even whole humans together in his morbid experiments. The vast majority suffering agonizing prolonged pain before dying."

"That's right, Lucci, and they did all that to prove the supremacy of heredity and thus bolster the superiority of the blonde-haired, blue-eyed Aryan race." Dorothy's dark eyes were ablaze with anger as her fist struck the desk with a thud, sending the mountain of smoldering butts cascading off the ashtray and onto her desk.

"Are you familiar with the Lebensborn program, Lucci?" She said while sweeping the butts onto a tissue and throwing them into her wastebasket.

"No, can't say that I am. Sounds German."

"Darwin wrote about the breeding of fancy pigeons mostly. He was well aware of farmers breeding livestock for prize bulls and racehorses."

"Ahh, and the Nazis decided to do it with the breeding of people to develop their 'master race', I bet."

"Yes, *Übermenschen* in German. Lucci, there's hope for you yet. Those Germans who were deemed, by examination, to be racially pure, could breed. The Schutzstaffel ran the show and got first crack at many single girls. Extramarital relations were encouraged. Marriage—"

"Schutzstaffel?" I interrupted, not being familiar with the term.

"Let me finish, Lucci. Didn't your mother teach you not to interrupt?"

"Schutzstaffel—the SS! Didn't you learn any history in school, Lucci?" She swiveled a bit in her chair. "Marriage—as I was saying before I was interrupted—was not a requirement. About 60 percent of the women in the program were unmarried. Those who did marry SS officers, and had racially healthy babies, underwent Nazi baptisms, Swastika flag and all! The unhealthy were to be . . . ah . . . disposed of."

"What?" I bounced up from my chair. "All this to *prove* the evolutionary superiority of the Aryan race?"

"Yes. Hitler was enamored with the evolutionary concept through the writings of Ernst Haeckel, a German biologist who promoted Darwinism and was a fanatical supporter of eugenics."

"I know this guy. He was the charlatan who faked the embryo drawings that are still in textbooks today. 'Ontogeny recapitulates phylogeny.'"

"Ontology, what?" She looked lost.

It was my turn. "Dorothy, didn't you learn any biology in school?" I queried, giving her a quirky expression.

"Since you are *a lot* older than me, Lucci," she zinged me back, "my biology textbook had already removed the falsified theory, but you are correct, the drawings remain. They show embryos of a human, pig, chicken, and fish all at different developmental stages, suggesting they all evolved from one common ancestor," she exclaimed, exhaling smoke from her mouth and nostrils. "The point I'm trying to make, Lucci, is that Haeckel wrote a book titled *Wonders of Life*, in which he proposed the 'destruction of abnormal newborn infants' could not 'rationally be classed as murder', because these children were not yet conscious."

In a flash, I stood up again. "Is Peter Singer a re-incarnation of Haeckel? He's the chair of bio-ethics at Princeton and is advancing essentially the same garbage, suggesting that parents should have the option of terminating newborns up to several months old— since they have not developed self awareness yet!"

Dorothy swiveled back and forth, her cigarette clasped between her fingers on the arm of her chair. The smoke zig-zagged up in sync with her back and forth movements. She continued, "And Haeckel didn't stop there, and neither did Hitler's admiration of him. Haeckel proposed, and Hitler put into practice, that all defectives, lunatics, and even cancer patients in Germany be eliminated or sterilized according to the 'laws of evolution.'"

Unable to remain still any longer I started to pace. "*Of course*, according to evolutionary theory we are all just highly evolved pond scum. If you take evolution at face value, why not advance it by *artificial* selection rather than slow natural selection. Eliminate the undesirables. Hey, if farmers can stud out their prize bulls, why can't a nation, through selective whoring, attain Aryan supermen and superwomen? How did you say it? The Übermenschen?"

"And, Lucci, do you know where Hitler got the particulars on how to go about putting this into practice?"

"No, where, Dorothy?"

"The United States of America!" She coolly sat back on her swivel chair, took another drag of her cigarette, inhaled it deep into her lungs, while watching for my response.

CHAPTER FIFTY-TWO

THE CUCKOO'S NEST

was still staring at her as I was thinking; *The United States of America was involved back then, with all that perverse evil. It's unthinkable. Something is wrong here.*

Dorothy got up from her chair and walked over to a small micro-refrigerator in the corner, which I hadn't even noticed due to the clutter surrounding it. "Would you like a soda or bottle of water? I'm parched myself, from educating you."

"I'll take a water," I said standing to accept the bottle of water, and then I walked over to look out the window. Suddenly I heard the pssssh of a can of soda being opened. I turned to see she had selected a cola.

"Dorothy, between the soda and the cigarettes, you're going to kill yourself. And don't give me that 'Well, we all will die from something' routine."

"No, Lucci, in fact I'm going to praise you on the stance you took the other week with Dietrich, right in front of the cameras. Ballsy approach and it worked."

"Well thanks, Dorothy," I said knowing she doesn't give out compliments lightly.

"At least I'm paying my way with my own health insurance coverage and not asking the taxpayer to do it for me. And if at some point they decide to drop me—so be it. This country was conceived in freedom. Too bad we're losing it. I'll take responsibility for my actions," she chided as she chugged down some of her soda, cigarette still in hand.

"So you agree with me, I take it," I stated, still wanting to confirm her position.

"Yes, Lucci, if one wants to trash and destroy their body on alcohol, cigarettes, and drugs, that's their decision. Did you know at one time, up till the early 1900s in this country, one could walk into a chemist, we now call pharmacies, and order virtually anything they wanted off the shelf—cocaine, opium, whatever, without a prescription? It was at the chemist's discretion whether to sell it to you or not."

"Yes," I said, taking another swig of my water. "I am well aware of that freedom Americans once had. And if they got sick, their family, community, or church would help if they could. If not, sayonara!" I gave a half military salute-wave goodbye.

Dorothy again turned back and forth in her chair. "Now nanny government steps in to control everything and everybody and promises health care until death due you part—from them—in exchange for votes, of course. It's up to the states, *not* the federal government, dammit, what health care to dispense, if any!"

"Father Ed and I have been through this discussion before," I replied.

"This is not going to last much longer," she predicted, taking another gulp of soda as she puts out her cigarette, which had burned down to her chronically scorched fingertips.

"How so?"

"Lucci, I also did mental health in the Emergency Department for a while. If the taxpaying public only knew."

"The same patients cycle through over and over again. *I know,*" I replied.

Dorothy placed her soda can on the desk and lit up another cigarette. "They don't take their medicine, don't follow up with their psychiatrist, and blow their disability and welfare checks on street drugs and alcohol. They cause a calamity—assault, a domestic whatever—police are called, and they are brought to the Emergency Department."

I jumped in. "Then I get to see them for the one thousandth time, for medical clearance, and afterwards, I send them over to you in the rubber room."

"Right," she said, sitting back again in the swivel chair. "Then I get to process them again for the one thousandth time and try, with much difficulty due to lack of space, to locate a mental health institution where they can be treated for the proverbial one to three days. They shove some more pills down their throat, then give them their prescriptions and an appointment to follow up with their psych doctor, which of course doesn't happen. And the cycle begins again."

"Tell me about it," I answered bitterly. "These people need to be locked up for a long, long time—no booze, no cigarettes, no alcohol, and no street drugs. Of course our bleeding heart liberals don't want them put away in some institution because some Nurse Ratched may hurt their feelings."

"Funny movie, *One Flew Over the Cuckoo's Nest*, although a bit unrealistic and over the top." Dorothy actually laughed, reflecting on it as she spoke. "What the public doesn't realize is that we really need to re-open, and if necessary to construct, more of these long term facilities, *but*, and it's a big but, they must be controlled by the states, and not the feds."

"And when you crunch the numbers," I added, "it would cost the taxpayers a hellava lot less money to keep them locked away, than roaming wild on the streets abusing the taxpayer's money on street drugs and alcohol and causing mayhem. Of course, locked away it's kinda hard to vote for your freebies."

"Do you know what is about to happen, Lucci?"

"No."

"Ed is not the only one with contacts high up the chain of command. Since the federal government is controlling it all now, they have finally discovered the best, not the only, but the best way to eliminate the Second Amendment—and with the people's blessing."

"Dorothy, are you talking about confiscation of all personal firearms by the fed?"

"Yes, I am—absolutely!"

"And the public is going to support this?"

"Without a doubt!"

"This I have *got* to hear." I moved again to sit on the visitor's chair. "By the way, how come you don't do psych in the ED anymore?"

"Oh, a patient punched me in the face."

"And?" I asked.

"I slugged him back, so they fired me. Said I wasn't being professional," she stated matter-of-factly as she calmly exhaled a plume of the carcinogenic gases into the air.

CHAPTER FIFTY-THREE

THE QUEEN B

"What a joke," she exclaimed, remembering the awful event. "What would happen to you, Lucci, if you spat on, cursed at, or hit your parents?"

"Let's just say, I wouldn't be here to tell you about it." My thoughts immediately went back to my dad, who was a strong disciplinarian.

"Oh, so your parents weren't being . . . professional?"

"I never thought of it that way."

When Dorothy realized her can of soda was empty, she proceeded to get up to get another one, leaving her cigarette in the glass ashtray. She returned, to her desk with another can, placed it on her desk, popped it open, and sat down again. "So, therefore, I guess its okay for those street punks to spit on and throw rocks at police without significant repercussions. And if the police retaliate they are not being professional."

"You've got a point there, Dorothy."

Still very curious about what she had to say regarding the Second Amendment, I asked, "So how is the government going to get the general public to actually *want* the government to seize their firearms?"

"From what I'm hearing through the political grapevine, my colleagues in the mental health field tell me that the government's strategy is to make sure their bootlickers in the liberal media

continue to pump out stories of psychos who use firearms to kill."
She took a big gulp of her second cola.

"Go on." I prodded her.

"Don't rush me, Lucci. Instead of the media pushing for more mental health institutions to chamber these deviates to begin with, *before* they start their killing sprees—at schools, churches, and other venues—they only wish to remove the weapons from their possession. Sounds logical, doesn't it?"

"Yes," I said, but I was still unsure of where Dorothy was going with this. And she saw the puzzled look on my face.

"Lucci! Follow me closely," she said, pointing two fingers toward her eyes and then back to mine with frustration.

"The feds plan to start with the schizophrenics, major depressives, and the bipolar. People in those categories who own weapons will be made to cough them up. The general public will fully and totally back this."

"Ahhh, then quietly—"

"Do not interrupt, Lucci; it's not polite."

"Okay, Okay." I respond indifferently.

She then repeated my words. "Then quietly, slowly they move down the ladder to anyone who has taken even one valium tablet, or who even *lives* with someone who is on psychotropic meds or anti-anxiety drugs. All this under the guise of public safety."

"And the public won't even realize what is happening until it's too late. The Matrix at work—big time."

"Bingo, Lucci. You finally got it through that thick Italian skull of yours," she uttered, sitting back and savoring a long drag on her cigarette.

"Well, *you're* sorta half Italian, Dorothy."

"By injection only, my friend. By injection only."

She stopped swiveling and sat up directly confronting me. "The *ultimate* power and control, is to leave ones' citizens defenseless. Why the hell do you think Paul Revere and William Dawes made that ride? It wasn't to trollop around at midnight to look at the stars."

"The Minutemen of Lexington and Concord needed to be warned that the British were on a forced seventeen mile march from Boston, after rowing across the Charles River, to confiscate their weapons and ammunition. If the British had been successful, the Revolutionary War would have ended before it even started—strangled in its crib."

"And we'd all still be drinking tea instead of soda," Dorothy quickly added, while chuckling and taking another sip of her second cola.

I succinctly added. "And the Minutemen were a militia made up of any able bodied men, which is why our Founding Fathers wrote about a "well regulated militia" in the Second Amendment. The libs have twisted and revised it to mean the modern National Guard or something of that nature—in other words, the *government!*"

The Dorothy dragon was ablaze. "They dumb the kids down with that Common Core, or whatever the hell they call it now. Our Founding Fathers are doing back-flips in their graves. The youth today don't even know we were fighting against our own government. We were British subjects."

Searching my tablet, I found a quote. "Dorothy, check this out. George Mason, the father of the Bill of Rights, who kinda ought a know a few things regarding the Second Amendment, stated, 'I consider and fear the natural propensity of rulers to oppress the people. I only wish to prevent them from doing evil. . . . Divine Providence (God) has given to every individual, the means of self defense.' Mason was saying that we the people had a God-ordained right to protect ourselves against our own government."

"Lucci, you just brought something out that most of the liberal Marxist crowd has never considered."

"Which is?" I asked, looking at her wondering if I unintentionally missed something.

"You're trying to educate the kids that there is a God and that He's the God of the Judeo-Christian Bible, correct?"

"Okay." I drawled, still wondering the direction Dorothy was going in.

"It's staring you right in the face, Lucci—wake up! Our Founding Fathers said our rights come from God. No God leaves *only* our *benevolent* government the ability to bestow rights on us. What government grants, government can also take away—*if* there is no God. Remember what you said to the World Ecology Flag crowd?"

"I almost forgot, that's right. I did subtly allude to that point."

"Here's a tidbit for you, Lucci. The word *ecology* was coined by none other than Hitler's favorite little racist, Ernst Haeckel."

"He's the same weirdo who falsified the embryonic drawings and called for racial purity for the German people, as dictated by the inexorable laws of evolution."

"Why do you think our government, with collusion from media and academia, is ramming this 'Mother Gaia birthed us' evolution hogwash down our throats, and permits no dissention?" as she slams the soda can on her desk and more butts go flying all over the place again.

"Power and control!" I immediately responded. "They want to be the sole power and the glory forever and ever. They must marginalize and ultimately destroy the Judeo-Christian God and His laws of life."

"And put that head of yours on the silver platter," Dorothy said, and we both started to laugh.

"One more thing. How did Thomas Jefferson put it?" I asked while scrounging on my tablet trying to find the quote. "Ah, here it is. 'A government big enough to give you everything you want, is a government big enough to take away everything you have.' Dorothy, I totally agree with you, once the feds hijack our means of self defense, it's over! Yep, it's all about power and control."

I looked at my watch. "Geez, it's getting late. Emily will be wondering why I haven't called her yet."

"I need to hang around. Vince still has a Tai Chi class, and afterwards he's promised to take me out to dinner tonight. He's a real softy."

"Walk me to my car," I requested of Dorothy.

"Why? Do you need me to protect you, Lucci?"

I shook my head and rolled my eyes at her. "No Dorothy, I wanted you to explain to me how the United States initially became involved with eugenics and sterilization. You intimated that the Nazis followed *our* lead."

We opened her office door and headed down the hall to the stairway. I finally could breathe again. "So which Americans were involved with this eugenics stuff?" I turned to her and asked.

Casually, she looked at me somewhat surprised and said, "None other than the Queen B herself—Margaret Sanger, founder of Planned Parenthood."

My mouth dropped open. And before I had a chance to speak, she followed through with "And the Supreme Court of the United States."

I stopped dead in my tracks.

CHAPTER FIFTY-FOUR

THE OFFICE

"**W**hat's your problem, Lucci? Got glue on your feet?"

"I didn't realize how tied into the eugenics movement Margaret Sanger and even our judiciary were."

We were about to descend the same stairway that I had initially come up from the building's entrance.

"Well, while we wait for you to unglue yourself, do you know whose office that is across the hall, opposite these stairs?"

"I haven't the foggiest idea."

"That's the office of your favorite gay social justice bureaucrat." She said smiling in a sly way while nodding her head.

"Dietrich's office? That's it?"

"Yes, he expropriated it from one of our department heads, tore down the walls on each side, and expanded into those office spaces as well. Had it completely remodeled to his liking. It's immense. Even Dean Avery's office could fit two and a half times into Dietrich's."

I walked over to his door. There was a very large thick brass-plated slab of a sign. His name was deeply engraved in black on the plaque. Marvin Dietrich, PhD was on the top line and beneath it read Chairman – Department of Social Justice.

"Holy cow! He really is an arrogant—" I paused searching for the right word.

Dorothy leaned over and, with her hand aside her mouth as if to whisper to me, said, "Lucci, you can say it. No one's around. They've all gone home, and I don't have the cussin' jar. Say it . . . *bastard!*"

"Well, you know . . ." I said sort of embarrassed and shaking my head.

"Actually, in his case, it would be the correct term. He truly is an illegitimate child. And you can appreciate this, Lucci, the term is also biblical."

I really think she enjoyed using the word since Dorothy obviously reviled him anyway. And the illegitimacy thing was a welcomed point of irony.

"Do you remember the large tall expanse of windows just above the entrance you came through?"

"Yes."

"All that is his office. The entire bank of windows was altered and augmented to his specifications with the very best low E-rated metallic oxide coating, of course."

"Hey, the best taxpayers' money can buy, right, Dorothy?"

"His vista, which is opposite of mine, has a clear shot down the walkway to the flagpole and the statue of Mary beyond. And he hates it. Every time he looks out, he is required to look upon our nation's symbol—which he despises—and then the statue of Mary—a reminder of our country's religious heritage."

"Lucci, this guy is slime of the worst order. One of the cleaning crew guys, making his usual rounds to all the offices on this floor, unlocked Dietrich's office door one evening. He caught Dietrich fisting Erik."

"Holy crap! Is Dietrich a Kevin Jennings acolyte?"

"Who?" Dorothy asked.

"Jennings was Obama's Safe Schools Czar. He's the founder of GLSEN—the Gay, Lesbian, Straight, Education Network. He was the keynote speaker at his own GLSEN conference that discussed the subject of homosexual activists with school kids."

"Did you say Safe Schools Czar, Lucci? Holy Mother of God!" she exclaimed, shaking her head violently, in total disbelief. "All I know is that this worker was just trying to do his job, cleaning offices. He happened to be in the wrong place at the wrong time. Dietrich reamed him out and tried to get him fired. It was the talk of the campus his first year. I counseled the poor fellow for a while."

As we started down the stairs, Dorothy was ahead of me mumbling something about, "That S.O.B. probably can't get it up, anyway."

CHAPTER FIFTY-FIVE

DECADENCE

As we exited the social sciences building, I had to turn around to see those windows of Dietrich's. They *were* impressive.

"So Lucci, pay attention! You wanted to learn about the eugenics movement in the U.S."

"I'm listening," I said, turning my head and eyes back to Dorothy.

"What was the *full* title of Darwin's first book?"

He titled it, "*On the Origin of Species by Natural Selection.*"

"There was a sub-title you know. What was it?"

"Umm . . ." I thought for a few seconds. I knew it. Just needed to dredge it up from the deep recesses of my memory. "*Or the Preservation of Favored Races in the Struggle for Life,*" I finally blurted out, smiling at her with a "See, I knew it" attitude.

"I don't know what you're grinning about, Lucci. It's nothing to smile about." She looked like she was digging for a cigarette in her bag. "Repeat it slowly to yourself and you'll get the answer you're looking for."

Half under my breath I muttered, "Or . . . the . . . Preservation . . . of . . . Favored Races . . . that's it! *Favored Races*! Wow! If that isn't a racist title, I don't know what is."

"And if there's any doubt in your mind, Lucci, his second book, *The Descent of Man*, should seal it for you." Dorothy was still digging in her bag.

"I thought you only smoked in your office?" I asked, leaning over, making it obvious I was looking down into her bag along with her.

"Okay, Lucci. I do cheat once in a while. But you're right. I'll be good." She closed her purse and slung it over her shoulder again.

"Why don't you take that little government spy box of yours and bring up some of Darwin's misogynistic quotes."

Typing on my tablet as we walked, I searched. "Here's a good one: 'A woman is merely a stunted man.' And this: 'The average of mental power in man must be above that of woman.' Oh, this is a good one: 'The chief distinction in the intellectual powers of the two sexes is shewn by man's attaining to a higher eminence, in whatever he takes up, than can woman.'" I started to laugh heartily, silently reading the next quote.

"Okay, Lucci, your chauvinism is showing. Which quote are you laughing at?"

"Writing of a future wife he wrote: 'An object to be loved and played with—better than a dog, anyhow.'"

"That's enough of Darwin's female bashing. Why don't you research some of his statements regarding anyone who was not Caucasian—his racist quotes?"

We had reached the quadrangle's flagpole, and I suggested to Dorothy that we sit on the little wall that surrounds the flower beds while I touch base with Emily, so she doesn't worry.

After my quick call, I noted, "Looks like the monks have repaired the mess Erik and his clodhoppers made a few weeks ago trampling over the flowers. You can't even tell that one bloom was disturbed," I said admiring their work.

Dorothy gave me a dirty look, for me to get back on point.

"Yes, the racist quotes," I scrambled quickly. "Wow! This about sums up his entire attitude: 'At some future period, not very distant, as measured by centuries, the civilized races of man will almost certainly exterminate, and replace, the savage races throughout the world.'"

"Go on, it gets even better," Dorothy cajoled, her face showing a mixture of irritation and outrage.

I proceeded. "'At the same time the anthropomorphous apes . . . will no doubt be exterminated. The break between man and his nearest allies will then be rendered wider, for it will intervene between man in a more civilized state, as we may hope, than the Caucasian, and some ape as low as a baboon, instead of as now-'"

"'—between the negro or Australian and the gorilla,'" Dorothy finished off the quote from memory. "You realize, Lucci, that Darwin equates the black man with the Australian aborigine and that of the gorilla. At best, maybe a step above the apes."

"I want you to locate Darwin's statement regarding 'the weak members of society,' and you will see Dr. Mengele, Ernst Haeckel, Hitler, and Planned Parenthood all rolled into one."

"I believe this is the one you are referencing: 'Thus the weak members of civilized society propagate their kind. No one who has attended to the breeding of domestic animals will doubt that this must be highly injurious to the race of man. It is surprising how soon a want of care, or care wrongly directed, leads to the degeneration of a domestic race; but excepting in the case of man himself, hardly anyone is so ignorant as to allow his worst animals to breed.'"

"Incredible! Unbelievable! I must bring this up in my class. Students, and the public in general, have absolutely no idea what the underbelly of evolution is really all about."

"Lucci, now that you understand the basis for this decadence, I will present the face of evil to you in the figure of Margaret Sanger."

CHAPTER FIFTY-SIX

IN THE DARK

Still reeling from Darwin's statement, I repeated the phrase, "'As to allow his worst animals to breed.'"

"Lucci, Darwin equated humans with animals! And so do many leftists in academia and the government." Dorothy stopped and leered at me, as if to attempt to infuse her thoughts into my mind. "No soul, no spark of divinity in us. And why should they? Everything just evolved *somehow* from the slime pit. Amoeba to man. Fish to philosopher. Ape to Caucasian . . . excuse me . . . to Aryan—the pinnacle of evolution."

"The secular humanists will say that they don't believe in social Darwinism any more. How do you respond to that?"

"Nice talking point, Lucci. Good sound bite! But it doesn't cut it in the reality of everyday life. The abortion mills are still cranking. The fetal body parts are still shipped to science labs for experimentation. They use clean sounding words and expressions like 'embryonic stem cell research,' 'harvesting for *possible* cures'— all in the name of humanity. It's Dr. Mengele's human flesh on a massive microscopic scale, that's all."

"And the public," I responded immediately, "doesn't know or doesn't care to know the difference between embryonic and adult stem cell research. Of course, *only* adult stem cell research has given us over eighty treatments and cures, while embryonic haven't produced a one."

Dorothy began to dig into her bag and then remembered. She angrily threw her bag down onto the little wall next to her. Very agitated Dorothy stood up and lamented, "The tortured screams are muffled now; they're in the womb, not in the gas chambers," as she paced in circles. "Lucci, drum up Thomas H. Huxley on your little nefarious tablet."

"Wasn't he Darwin's bulldog, a staunch defender of Darwin's theory? He went head to head with Bishop 'Soapy Sam' Wilberforce in the first Creation-Evolution debate barely seven months after *Origins* was published. Huxley soundly pummeled 'ole Soapy Sam; and the atheists have been riding high ever since."

Dorothy, still pacing in circles reminded me, "Karl Marx glommed on to what he perceived would be a good thing to underscore his Communist philosophy. Darwin's family was not happy with Karl trying to buddy up with Charley by dedicating *Das Kapital* to 'his friend.' They felt their friends and church members would not look kindly on the matter. Lucci, do you have arthritis in your fingers? Haven't you found Huxley's quotes yet?"

"Got 'em."

"Okay, check out the one that starts out," Dorothy's eyes searched skyward as she tried to remember the beginning of the quote. "Yes . . . 'No rational man'."

"Got it: 'No rational man, cognizant of the facts, believes that the average Negro is the equal, still less the superior, of the white man.'" I looked up from my tablet.

Dorothy had stopped pacing and stood with her arms on her hips, favoring her right side. "Yeah, and I guess the leftists will concede the exceptions being Dr. Ben Carson, Thomas Sowell, Deneen Borelli, Dr. Walter Williams, Star Parker, and a number of other current conservative black leaders," she snidely stated. "Now for the Queen B," she fired back at me, pointing to my tablet.

"Give me a second," I implored trying to retrieve Sanger's quotes. "Ah, here are a slew of them, and boy, do they make Sanger look culpable. She said: We 'are seeking to assist the white race toward the elimination of the unfit [blacks]'; 'Birth control to create a [white] race of thoroughbreds.'"

"Listen to what Sanger says regarding her Negro Project," I cried out, forgetting momentarily that Dorothy was well aware of the quote. "'We don't want the word to go out that we want to exterminate the Negro population and the [black] minister is the man who can straighten out that idea if it ever occurs to any of their more rebellious members.'"

"And the final icing on the proverbial cake: 'I accepted an invitation to talk to the women's branch of the Ku Klux Klan.'"

"There are some additional statements in this article that her racism was not limited to blacks only. She despised Catholics, Jews, and many immigrants from Europe; 'human weeds,' she called them. The Nazis had become sympathetic to her writings. I see now why you call her the 'Queen B'," I expressed with implicit incredulity, as I faced her and raised my eyebrows.

Dorothy resumed her pacing and confessed with distain, "And many of my *very own* black colleagues are dumb and blind to the facts. The liberal media and Common Core are keeping the average schlub in the streets, or in the government universities, ignorant of all this."

CHAPTER FIFTY-SEVEN

SUSTAINABLE DEVELOPMENT

"**S**anger established her first full service 'clinic' in Harlem in 1929," Dorothy somberly stated. "The first of many to come into the Planned Parenthood organization. What a deliberate euphemism: 'Planned Parenthood'. It's meant to keep people blind to the truth." She continued through gritted teeth, "Just like when the Nazis cajoled with 'We're taking you to the showers now.'"

Our minds went to the horrors of the holocaust for a moment as we stood there in silence. Dorothy's anger seemed to mollify a bit, but her eyes revealed her inner feelings. I tried not to notice them slightly reddened and welling up. "There's some info in this article of Sanger's impact during her lifetime. In the United States, the eugenics movement was responsible for over sixty thousand compulsory sterilizations, mostly in the 1930s and 40s. And . . . Oh my God, 'The Rockefeller Foundation helped fund the eugenics movement in Germany and was a benefactor of a program for . . . *Dr. Josef Mengele!*' Whoa, and here's the title of an article from our own Dr. Peter Singer at Princeton: 'Killing babies isn't always wrong.' He wrote it in 1995. Mengele would be proud of him."

"Lucci," Dorothy blurted out trying to contain herself best she could. "Look up *Buck vs. Bell.*"

I started to read it to myself, when Dorothy exploded: "Read it out loud! My blood pressure hasn't risen sufficiently enough."

"Okay, Supreme Court Justice Oliver Wendell Holmes, Jr. in the *Buck vs. Bell* case in 1927 stated that, 'three generations of imbeciles are enough.'"

"Read his Supreme Court decision," she emphatically roared at me.

"I've got it right here," I spit out, getting a bit edgy myself, "'a state statute permitting compulsory sterilization of the unfit . . . for the protection and health of the state did not violate the due process clause of the Fourteenth Amendment.' It also says in this article that the Supreme Court has never expressly overturned *Buck vs. Bell*."

Dorothy summarized my last words. "For the protection and health of the state . . . and the Court has never expressly overturned *Buck vs. Bell*," she said slowly, shaking her head in disgust. Even his eminence Bishop DiLorenzo, of the Richmond Diocese, declared in 2005 that, 'the Church does not need to fear the teaching of evolution as long as it is understood as a scientific account of the physical origins and development of the universe.' Of course, if he was privy to our discussion, I'm sure he would say, well, not social Darwinism."

I piped up. "One can't separate social Darwinism from evolutionary Darwinism. Ignorance is one thing. But when the supposed intelligencia refuse to evaluate this philosophy properly, they are just plain *stupid*—which is the permanent deal!"

We started to walk again toward the parking lot. I turned to Dorothy and asked, "And what about the evolution-Mother Gaia link?"

"Do I have to spell everything out for you, Lucci? If evolution is true, then we are all related. The biology textbooks claim we are related to worms, and ultimately to the protozoa. Mother Gaia birthed us, and we must defer to her. All of creation, therefore, was not God ordained—there is no God. Religion by default, then, is irrelevant and passé. All religions must bow before her. We are slime, not souls."

"Got it, Dorothy! Man is the usurper. Man is the parasite. We must adhere to the U.N., and the government Matrix's sustainable development and Agenda 21, now called Agenda 2030, and bring our population down below one billion. Due to our own apathy, ignorance, and stupidity the entire human race has become enamored with Ernst Haeckel's 'ecology' and Darwin's 'evolution,' synthesized together under the banner of Mother Gaia. We must protect the . . . the . . . mosquito, our ancestor. We must save Mother Earth at any and all costs. We've signed our own death warrants! Maybe that's why Glenn Beck's *Agenda 21* books were so popular."

"*Finally*! You've finally put it together, Lucci!" I sensed a tinge of sarcasm in her voice. "And Pope Francis had also signed on to all of this!" Dorothy exclaimed, as she picked up speed with those sneakers of hers.

Trying to catch up with her I called out, "That's right, his encyclical Laudato si'."

"Lucci, do you know who advised him on that?" she asked, really shifting into overdrive with the sneakers.

"No!" I said, huffing and puffing trying to keep up with her.

"Hans Schellnhuber, professor of theoretical physics at the University of Potsdam, was most likely the Pope's primary advisor on the encyclical."

"Your point?" We slowed our pace to sub-light speed as we reach the parking lot.

"The professor is an atheist and advocate of population control. He favors a reduction of the earth's human population to below one billion from its current seven billion. Perhaps Hans will be first? *And,* he's a member of the esteemed PAS."

"You've got to be putting me on, Dorothy." We stopped by the vehicle and I had to catch my breath. "The Pontifical Academy of Sciences, the PAS, which advises the Pope and the College of Cardinals?"

"Yes, the very same one that Steven Hawking is also a member of." Dorothy affirmed. "Hawking, the wheelchair astrophysicist who is also an acknowledged atheist—and a patron of the London strip clubs," her lips curled with revulsion.

In a daze by all this revelation, it took me a moment to come around. "Dorothy we are at your car, not mine."

"Well, Lucci, whose fault is that?"

***

I parked my tank in the garage and entered through the kitchen door, as usual, and attempted to give Emily a kiss.

She pushed me away before I had my chance. "You smell like a stale tobacco factory. Were you in a bar? Go to the mudroom and remove all your clothes. I'll need to wash them, or bring them to the dry cleaners. You stink!"

"I was in Dorothy Mecurio's office," I said, and then suddenly it hit me. "She removed her implants."

"What? Dorothy had implants removed?" Emily gave me a strange look.

"No, No. Maggie removed them," I replied.

"What? Maggie removed Dorothy's implants?" Emily asked, shaking her head in confusion.

"No, Maggie removed her own implants!"

"What? Right in Dorothy's office? Did Dorothy call you to stop the bleeding? I knew that girl had mental problems but . . . did you call 9-1-1?"

"No, no! Stop, stop! You're all mixed up."

"I'm all mixed up?" Emily was becoming belligerent.

"Emily, I'll explain it all to you slowly and calmly over dinner, okay?"

"Okay!" She hotly responded.

"Okay. Good! I'm starving. What's for dinner?"

"Fresh plump chicken breasts."

"Oh brother," I moaned, rolling my eyes.

CHAPTER FIFTY-EIGHT

T-CHIP

I entered the class with Tom on my heels. The students were already abuzz and animated about something. I got them quieted down, somewhat. We proceeded with the pledge, with Ali seated quietly, although his arms were on his desk and not folded across his chest. *Hmm,* I thought, *perhaps he is opening up a little.*

As I set the cussin' jar in its usual place of honor on the lab table, I asked them, "What's all the hubbub about?"

Juan excitedly burst out, "Doc, everyone on campus is getting one of these cool T-chips, and for *free*! For free, man!"

"I'm sorry Juan, as you guys know, I'm not a tech head. I got as far as the abacus and stopped there."

"Abacus?" queried Juan, looking at me cross-eyed.

Nate jumped in. "You know the ancient rectangular wood framed thing with rods of beads on it that are moved to do math calculations."

"No," Juan thoughtfully answered, still looking confused.

"Never mind," I said. "What's with this T-chip deal?"

Nate picked up the ball. "The government, in conjunction with all the wireless phone companies and credit card companies, is offering students this one-time deal for the next month or so. If you sign on right now, you get the T-chip for free and 50 percent off your monthly cell phone bill for the next twelve months.

And 15 percent back on whatever purchases you make over that twelve months. Cool, huh?"

"Okay," I drawled. Looking at Nate and the class's obvious excitement about this new development, I asked, "But what *is* a T-chip?"

Matt jumped into the fray. "Doc, you need to get with it, man. This is the coolest thing since sliced bread. You can make hands-free calls and charge stuff without having to carry your credit card around, worrying you'll lose the dumb thing. Too much of a hassle. We can voice text. No more wearing our fingers to the bone texting. This is the bomb."

"Could someone show me what this T-chip device looks like?" I asked.

Several students looked at each other perplexed; then answered almost in unison, "We can't."

"Why not?"

Philip explained, "The RFID transmitter is implanted under the skin of our hand; you know, that fleshy part between the thumb and index. The receiver is inserted in the soft tissue behind our ear."

"T-chip—Talk chip. Now I get it. I was wondering why some of you were acting like Dick Tracy or James Bond when I came into the room."

Santi scratched his head, then turned around to his cousin Juan and asked, "Quien es Dick Tracy?"

"Cállate, hombre. He's a comic strip dude."

Addressing the class, I ascertained, "And the transmitter in your hand can be waved over a scanning unit, like at the grocery store, to make your purchase?"

"Yeah, that's it, Doc. Way cool, huh?" Matt continued, "We can even pass our hand over the QR barcode readers on our cell phones to make purchases."

"So you still need access to your smart phones, correct?"

Philip answered, "As long as our cell phones are within ten feet or so of us, we can at least voice text or make or receive calls."

Standing behind my lab table, I stroked my chin and recalled Revelation 13:17: 'And that no man might buy or sell, save he that had the mark, or the name of the beast, or the number of his name.' Then I asked the class, "And for those people that don't opt to get this microchip implanted sometime during the twelve-month period?"

"Oh, after that it becomes a requirement. But then you don't get any bennies or freebies, and you will pay retail for it." Matt added with that used car salesman mug of a smile.

"Are any of you familiar with the number 666?"

Jim raised his hand and answered, "That's some kind of old timey superstitious devil number in the Bible or something."

"Yes, Jim . . . or something," I responded with a very slight shake of my head. "And I bet this thing has GPS capability as part of the deal, right?"

"Oh, yeah," Matt enthusiastically replied. "Don't have to worry about getting lost."

"Yeah, the government will be sure to find you. You can run, but you can't hide." I was still shaking my head.

Claudia raised her hand, and I recognized her. "My mom had one of the first archetypal chips put into my grandmother, over ten years ago. She had Alzheimer's, and at times had been found wondering around on the streets. Also, all of our Afghan hounds are micro chipped. They are pedigreed, of course."

"Of course." I offhandedly replied. I then remembered about Claudia's aversion to anything coarse or brutish. "Claudia, did you get chipped?"

"Ah . . . no . . . not yet. But I am considering it. My parents want me to get it. Security and all. Ransom. That sort of thing."

"I totally understand." I nodded my head in affirmation.

"By the way, what happens if someone refuses to be chipped after the twelve months?" Leaning on my lab table on both outstretched arms, I scanned the class.

Most of the students looked at each other somewhat confused. They hadn't thought that someone might not want to get chipped. Tom, our pre-law 'counselor', raised his hand. "Some of my law professors have said that no one will have, in effect, the choice to opt out. If they don't get chipped, they will forfeit their government paychecks, social security checks, welfare checks, and any entitlement checks they have been receiving. They will eventually be unable to purchase anything—gas, food, clothes . . . nothing. Also, they will not be able to receive any medical care, nor perform in-person banking transactions, and they won't be able to vote."

"And let me guess, Tom. In the event you are arrested or detained for any reason, the chip will be forced upon you?"

"Yeah, I just found that out late yesterday. How did you know?" Tom looked baffled.

"Tom, you need to study more about the Nazis and Communism!"

Pete, who had been taking all this in, raised his hand. "Doc, are you going to get chipped?"

Without thinking, I exploded. "The hell I am! Oops. Sorry, guys." I took a dollar from my wallet and placed it into the cussin' jar.

CHAPTER FIFTY-NINE

CHAPERONES

"Jude." I acknowledged his raised hand.

"About the cussin' jar. At the end of the year, what will *you* do with all the money?" He said it in a snarky way, implying I would keep the funds for myself.

"Well, Jude, the class, as a whole, will decide which charity or charities to donate the money to."

Nate turned around and said to Jude, "And I'm sure that will meet with your standards and approval." He then turned back around with a smirk on his face. Others in the class smiled and nodded. Jude sat silently with his famous "weaned on a pickle" look.

I broke the momentary silence. "So, I gather all of you don't have one single challenge with this T-chip device?"

Thad, our journalist/astronomer spoke up. "Doc, Claudia is correct. The basic RFID prototypes on this came out well over ten years ago. Initially, they were implanted in pets, grandma, or even young children. The government supported the sale and distribution of these things for personal security reasons."

"And yourself, Thad?"

"I've declined for the present to have one implanted in me. Not for any religious reasons . . . just some apprehension."

"Would you mind explaining that to the class, if it's not too personal," I requested politely.

"Sure, Doc. It's really simple. I just don't trust the government. And with every passing day in this class, and accompanied by my research for the Matrix Exposed columns I've been writing, let's just say I've come to trust the government less and less. And besides—"

"The government," Jude boorishly interrupted, "has been kind enough to work out the arrangements with cell phone companies and credit card bankers to provide a deal for the people that's too good to be true. And all you can do is criticize and bad mouth their Herculean efforts?"

Nate pivoted in his seat again. "God, you sound just like Chris Matthews. Listen to your liberal self, for once."

Jude, not to be besmirched, leaned over in Nate's direction. "Ooh, Nate you took God's name in vain. Didn't you?"

Nate abruptly stood up and stomped toward the front, mumbling under his breath, "Guy's a pain in the . . ." he caught himself as he stuffed a buck into the jar and stomped back to his seat.

"Okay, then," I commented, "switching over from the T-chip and onto our trip. We will be leaving next Monday morning at 7 AM sharp from the student parking lot. I've arranged with Brother Francis to do the driving for us on one of our ICC buses."

Moans came from around the room. "Seven! My eyes don't even open until 8," spouted Matt.

"Well, you can get your beauty sleep on the bus then," I replied. "Oh, and by the way, Fred and his wife, Cindy, will be accompanying us."

"Chaperones?" Tom injected with a caustic tone. "We're adults, not little kids."

"And that's exactly why you *need* chaperones. If you were little kids, I'd bring along babysitters." Several around the room laughed, including Maria and Maggie. From Tom's expression, I gathered he did not find it funny.

"Cindy will be bunking with the girls, and Fred, myself, and Brother Francis will each be assigned to one of the guys' rooms."

"With the T-chip and announcements behind us, I guess we should start today's lesson, late as it may be. I've titled it, Smoke and Mirrors."

CHAPTER SIXTY

SMOKE AND MIRRORS

I had already placed a number of fossils on the lab table, as well as some props.

"What I wish to cover today is the fact that some government agencies, including the Department of Education at the Federal level, and some of their outside supporters, are not being completely honest with us regarding science. And thus the truth must be suppressed by them."

Andy raised his hand. "Are you saying, Doc, that the Matrix also wants to control us by distorting science somehow?"

"In a word—*yes*! If one doesn't toe the party line, there are repercussions. By deciding who does and who does *not* get grants for certain projects, is one way. Putting pressure on institutions and universities to demote or fire professors that are bucking the conventional evolutionary Mother Gaia line is another."

"My dad," Nate interjected, "has shown me a number of articles where professors were harassed or fired, including a guy with *two* PhDs—Dr. Richard von Sternberg from the National Institutes of Health with ties to the Smithsonian Institution—who wrote an article mildly critical of evolution; and he has shown me other write-ups on grants being given primarily to those only supportive of global warming."

Juan's hand shot up. "Yes, Juan," I acknowledged.

"Doc, you are right. Follow the money, which leads to power and control—over us."

"Santi," I called, waving my finger in his direction as he wished to contribute something.

"Madre de Dios. These evil gente . . . people . . . these Nazis, must destroy God, so they can be gods themselves—as my prima, Juan said—over us."

I nodded my head at Santi. *They are beginning to catch on, I* thought. *But they need the tools, the hard evidence to support their new positions; otherwise, the atheists, liberals, and secular humanists will have them for lunch.*

"Okay gang, we are about to attack the belly—no, the heart of the beast. The first and last thing the progressives and leftists will hold onto down to their fingernails is the age of the earth and universe. This is their ace in the hole. The concept of millions and billions of years is required for evolution to happen; that alone destroys the Judeo-Christian concept of a God. This is important—"

Jude immediately countered, "Oh, spare me. Bunch of flat-earthers. Of course millions of years destroys God . . . because it's true! That is why only the elite intellectuals should control education, and direct society and its goals."

"Like in Plato's *Republic*," I replied. "The philosopher-king and the guardians ruling over the proletariat."

"Ah . . . yeah, right," Jude answered, a bit unsure of the reference. "A ruling class to make everyone and everything fair and equal. This is needed to guide the people, as no one anymore believes in a God; and everyone doing their own thing is getting way out of control with civil unrest, robbery, murder, clash of religious beliefs—"

"Excuse me, excuse me," Ali interrupted, waving his hand rapidly. "We Muslims believe in Allah, praise be his name, and Sharia Law keeps everything under control."

"Sorry, Ali, with the exception being the Muslims," Jude backpedaled on his position somewhat.

Maria jumped right out of her chair and turned toward Jude, who was at the back of the room in his usual corner by the windows. Her dark eyes aglow as she pointed an accusatory finger at him. "Yeah, an elite class, just like the "enlightened" of the French Revolution. And I suppose you'll elect yourself like Robespierre, the philosopher-king, to mandate a 'share the wealth' executive order. I should lop your damn head off—personally."

There was stunned silence. Maria was becoming quite feisty. Realizing what she had just said, she quickly advanced to the cussin' jar, dropped a dollar into it, and returned to her seat. She leaned forward with her head bent low and clutched her cross, perhaps doing a mea culpa.

"I think we've gotten a bit off track. Can we advance this discussion without all the drama?"

Philip raised his hand, and I was happy to recognize him.

"Doc, Jude is correct. And the millions of years is one of the main reasons I'm an atheist. I've studied a little of your Christian religion, and originally it held to a roughly six thousand-year-old creation. All your church fathers and doctors of the church adhered to this, including Augustine. But with the advent of what Hutton, Lyell, and Darwin wrote, the church capitulated and has agreed with the millions of years theory themselves, since the late 1800s."

"That is absolutely correct, Philip." Jude was smiling smugly with his arms crossed.

"Besides," Philip continued, "nothing personal . . . but I've found that most of you Christians don't even understand your basic theology of what you're suppose to believe in."

"How so? Please elaborate for us, Philip."

"Well, if millions of years exist, which is what even you Christians believe now, that puts trillions of animals that lived and died prior to man—or Adam, as you like to call him—coming on the scene. Correct?"

"Good analysis, Philip." Jude sat up, rubbing his hands gleefully.

"I'm not finished. That puts death and suffering *before* your Adam even existed and therefore *before* he sinned. And according to your Christian teaching, Adam's sin of eating the forbidden fruit is supposedly what brought death, suffering, starvation, predatory animals, poisonous insects, and a host of other maladies into the world. Is that not so?"

"Right again, Philip." Jude could hardly contain himself.

"So what do I need a savior for? To save me from what, Doc? If death, suffering, and disease have been ongoing since the earth was a simmering molten mass, what's the point?"

"Are you agreeing with Jude," I asked Philip, "that we need a big nanny government babysitting us, then?"

"Not necessarily. I don't like anyone telling me how to live, not the feds not the illuminati or whoever. But since we have millions of years of death and suffering behind us, and apparently millions of years of the same ahead of us, I just don't have an answer. It appears to me that this original sin thing with some Adam character was also created by men to control us."

Maria nervously squeezed her cross and Maggie pensively looked at me, waiting for me to fire a magic-bullet comeback at Philip. Jude was just glowing.

CHAPTER SIXTY-ONE

THE BIG IF

"**D**oc," Philip continued, "I'd like to read something from one of my atheist colleagues, which I believe sums this all up."

"Sure, go ahead," I replied.

Philip cleared his throat and proceeded to read from his tablet.

"'Christianity has fought, still fights, and will fight science to the desperate end over evolution, because evolution destroys utterly and finally the very reason Jesus' earthly life was supposedly made necessary. Destroy Adam and Eve and the original sin, and in the rubble you will find the sorry remains of the son of god. Take away the meaning of his death. If Jesus was not the redeemer who died for our sins, and this is what evolution means, then Christianity is nothing!'"

"That was a quote by G. Richard Bozarth from his article, "The Meaning of Evolution," in *American Atheist* magazine from February 1978. If there was no Adam for God to create, then Jesus didn't need to die for our sins. As I was saying Doc, this makes your Christ's death and resurrection completely unnecessary."

The class was absolutely silent. All eyes were on me waiting for me to counter with a diametrically opposed argument.

"Philip is right, and so is Bozarth. *If...*" I paused.

Jim animated and fired up as usual, responded. "So my religion means *nothing* with this millions of years thing." He momentarily reflected. "Yeah, that's right, trillions of deaths of animals and hominids before Adam was created, or evolved."

Nate raised his hand. "Adam's sin supposedly led to death, disease, and suffering. But if death and suffering have already been ongoing for millennia, there *is* no sin, so to speak. We're back to relative morality and everyone doing his own thing. And since there is no God to save us from ourselves and the chaos we've created, that leaves only the governmental Matrix to turn to for help."

With that there was a hushed muffled exchange of ideas and feelings swirling about the class—and a feeling of abject hopelessness.

Finally, Jim again spoke, and revealed what everyone was thinking and saying. "Doc, there is no hope, no future for us, just millions of more years of the same weary existence: pestilence, war, famine, and death."

I looked around the room at these fresh young faces now without promise or hope for the future.

"*Good*, you now understand," I said forcefully while leaning on the lab table.

"Good? How is millions of years of suffering, still ahead for mankind, good?" Jim posited still wired up.

"Maybe you should take an antidepressant. That's what people do who have no hope, and, as you said, Jim, the millions of years kinda puts the icing on the deal." I looked at Maggie and gave her a wink and a smile. She smiled back.

"I said *if* – remember?" I paused again.

Philip picked up the banter. "If . . . if what, Doc?"

"Only *if* the millions of years truly exist is there no hope. But *if* the entire universe and earth is really around six thousand years old . . ."

I paused, yet again, for added affect.

". . . Then the Bible is accurate and correct," Maggie finished my thought for me. "And that is why the atheists and leftists must fight tooth and nail to preserve their millions and billions of years. It's their last straw to control us. It's the only thing they've got, because evolution of all plants and animals *definitely* can't take place in a short six thousand-year time span. Nate, what was the name of that double PhD guy who was demoted or whatever?"

"Dr. Richard von Sternberg," he replied to Maggie with a smile.

Maria followed through. "And if the Bible is correct regarding creation, then we have a God we can look to for guidance—not the Matrix government bureaucrats, not Plato's illuminati, nor the French Enlightenment's Robespierre."

"And, may I add to what Maria said, we have a bright future as well. But, you would need to read the last chapter for that."

Jim, happy now, piped up. "Well, what the devil are we waiting for, Doc? Let's see this evidence you have for our young earth and universe."

"You said it, Jim, the devil—old scratch, Beelzebub." Jude was just sitting and pouting, very leery and apprehensive about what the evidence may show.

CHAPTER SIXTY-TWO

MILLIONS AND BILLIONS

"I need to bring some of you up to speed on this young earth topic." I said, as Claudia nodded her head, along with some others.

"The Judeo Old Testament and Christian New Testament writings, together comprise what we call the Bible. The Protestant Bible is composed of a series of sixty-six books—the Catholic Bible has seventy-three books—written by over forty men, over a period of about fifteen hundred years, in three different languages, on three different continents. The first five books of the Bible—Genesis, Exodus, Leviticus, Numbers, and Deuteronomy—were written by Moses. Genesis covers the history of the early earth and universe. Other books have different authors and cover various aspects of our history, as well as other topics."

"That Moses guy," Juan said, raising his hand, "was he the same dude that parted the Red Sea and received the Ten Commandments from God?"

"That's also just another bunch of B.S." Jude interrupted.

"B.S.?" Nate exclaimed, turning to Jude wanting some cussin' jar payback.

"Yeah, Barbra Streisand, Nate. You've heard of her, haven't you?"

Nate turned forward again in his seat, mumbling under his breath.

"Look fellas, all this bickering and back biting is not going to get us anywhere. If you wish to disagree with a point, raise your hand and present your evidence. To answer Juan's question - yes, Moses lived around 1400 BC, or around thirty-four hundred years ago."

I continued. "The Bible doesn't directly come out and say six thousand years old for the earth and universe; one need only to add up the 'begats'."

"Pregunta," Santi said, now raising his hand. "Que es 'begats?'"

Juan tapped Santi on the shoulder, and then made a circle with the thumb and index finger on his left hand, moving the index finger of his right hand in and out to illustrate 'begating' to his cousin.

"Oh," Santi exhaled and turned back around somewhat embarrassed. The class chuckled.

"Well, now that we all know what 'begat' means, the Bible, starting with Adam, goes through the lineage of man. Adam begat Seth who begat Enos who begat . . . and so on through Noah, and continues through to Abraham and his sons Ishmael and Isaac. That led to—"

Ali was extremely agitated. He waved his hand so violently I stopped mid sentence to acknowledge him.

Ali stood up and very angrily stated, "Ismael is the *first* legitimate son of Abraham. Isaac, the liar and cheat, stole his birthright. Allah will have his revenge on those Jew dogs."

"Okay, Ali, cool your jets," I stated forcefully, pointing a finger at him. Matt's face tightened up. Ali sat down with a thump onto his seat.

The class appeared tense and confused. "What Ali is alluding to is that Abraham's wife Sarah could not conceive. She encouraged Abraham to have relations with her servant Hagar. She bore Ishmael, whose tribe became the Arab nations."

Juan was beside himself, "Man, like you could have sex with a servant girl back then in biblical times? God permitted this?" Some sporadic chuckles played about the room.

"Only to propagate your lineage, Juan, or your family name would die out," I explained. "God permitted it only under these specific circumstances."

Jim jumped in. "And then afterwards, Abraham's wife Sarah did have a son, Isaac, and his offspring led to the nation of Israel - and the two have been fighting like cats and dogs ever since." He then sat down proud that he remembered some of his biblical history.

Thad raised his hand. "So all this ongoing conflict in the Middle East goes all the way back to these two sons of Abraham?"

"That's about it in a nutshell, Thad."

"What an incredible series I could incorporate into my news articles."

"What an incredible *history* of the Middle East, if people actually just read the Bible," I asserted.

"Wow! The Bible as *real* history, I never thought of it that way, Doc," Thad very introspectively replied.

"Let's finish up this synopsis of the begats; it continues through the House of David, where, at that point, the linage splits. One line leads to Jesus, and the other to Mary, his mother—which this college is named after."

"This is the *original* Ancestory.com. From your great-great-great granddad Adam to Abraham, when one adds up the lineage of the begats, is about two thousand years. From Abraham to Christ is another two thousand years. And from Christ until the present day is the final two thousand. Voilà, six thousand years of earth history, plus the six days of God bringing the earth and universe into existence prior to Him creating Adam and Eve on that sixth day."

Philip forcefully interjected. "That's fine, but how do we know that the days of creation were only six? Maybe they represent the millions of years of earth's evolutionary history before Adam really evolved, and therefore was *not* created by your God from the 'dust of the ground,' to quote your Bible."

"Philip has a good point, Doc," Tom aired directly. "The millions of years must exist. Hundreds of thousands of layers of rock contain fossilized death representing billions of years before Adam, or man, came on the scene. How do you explain that in light of Christianity like Bozarth wrote? Or is your God an ogre, and likes death?"

Addressing the whole class, I explained, "What evidence is out there in the world today that shows this millions of years of death?"

"The geologic column, of course, and that's some cold dead *hard* fact—literally" answered Pete, our geology major, who chuckled a bit.

"And what would that cold dead *hard* fact be, Pete?"

"Well, the single biggest and best example would be the Grand Canyon. That carved out hole is the best evidence for the geologic column, which illustrates clearly the millions of years. The layers of the canyon contain thousands upon thousands of fossils embedded in them—the death Tom mentioned."

"Philip, I remember you saying early on that the facts determine right and wrong?"

"Yes, I did. Facts speak for themselves," he said hesitantly, looking at me suspiciously, knowing I'm going somewhere with this.

"Remember our discussions in the early days of the class when we were talking about one's worldview and how it impacts a person and his decisions?" I asked the class as a whole.

Many nodded that they remembered. "This is where it comes into play now. Christians and atheists, or evolutionists, both have the *same* facts. The *same* Grand Canyon, the *same* earth, and the *same* universe. Each group *interprets* those facts according to his or her worldview."

Pete stopped me. "Doc, you're losing me. When I look at the Grand Canyon, it's obvious that it took the Colorado River millions of years to chisel that mile deep trench."

"Pete, and all of you, think for a moment. You are saying that basically a little bit of water over a long period of time carved out the canyon. Did you personally *observe* that happening? In other words, do you *know* that for a fact, or did you memorize it from a book?"

Jude arrogantly jumped up. "You didn't observe it happening either - right?" he questioned, pointing his finger at me, the sun's rays bouncing off the fake emerald on his pentagram ring.

"You're right, Jude. I didn't *personally* observe the formation of the Grand Canyon."

"Damn straight, I'm right." His mouth almost dropped open immediately.

Nate reflexively whipped around. "That'll be one dollar for the kitty, Jude."

"I don't have it on me," he smugly replied, and sat down.

"Oh, big man doesn't have a dollar. Daddy not send you your allowance this month?"

Jude just sat silent, his dead eyes staring full of animus at Nate.

"Okay, then," Nate said as he got up and walked to the front of the room. "That'll be one greenback you owe me." He dropped a dollar into the cussin' jar.

As Nate walked back to his seat, I remarked, "Let's get back on track. You guys will have to work out your finances on your own time. Philip, what *is* the proper and correct definition of science?"

CHAPTER SIXTY-THREE

EVIDENCE VS. OPINION

Philip, who had been leaning back in his chair, sat up straight to address the class. "Science must be observable, repeatable, and verifiable or falsifiable." He then resumed his usual position.

"Thank you, Philip. From now on, most of what we will be covering is not under the realm of the pure definition of science. Anything that has occurred in the *past* cannot be observed, nor repeated directly."

"Tom, you are our legal counselor here. In a murder trial, does the state really *prove* that John Doe committed the murder, or do they try to present overwhelming *evidence* to convict him?"

"Doc's right. We can't observe the murder directly; the dude is dead. All that CSI testing provides is *evidence,* not proof that John Doe committed murder. Even a videotape can be tampered with. Hopefully, it will be the weight of the evidence that convicts the murderer."

Some in the class still had deadpanned looks, and Maggie picked up on it. She turned to address the class. "If I claim that I have discovered the formula to turn lead into gold, any scientist worth his salt should be able to attempt to duplicate the process; and therefore verify my formula, or falsify it and call me a charlatan."

The class nodded in agreement. I thought they were starting to understand the difference between proof—which is repeatable observable science, versus evidence—which is historic past events.

Pete was still focused on the geological argument. "So, getting back to the Grand Canyon, you can't *prove* your position either; so, you're going to provide evidence. Am I correct?"

"Correct a mundo, Pete. We creationists who believe in a young earth, can't *prove* what happened in the past, any more than the evolutionists can."

Pete's eyes lit up. "So, Doc, are you saying that you are going to present a weight of evidence that outweighs the evolutionary evidence?"

"Correct again, Pete. Anything that has happened in the past, like the John Doe murder, cannot be *proved* using the correct definition of science. Only by the weight of evidence will the jury, or our class, decide who wins. Hopefully, my worldview that God did it, will outweigh the evolutionary millions of years worldview that Mother Gaia did it."

"Ding, ding . . . round one," exclaimed Nate. "God versus Mother Gaia! Which worldview will win?" The class erupted in loud clapping and hooting.

After they quiet down, Pete asked, "So, Doc, what's your evidence for the worldview that God created that 270-mile-long, one-mile deep canyon?"

"Pete," I said as I panned the entire class, "could the fact be that perhaps a *lot* of water, over a *short* period of time, excavated that gorge in a matter of a couple of weeks, at most?"

"What!?" Pete practically yelled almost leaving his seat. Others joined the chorus as well. "That's impossible! There is *no* geologic process which could have accomplished that massive a result in such a short span of time." Many in the class nodded their heads in agreement.

I electronically dropped the Insta-Screen down in front of the whiteboard, and with my tablet, I integrated with the screen, bringing up a canyon with a river at the bottom.

"So Pete, tell me what you see?"

"A standard run-of-the-mill canyon with multiple rock layers, and a river at the bottom. Obviously similar to the Grand Canyon. So what?"

Photo of a canyon with a river at the bottom
Photo credit: Dr. Steve Austin

"Any idea how old that canyon may be, Pete?"

"I'd have to send rock samples off for analysis, but it should be several million years old—at the very least."

"The North Fork of the Toutle River carved out that canyon only forty plus years ago, in one day."

"What? No way!"

"Really, Pete? Ever hear of Mount St. Helens which erupted in 1980? A mudflow on March 19, 1982, carved out that 150-foot-deep sucker, in one day. Go ahead and transfer it to your own tablets for a closer look, if you wish."

Photo of man standing at the bottom of canyon with layers of rock behind him. Photo credit: Dr. Steve Austin

The entire class is rapidly scrambling to investigate Mount St. Helens, and the subsequent lahars or mudflows that created the canyon.

"Now, I can't *prove* that it was created in one day, as I was not there to observe it. However, after the smoke cleared, pun intended, a canyon was formed that was not there prior to the event, which is pretty strong evidence."

I then added, "Check out Burlingame Canyon in Washington State. It's another rapidly formed canyon; made in six days."

"We studied a little about Mount St. Helen's in geology," Pete responded, "but not from your point of view. Why not?"

Maria had her hand up; she turned to address the group. "Why not? Why not?" She exclaimed, raising her voice each time. "Give me a break. What has Doc been trying to get us to do?" she asked looking directly at Pete.

"He wants us to think, not just memorize," Pete replied.

"Didn't Doc just present us with the first chink in the armor of the millions of years scenario we are constantly bombarded with? Can't have people thinking and challenging Mother Gaia's millions of years—heavens, no! The Matrix, which controls our education and our thinking, may not like us analyzing independently from the slop they are feeding us."

Jim put his hand up. "Doc, I'm getting ticked somewhat. I decided to major in ecology because I thought science was the search for the truth. Why haven't we been at least *exposed* to this different point of view?"

"Jim, science *is* a search for the truth. What you are just beginning to realize is that evolution and its millions of years is a philosophy, not a science. Remember the definition of science - it must be able to be observed and duplicated."

Jude was pumping his hand in the air. I waved my hand for him to speak. "Well, your young earth creationism is a philosophy, also! Correct?"

"Absolutely, Jude. What you have just discovered is that this is not religion versus science; it's one philosophy versus another philosophy, because evolution, or creation, took place in the unobserved past. This is not ironclad proof versus alchemy. This is weight of evidence versus weight of evidence."

I recognized Thad. "I get it now. Science is duplicable stuff that can be directly tested, then verified or falsified. Things like what Maggie said. Lead to gold. Or snake oil. Or rockets, computers, antibiotics—or even toasters." Which got the class laughing.

"Philip," I said, acknowledging his raised hand.

"I've been analyzing this, and evolution doesn't even meet the definition of a theory—of course, neither does creation. It more properly should be the evolution model versus the creation model."

"Excellent deduction, Philip. You are absolutely correct."

Jude jumped out of his seat and almost screamed at Philip. "It's called the theory of evolution, and as far as I'm concerned, it's still a fact!"

Philip, still lazily reclined in his chair, barely looked at Jude. "You can call it anything you want, buddy; it's your opinion. And we all know what an opinion is."

CHAPTER SIXTY-FOUR

PROFOUND REALIZATION

Jude's mouth hung open, but nothing came out. He realized his mental acumen was no match for Philip. He sat down in a huff.

The class was quiet for a moment. Pete broke the silence. "Doc, you never did tell us what process or event could possibly have sculpted the Grand Canyon so quickly." His eyebrows narrowed with a big question mark on his face.

"As I said, a lot of water over a short period of time." I noticed Maria anxious to give Pete his answer. "Maria, why don't you tell the class?" She looked at me with her Mona Lisa smile.

"Noah's Flood, of course. Remember the correlation with the Mount St. Helen's event?" she stated, as she had turned in her seat to face the class.

The class was all chattering. Some pro, some con, some mystified, and some totally disconcerted.

Pete raised his hand. "But what about that—"

"Geologic column?" I completed his question.

"Yeah, Doc, that's suppose to *prove* that those layers in the Grand Canyon and strata around the world, for that matter, are millions of years old."

Andy, his brother looked across at Pete and tapped him on the shoulder. "*Prove*? Are you sure? It did happen in the unobserved past."

"Alright, alright—provides *evidence* that those sedimentary layers were laid down slowly over millions of years rather than quickly by Noah's Flood?"

"Pete," I said, really addressing the group, "who was responsible for the concept of the geologic column?"

"A geologist named Lyell came up with the idea in the early 1800s," he states immediately with confidence.

"Does anyone know who Charles Lyell was?" I looked back at Pete and the rest of the class.

Maria's hand went up again. "Yes, Maria."

Maria again turned in her seat toward the class. "Lyell was Charles Darwin's mentor." She let that point resonate with the class before continuing. "He personally gave Darwin a copy of his book *Principles of Geology* prior to Darwin's voyage on the *Beagle*. Darwin was then prepped and brainwashed in long earth ages, *way* before he arrived at the Galapagos Islands, where he did his finch studies and developed his evolution theory, excuse me . . . evolution model."

Maria momentarily turned back to me. "I'd like to add another point, if that's okay?"

"Sure, Maria. Go ahead."

She turned again to the students. "Lyell hated Christianity . . . all those stifling rules and regulations you know. He schemed to deceive the church into accepting his millions of years. And being Darwin's mentor and confidant, Lyell had tremendous influence on Darwin, similar to the Matrix with us. May I quote Lyell from my tablet, Doc?"

"Go on."

"In a letter to like-minded George Scrope, a fellow geologist, he wrote, 'I am sure you get the Q.R.,' he's talking about a journal called the *Quarterly Review*, 'what will free the science from Moses, for if treated seriously, the party,' talking about the church, 'are quite prepared for it. . . . It is just the time to strike, so rejoice that, sinner as you are; the Q.R. is open to you.' Lyell was also an accomplished lawyer, by the way."

Pete was aghast. "Are you saying that he made up the whole thing? The entire concept of the geologic column with all its epochs of the Cambrian, Silurian, Devonian, Jurassic, and . . . and claiming each lasted tens of millions of years just . . . just came out of his head?"

Maggie then turned to the class. "Yes, Pete, the whole thing was just a crock to destroy the Noahic Flood, which Moses wrote about in Genesis. Up until then, the church, and many scientists, believed the Deluge laid down the fossil layers around the world, including the Grand Canyon!"

Maggie then turned back around, as Maria held up her hand to give her a high five. "You go, girl!" Maria praised. She then gave her another high five, as they laughed together.

I had a big puzzled look on my face. Maggie explained, "Doc, Maria and I started to figure out where you were going with much of the material and we decided to get a jump on it. Together we began to read a number of books and websites on these subjects, from, how should I say it, a non-conventional approach."

Matt was waving both hands in the air. "Yes, Matt."

"Even if all the names of the layers and the time frames between them were *made up*, they do show the evolutionary progression of fossils from the early period of earth up to the present." He then integrated an illustration of the geologic column on the Insta-Screen.

"Yeah, Doc," Tom joined in. "The deepest layer the . . . a . . ."

"Cambrian," Pete leaned over to inform him.

"Yeah, the Cambrian shows the basic primitive life-forms. Then as we move up the strata, or layers, the organisms become more complex. What gives?"

"So, Tom, what you are saying is that the bottom layers of strata are the oldest and contain the more primitive life-forms, and as we move up the geologic column through the millennia, the layers are younger and contain more advanced organisms. Is that right?" I asked.

THE GEOLOGIC COLUMN		Millions of Years Ago	Typical fossils
Eras	Periods		
CENOZOIC	QUATERNARY	2	
	TERTIARY	65	
MESOZOIC	CRETACEOUS	130	
	JURASSIC	180	
	TRIASSIC	225	
PALAEOZOIC	PERMIAN	275	
	CARBONIFEROUS	345	
	DEVONIAN	405	
	SILURIAN	435	
	ORDOVICIAN	480	
	CAMBRIAN	600	
	PRE-CAMBRIAN		

*Illustration of the Geologic column time scale
with animals and plants. Credit : UK Apologetics*

"Ah . . . yeah. Doesn't that show proof . . . ah . . . evidence of some kinda evolution going on?"

"Tom, what type of organisms do we find in that bottom Cambrian layer?"

Tom turned around to Pete. "Hey, man, help me out on this."

Pete, happy to help out, stated with certitude, "It's called the Cambrian Explosion because we find all kind of basic sea life like jellyfish, corals, brachiopods, sponges, worm tubes, and more." He smiled; proud he knew his geologic time scales.

"Pete, tell me—and the class—what is found in the pre-Cambrian layer underneath, or below the Cambrian."

"Nothing really, just single-celled microscopic protozoa and bacteria, where life began."

"That's right, Doc, I've learned the same in my ecology class lectures," Jim interjected.

"Okay guys, now follow me on this. The basement layer, the pre-Cambrian, has only microscopic, single-celled life and the very next layer above it contains fairly complex multi-cellular life-forms, such as the worms, corals, and jellies, which Pete alluded to. Does anyone see a problem with this?"

Several of the students consulted with one another; finally, Matt raised his hand. Apparently he had come to some conclusion.

"Doc, where are all the in-between life-forms? The bottom layer is micro single-celled and the next above it is complex gazillion-celled life. Where are all the . . . the . . ."

"Transitional one hundred or one thousand or ten thousand-celled organisms," Pete added with much consternation, as he had never questioned what his professors and books told him.

"Matt! Excellent! You have ascertained a critical point that many PhDs have failed to grasp," I exclaimed, giving Matt some well-earned kudos.

"I have?" He replied, somewhat astonished. He turned around to Pete, who had perceived the significance of what Matt had said and was staring at Matt in disbelief.

CHAPTER SIXTY-FIVE

ROUND ONE

Philip sat straight up in his chair putting all its legs on the floor. This did not go un-noticed by others in the class.

"Okay, Philip," I said, "I see you've discovered something very crucial. Why don't you share it with us?"

From his expression, he was not happy to have been called on. But I knew I was about to count on this atheist to again be honest.

"The significance of what Matt stated regarding the lack of evidence for transitional organisms carries with it the same weight as the failed Miller-Urey experiments."

Philip fidgeted as he talked, obviously very uncomfortable with this.

"Philip, please proceed."

"First, I must concede that I myself never paid much attention—no, not *any* attention to this extremely pivotal aspect of the pre-Cambrian and Cambrian portion of the geologic column."

"How so, refine your thoughts for us."

"Okay, we are all familiar with the rubric we have been taught to accept, that life started out as unicellular microscopic organisms which evolved to the invertebrates—those corals, brachiopods, worms and jellies Pete mentioned—then advanced to the vertebrate fishes, amphibians, reptiles, birds, mammals, and finally to man."

Jim, impatient and short-tempered as usual, boldly inserted himself. "Philip, what the H-E double hockey sticks are you talking about? Speak English, man!"

Philip responded in kind, looking at Jim. "Where in the H-E double hockey sticks are the missing links between the single-celled microscopic organisms and the gazillion-celled ones Matt mentioned? Over those millions upon millions of years, there should be at least some organisms that advanced and grew bigger, transitioning from a microscopic single cell to an intermediate-sized organism, before reaching the ginormous size—relatively speaking—of a jelly fish or worm. They are not there, which means they don't exist. Got it?"

Jim's eyes grew big as he began to realize the impact of this line of reasoning. There were still others in the class unsure of the implications.

Maggie came to the rescue. She stood up and turned to face the group. "C'mon guys, think, for heaven's sake; use your brains. Can anyone name one, just one example of a multi-cellular organism in between a one-celled bacterium or amoeba and the gazillion-celled coral or jellyfish or worm or clam?"

Nate stood up to answer Maggie. "OMG, there are none. I can't think of even one example." He then turned around looking for any feedback. "Does anyone know of any organism between the one-celled protozoa and the invertebrates? Anyone?" he asked, still petitioning his classmates.

"*That's why* it's called the Cambrian Explosion! I get it now," Tom exclaimed. "But the missing links—all the transitional fossils and organisms—are still missing between those two layers of the pre-Cam and Cambrian, even to this very day. Holy crap! But . . . but that alone is enough to destroy evolution and possibly the millions of years theory."

Claudia added, "Evolution is supposed to be some kind of slow advancement through the millennia. But all of a sudden there is this enormous jump from protozoa and bacteria to the invertebrates from the pre-Cambrian to the Cambrian periods. It's like leaping from a single brick to the Empire State Building, without any other structures of any other size in-between. Why didn't we all see what was undeniably missing?"

"Dr. Lucci, I'd like to add another observation, if I may," Claudia asked.

"Observe away, Claudia."

"It appears to me that if the Deluge of Noah caused all this, wouldn't we find sea creatures at the bottom layers of strata and land animals that could run from the rising waters of the flood toward the top layers?"

"A very canny discernment, Claudia." I then addressed the class. "Why don't you all transfer to your tablets that schematic of Lyell's geologic column itself to see if Claudia's assertion is correct?"

Several seconds later, the class was all abuzz. "Basically, Claudia's correct," Juan shouted out, his voice rising above the chatter.

The students were pouring over the schematics of the geologic column on their tablets and talking amongst themselves about what they saw.

Santi raised his hand, and I recognized him.

"If I now comprende this columna stuff; these estratos or layers of rock have to be either many millones or only thousands of years old. Correcto?"

"That right, Santi. We creationists believe it's thousands— Noah's Flood, which formed the 'geologic column of death,' was approximately 4400 years ago, which means death and suffering only came into the world *after* Adam."

The class was reflecting on what I said without fully understanding this absolutely crucial point, when I saw Santi's hand go up again.

"Dónde está . . . a . . . where is this grande columna?"

"Only in the textbooks. There is no place on earth that contains the *entire* geologic column. It would have to be one hundred miles high. Am I correct, Pete?"

"The Doc's correct. The entire column, as one entity, only exists in textbooks. Even the Grand Canyon only contains a small part of the column. Oh, I see you've brought up an accurate quote on the Insta-Screen, Doc, and from an evolutionist."

The "geologic column" is more of a concept than a reality. Eighty to eighty-five percent of Earth's land surface does not have even 3 of the 10 "geologic periods" appearing in correct consecutive order required by Evolutionism. Even the walls of the Grand Canyon include only about 5 of these "periods".

—Source: Edmund M. Spieker, evolutionist, John Woodmorappe, geologist and William Walsgerber, George F. Howe and Emmet L. Williams

*Quote/illustration on the geologic column
by Edmund M. Spieker Google*

Nate chimed in. "This is looking worse and worse for the evolutionists and their millions of years. But now *I've* got a question."

"From what I've been checking out here on my tablet, the way the archeologists figure this, even today, is they determine how old a fossil is by the rock layer it is found in. However, the geologists determine how old a rock layer is by the fossil that is found in that rock layer. This sounds like circular reasoning to me, or am I nuts?"

"Huh?"

"What did he say?"

"Come again?" Many students were confused by what Nate had just said. Several responded immediately looking for clarification.

Leaning on my lab table, again my arms outstretched, I said, "Look, you guys will probably not believe me, but you may believe an evolutionist himself. Punch up on your tablets the *American Journal of Science*, Vol. 276, January 1976, p. 53."

Pete was the first to bring it up and started waving his hand back and forth.

"Okay, Pete just give everyone a chance to find it. I want their eyeballs to see this at the same time you read it."

Pete paused until he saw everyone nodding their heads around him. "Got it" and "found it," echoed around the room.

"This statement is from J. E. O'Rourke, from his article "Pragmatism versus Materialism in Stratigraphy." 'The rocks do date the fossils, but the fossils date the rocks more accurately. Stratigraphy cannot avoid this kind of reasoning if it insists on using only temporal concepts, because circularity is inherent in the derivation of time scales.'"

Nate was jovially pounding his fist on Pete's back. "What kinda crap are they teaching you in geology? Rocks date fossils, but then fossils date the rocks!? This guy made that statement way back in 1976, and your colleagues and professors are still using this retarded circular reasoning? Are you kidding me?"

Pete turned around and tried to rebut Nate, but to no avail. All Pete could elicit was a bunch of incomprehensible utterances in defense of his chosen field, to the accompaniment of some jeers and heckles directed at him.

Nate then stood up and put his hand to his mouth, pretending to blow on a trumpet or bugle. "Da, da, da, dant, da, daaa!" Then, as if he was a ringside announcer, declared, "Round One goes to God and the young earth. Mother Gaia has taken some strong blows from Noah's Flood and is weaving . . . um . . . sinking dangerously."

"Santi wishes to add something before we go," I noticed. His expression was somewhat serious, but he also had a leprechaun smile on his face. He stood and turned to his classmates. "Creo que Dios . . . Juan help me." Juan whispers to him. "Yes, I believe God had, and has, a sense of humor *not* to have created those 'missing' in-between animales. I think He just wanted to mess with the atheist's cabezas'—heads. Mira, He even put the pink flamencos kneecaps on backwards."

With that the class doubled over laughing, including Claudia. I even saw a slight giggle erupt from Jude. Even he couldn't keep a straight face with that one.

CHAPTER SIXTY-SIX

EXTRA CREDIT

I started to pack up, preparing to exit the room, when I noticed the students in a huddle having a hushed discussion. Pete seemed to be taking the lead. He stuck his head up from the group and stated, "Don't leave yet, Doc." He put his head down into the huddle again. I stopped what I was doing, wondering what's up.

Shortly, the huddle broke up and Pete addressed me. "Doc, do you have any specific plans for this next hour?"

"No, nothing in particular. I'm meeting with Father Flanagan, but that's not until noon for lunch."

"Good," he replied. "We want to do another class session."

"Really?" I'm taken aback.

"None of us have any classes this period; and all of us want to continue the session."

"All of you?" I'm astounded and flabbergasted.

"Even Jude?"

Jude stepped forward stating, "I've read the *Art of War* by Sun Tzu. His premise is that in military strategy one must understand ones enemy's philosophy and tactics better than the enemy does himself in order to defeat him."

"Well, Jude, I never considered myself and Christianity your enemy. But let me warn you, one of our tactics is to win over your heart and soul from the dark side."

Matt, our adept sci-fi wiz, is enthralled with this. "Oh, way cool. The Matrix is the Dark Side versus Christianity, the Light. Is Mother Gaia the Death Star or should I say, Star-lette?" He laughed at his own joke.

The class booed Matt, and fake hissed at him while also laughing along with him.

"Actually, Matt, that's not a bad analogy. Okay then, we'll continue."

Maggie raised her hand. I nodded in her direction.

Maggie looked at me, but then turned to address the class as a whole. "Just so we are all on the same page," she said, pausing momentarily to look at me, "if I'm . . . we are to understand this Noah's Flood thing, you are saying that the Flood buried all the animals and plants that were on the earth, many of which fossilized. Is that correct?"

"Correct," I looked at Maggie, while speaking to all the students. "With the exception being those animals on the ark with Noah. That occurred about sixteen hundred years *after* God created Adam and Eve, or about forty-four hundred years ago."

Jim finally grasped the precept and stated, "Therefore, if the Deluge in Genesis truly happened, all the fossil layers represent death *after* Adam, and Moses and the Bible are . . . a . . . vindicated!"

Nate added, "But if the fossil layers, which represent dead things occurred millions of years ago, *before* man or Adam evolved, then the Bible is . . . a . . . Barbra Streisand from the get-go," he said looking at Jude. "So why believe the rest of the book?"

"So, if I got this straight," Jim said, thinking out loud, "those priests and theologians, who tell us we can believe the Bible *together* with the millions of years, don't know what the H-E double hockey stick they are talking about."

"And my former minister as well," Maggie added.

"Now I understand why my dad and mom barely practiced Judaism," Matt exclaimed, "with the exception of the tradition of the High Holy Days and Hanukkah. I know that my parents believe in 'millions of years,' my dad has told me as much. That's the reason why they felt Moses, Genesis, and the Flood were all bunk," Matt stated contritely as he reflected back on his childhood.

Matt was still looking down at his desk and continues to reminisce. "My parents had a 'do your own thing' philosophy with an open marriage, which ended in divorce. I now understand why."

The class was silent. The wheels were turning in their heads, and I sensed they were taking a decisive introspective and contemplative turn in their thought processes. Wanting to bring Matt out of his doldrums, I teased him a bit. "So what was it you were saying on that first day of class about only wanting to memorize books and notes?"

"Huh?" Matt grunted still in deep thought. "Oh yeah, this is much more fun using your brains." The stillness broken, several of the students around him started laughing.

"At the rate you guys are going, ICC will need to confer PhD's and D. Div. degrees on all of you."

Claudia raised her hand. "Dr. Lucci, I would like you to explain more about those layers of the geologic column from the viewpoint of the Flood, and how life was buried."

"As most of you surmised from Claudia's original observation, a world-wide flood would have covered the lowest and deepest animals and plants first—the sea life. That's why it's found in the bottom-most layers."

"Evolution says," Juan correctly determined, "that the next animals to evolve upward from those invertebrates of Pete's were the vertebrate fishes."

"Okay, Juan, can you give me an example of one, just one in-between animal found in the fossil layer—or alive, for that matter— that is transitioning or halfway evolving from an invertebrate to a vertebrate?"

Juan and the class remained silent.

"I see you've drawn a blank. How about between fish and amphibian?"

Silence.

"Amphibian to reptile?"

Silence.

"Reptile to bird? Bird to Mammal?"

Jude raised his hand. "What about archaeopteryx? The reptile becoming a bird?"

CHAPTER SIXTY-SEVEN

IF IT QUACKS LIKE A DUCK

"**A**h, yes, the ol' 'dinosaurs have evolved into birds' proposition," I responded to Jude's question about the missing link between reptiles and birds. "That archaeopteryx is the progenitor of the birds, the first to have evolved from the dinosaurian reptiles."

I brought up a picture of archaeopteryx on the Insta-Screen.

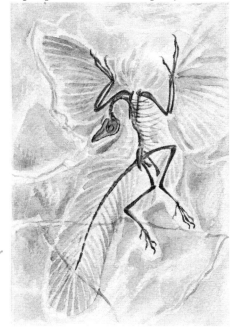

Illustration of fossil Archaeopteryx. Shutterstock

Illustration of bird Archaeopteryx. Shutterstock

"It has teeth and claws." Jude cried out.

"The ostrich and hoatzin and the touraco have claws on their wings. And extinct birds have been found with teeth. But let me ask you, does this bird have fully formed wings?"

"Yes." Jude answered.

"Does it have flight feathers?"

"Yes."

"Does it have an enlarged strong breastbone or sternum, which the flight muscles attach to?"

"Yes."

"Wouldn't this indicate a strong flyer?"

"Yes."

"Then it was a bird, Jude, an extinct bird, but a complete real bird in every sense of the definition; not halfway between reptile and bird. If it looks like a duck and walks like a duck and quacks like a duck . . ."

"It's a duck," Tom laughed as he glanced at Jude.

"Oh, a tiny piece of information the evolutionists like to leave out."

I stopped speaking to make sure I had 100 percent attention from the class. They were silent, looking and waiting for me to finish my thought.

"Modern bird fossils have been found in older deeper layers than archaeopteryx."

The class became animated.

"Andy," I announced, as I saw he wanted to contribute.

"Why don't they tell us this stuff? We never hear about dissenting evidence. That was an absolutely vital piece of evidence I don't think any of us have ever heard. What you have presented puts evolutionary theory . . . excuse me . . . the model, and the millions of years into serious jeopardy."

I noticed Jim becoming very agitated in his seat. His hand shot up.

"Doc, what about all these fossils of birds and fish and whatever they dig up every few years that they use to claim evolution is true? Then, in the museums they take us to, we see drawings and models of this stuff. I don't know what to believe anymore!"

"Jim," I briefly looked in his direction, while still addressing the class. "Remember the first day of class I explained that the Matrix has cobbled together science, religion, and politics to brainwash you?"

The class nodded in one accord.

Thad, our reporter for the *Veritas Beacon*, raised his hand.

"Doc said he would have to dismantle each one to expose and destroy the Matrix. The science is really evolution. The religion is Mother Gaia, and the politics is socialism/communism, which are all linked and intertwined together. Right, Doc?"

"An excellent concise analysis, Thad. Mother Gaia and Socialism/Communism use one thing as their primary support. Without it they vaporize into oblivion. What is that one vital buttress?"

Santi's hand was already up. I nodded at him.

"It's evolución."

"And the millions of years which give it that support," Juan added, patting Santi on the back.

"Way to go, you two. And right now we are covering much of my planned demolition of that brace, which is actually very weak when you scrutinize it honestly."

The class nodded in agreement again, with the only holdout being Jude.

"Now Jim has posed an important point about recently discovered fossils, and models and drawings in museums. Open any science journal, or newspaper, for that matter, and someone has discovered a new missing link for birds or reptiles or cavemen. The publication then has a photo or a drawing of it, with front page headlines."

"Yeah," Thad adamantly responded. "And six to twelve months later some other scientist is trashing the discovery as a fake or a hoax or just plain *scientific* baloney. I've followed a number of these 'discoveries' over the years, like Tikkalick, hoping to score a Pulitzer-winning article or even a book on one of these so-called discoveries. Check it out; several months later they are redacted or entirely retracted—quietly way back on page forty-seven."

Jim then turned around to face Thad. "What about the museums where they have the models and drawings of this stuff. They show fish growing legs, like the Tikkalick thing you mentioned, and reptiles and dinosaurs growing wings to become birds."

Philip slightly lifted his hand from his desk; then lowered it again momentarily, fighting with his conscience as whether to answer or not. I noticed from his eyes and strained facial expression that he had the answer.

"Philip!" I called in a commanding voice. He knew, I knew, he knew. The entire class turned and all eyes were focused on him.

"Okay, okay. These are museum models and drawings . . . if they had the *real* fossil, or even a replica of the fossil they claim *proves* a transitional organism or some provable aspect of evolution . . ." he took a deep breath, "wouldn't they *show* it to you?"

"Models, drawings, fish growing legs, dinosaurs growing wings." Jim smacked himself on the forehead and started to laugh. "I shoulda had a V-8." The entire class broke into hysterics as they realized the con game, and they are the patsies.

CHAPTER SIXTY-EIGHT

DINOSAUR TRICK

"Are any of you familiar with the British Museum of Natural History in London, England?"

Virtually all the hands went up. Pete then contributed, "That museum holds more fossils than any other museum in the world, I believe."

"Pete, have you heard of Dr. Colin Patterson?"

"Yeah, one of my professors mentioned in a lecture that he was a head honcho there. He has since died."

"Correct. Dr. Colin Patterson was senior paleontologist at the British Museum. Bring up on your tablets his personal letter written April 10, 1979, to Luther D. Sunderland. Patterson was one of the honest evolutionists."

"Pete, after you find it, start with the part of the quote which begins with 'I fully agree with...'"

"Got it." He cleared his throat first.

"'I fully agree with your comments on the lack of direct illustration of evolutionary transitions in my book. If I knew of any, fossil or living, I would certainly have included them. You suggest that an artist should be used to visualize such transformations, but where would he get the information from. I could not honestly provide it, and if I were to leave it to artistic license, would that not mislead the reader?'"

Pete looked up and around at his classmates. They are just shaking their heads in disbelief.

Jude half mumbling, but audible enough for all to hear, muttered, "That's just one guy's opinion."

Pete slowly stood up, and did not even bother turning to face Jude. "Just one guy's opinion?" he said in a restrained tone. "Just one guy's opinion?" he boomed. "Senior paleontologist at perhaps the most prestigious natural history museum in the world that has amassed, I don't know, a million fossils? That was not an ignorant statement - that was just plain *stupid!*" He sat down quietly without ever turning to face Jude.

The class was silent for a moment, watching Jude and looking back at Pete.

"Yes, Tom." I said, recognizing his raised hand.

"What was the *name* of Dr. Patterson's book that he responded back to Sunderland about?"

"*Evolution.*"

The class broke into intermittent chuckles.

"Before we move on, here's a little obtuse tidbit I think you'll like. You are all probably familiar with T. rex and the fast-moving velociraptors, and of course the low-slung, tank-like stegosaurus, if you've ever seen any of the Jurassic Park movies."

Matt commented, "I just love those movies, especially the blood thirsty raptors."

"Here Matt, come up to the lab table and pick up this velociraptor skull and pass it around."

As he walked back to his seat with the skull, he questioned, "This thing turned into a bird? Weirdest looking bird skull I've ever seen."

In the meantime I brought up pictures of a stegosaurus, a T. rex, velociraptor, and a turkey on the screen.

Illustration of steg and T-rex together fighting Credit: Joseph Laudati

*Illustration of velociraptor
Shutterstock*

Photo of a turkey. Google Photo credit: Mike Baird

"Now I want you all to picture this turkey clearly in your mind. The evolutionists claim that dinosaurs evolved into birds. The T. rex and velociraptor have a type of pelvis called saurischian, or lizard-hipped pelvis in English. The stegosaurus has an ornithischian or bird-hipped type." Using my laser pen I pointed to the hips of each, illustrating the comparisons. "Which one evolved—?"

"—into the birds," Matt excitedly broke in. "That's easy the orni . . . the bird-hipped one. The raptor types became birds," he said as he turned around nodding to his classmates with his big cheesy smile plastered all over his face.

"Hey, Matt," called Nate. "Better look at Doc."

Matt turned to the front, only to see me slightly shaking my head - no.

"What! Give me a break." And he pleaded, "No way, no way!

"Yes way, Matt. You weren't listening carefully. Because the tank-type stegosaurus has the bird-hipped pelvis; that type evolved into the birds—evolutionists claim, *not* the raptors."

"What a bunch of messed up retards."

I saw Santi wanting to add something.

"I think Dios—God—is just screwing with their cabezas again."

CHAPTER SIXTY-NINE

MARX AND LENIN

Thad's hand went up. "Doc, I still can't put together why one scientist will find some scrap of bone and claim it's a missing link, usually evolving to humans. It's splashed across the headlines and on TV for a while; then six months later, as I have discovered, it's quietly denounced by some other reputable scientists. Yet they *all* continue to claim evolution and millions of years are real and the truth."

Jim, who had been turned in his seat facing Thad while making his pronouncement, swiveled back around and bemoaned, "Thad's right, like that 'Ardi' and 'Sediba' apes; and 'Ida', that looks to me like some lemur monkey-like creature; and others since. There's initially all that ballyhoo and now I hear very little about each of those creatures."

"Excellent, you two are really using your heads and questioning the Matrix that wants to control you. That's potentially very dangerous thinking that you possess."

Maggie was eager to respond to Thad and Jim. She was very street savvy. I believed she would have the answer for them.

"Look guys," Maggie said, turning to address them. "What's it about . . . *all* of the time?"

Jim answered her. "The money!"

Thad responded right after him. "Power and control!"

Jim smacked himself on the forehead.

Thad rebounded, "Government research grants! Of course! The money! The socialists in power are not going to give money to someone doing creation research. It's been staring me right in the face all these years, and I failed to see it. Of course, they would use the argument that they only give money for science research and don't want to give money for religious purposes. Evolution being the science and creation being the religion."

Thad slowly closed his eyelids, and his forehead wrinkled in deep anguish.

Jim's temper flared as he pounded his desk. "The old separation-of-church-and-state excuse. However, in this case it's really philosophy versus philosophy or religion versus religion. Why don't they see it?"

"Some in power do, Jim," I answered. "And others go along and support this because . . . well they want to; those are Lenin's—"

"—useful Idiots." Maria finished my statement.

"Look, I wanted to discuss Noah's Flood to demolish the millions of years," I said, "but this is just as important, as part of the overall process of destroying this concept; the ultimate goal of which is to control *you*."

"C'mon guys," I encouraged the class, "Marx and Lenin's rationale and raison d'être is right in your faces. Just back up a bit and see the forest for the trees."

Maggie was on it. "In order to control the masses in their country, Russia—which originally was a Christian nation like ours was—Marx and Lenin needed *scientific* support for their 'share the wealth' philosophy. And whose *scientific* writings did they use for this?"

Jim still agitated, almost screamed out, "Darwin, *The Origin of the Species*! And by then, Darwin's buddy Lyell with his 'millions of years' lie had already been accepted by the church—the religious fools had planted the seeds for their own destruction."

Maria stood up and turned to face her classmates. "In order to control people completely, you must destroy God. Our Constitution tells us our rights come from God and—"

"—our Constitution is a secular godless constitution!" Jude bellowed out.

"Good point, Jude. That is another lie that will be addressed by me in a future session of this class. For now, assuming that your assertion is true, if our Constitution has no biblical basis, we are back to fallible man deciding what is right and wrong."

Both Thad and Nate tag-teamed Jude.

"Do you want another Robespierre with the French Reign of Terror?" Thad shot out.

"Or another Hitler or Stalin or Mao Zedong?" added Nate.

"All those societies killed millions of their own people, using their own man-made laws, having eliminated God and replaced Him with Darwin," reinforced Thad.

"Jude, c'mon, do you want that happening to us here in the U.S.?" challenged Nate.

Jude did not respond. He sat silent with his arms crossed, facing forward, and his dark eyes appearing blank and dead.

CHAPTER SEVENTY

MEGA SEQUENCES

Thad's hand went up. "Doc, I'm tying it together now. Nate brought to our attention the disciplinary action taken against Dr. Richard Sternberg and others—the old publish or perish thing. Everyone in the sciences knows the game and how it's to be played. They will all turn on a researcher who does not play by their rules, and like rabid dogs devour and destroy even a hardcore evolutionist's discovery of some *evolutionary* fossil, knowing its Barbra Streisand anyway." Thad looked at Nate and gave a little chuckle.

The class joined him, laughing at the double entendre.

"Right, Thad. There are a limited amount of grant monies; the economy being very tight. Most of these scientists know that evolution is a farce; its heyday is over, but it's the only game in town. They will destroy anyone, even one of their own, for a piece of that grant money."

"Got it, Doc. The powers that be, the government Matrix, which dispenses those monies in many cases, will do so for only those scientists supportive of an atheistic agenda," Thad explained. "Providing evidence that the Judeo-Christian God exists doesn't bode well for the Matrix and their Mother Gaia one-world government."

The class buzzed with discussion at a fever pitch. They were starting to understand. Jude was still sitting in the back corner, arms crossed, and his face turning purple.

Jim jumped right out of his seat. Sometimes I really thought he was a re-incarnation of Patrick Henry. "How do we fight this, Doc? We've got to do something to save our country." He stood there flummoxed.

Maggie came to the rescue as she turned to address Jim. "Truth and real knowledge, not the claptrap junk the governmental Matrix force-feeds us through its Common Core. Why do you think they are trying to brainwash us? Remember what Doc said about Hitler and controlling the youth. Now our government takes education out of the hands of the people and the local communities for their own evil designs of dumbing us down."

Maria turned around, and giving Maggie a smile, added, "Yeah, show me in the Constitution," she glanced at Jude, "where it says that our government, the Matrix, is suppose to be in charge of education. Show me!"

"Excellent ladies. Way to go," I encouraged. "Okay, Jim, Maggie said it—truth and knowledge."

"So what are we waiting for, Doc?" Jim asked still standing beside his seat like some senator giving a proclamation. "Let's rip that solitary support of the millions of years out from under Mother Gaia's evolutionism and all the other 'isms which it supports— communism, socialism, Nazism, and fascism."

"I agree," Claudia spoke at the same time she raised her hand. "Dr. Lucci, you must give us the mental tools, that young earth evidence; otherwise the libs on campus, and our friends, will be calling us flat-earthers and worse."

Wow! And this coming from one of the big libs herself, I thought.

"Claudia is right," Juan added, "let's learn more about evidence for Noah's Flood."

"Claro," Santi remarked. Heads were bobbing around the room as everyone was ready to take this on.

"Okay gang, let's rock and roll. Or should I say rocks that roll." The class heckled and jeered. "Hey, I'm allowed one bad joke per class session; it's in the by-laws."

"How many of you like pancakes?"

Many hands went up. "Think of those pancaked layers at the Grand Canyon and around the world. We'll be seeing many of those strata, on a much smaller scale, during our trip next week."

"Really?!" Matt excitedly responded. "Way cool!"

"Keep in mind that Noah's Flood laid down those pancaked layers. It wasn't until after the flood subsided and the waters receded that the Grand Canyon was formed and left the Colorado River. A lot of water over a short period of time."

"Now the long-age geologists like Hutton and Lyell," I continued, "believed each tiny layer formed slowly over eons, perhaps ten to one hundred thousand years for each small layer, with the Colorado River *afterwards* grinding out the canyon one sand grain at a time."

Pete's hand was up. "Some of my geology Profs say that possibly many small local floods may have laid each layer down over millions of years around the world."

"Sounds like they are slowly coming around to the concept of catastrophism. So if I understand your professors correctly, they believe in multiple small floods around the world, multiple upon multiple times, laying down a sedimentary stratum here and another there, slowly, over millions of years. Am I correct?"

"Ah yeah, Doc," Pete answered.

"Wouldn't it be easier to believe in the *one* all-encompassing global cataclysmic event called Noah's Flood, rather than innumerable small regional floods around the world?" I asked. "Oh, I'm sorry—one big hydraulic catastrophe would mean the Bible is correct and that there is a God who destroyed the world and punishes sin. Can't have that, can we!?"

"Wow! Never looked at it that way, Doc."

"Pete, what is the lowermost sedimentary layer of the Grand Canyon?"

"Uh, it's the Tapeats sandstone, which is part of the Sauk mega sequence."

"Are you aware that there are six mega sequences? Some of these strata extend across the United States into Canada and Greenland. Does that sound *local* to you?"

Heads were shaking around the room.

"Anyone familiar with the White Cliffs of Dover?"

"My great-grandfather was British," Nate proudly remarked. "He was a pilot in the RAF during WWII. He flew his Spitfire out of RAF Hawkinge to fight the Nazis during the Battle of Britain. He told my dad that he downed many a Messerschmitt into the sea by the White Cliffs of Dover."

"Thanks, Nate. Is anyone aware that the White Cliffs of Dover is also a sedimentary mega sequence which can be traced across Europe into the Middle East and extends into Australia? Another little *local* flood, I'm sure."

"Thad," I recognized his waving hand.

"Doc, where did all the water for the flood come from? There's not enough water in all the clouds over the earth for it to rain deep enough to cover all the mountains."

"I'll answer your question. But first let's modify it a bit. Pete, where do your professors say all the water came from, for all these multiple, multiple local floods, repeatedly over millions of years?"

"The oceans came over the land."

"Multiple, multiple times? What triggered them *each* and *every* time?"

"There are multiple, no pun intended, theories on this."

The class booed and hissed at that one.

"Hey," Pete said, "Don't shoot the messenger; they're not my theories."

"Okay Thad, *now* I'll answer your question as to where all the water from the flood came from."

CHAPTER SEVENTY-ONE

KOLA BOREHOLE

"**B**ring up on your tablets Genesis 7, verse 11. And Thad, please read to the class where it begins 'in the second month. . .'"

"Okay. '. . .in the second month, the seventeenth day of the month, the same day were all the fountains of the great deep broken up, and the windows of heaven were open.'"

"So Thad, where did *most* of the water originate?"

"The 'fountains of the great deep', but what are they? Where are they?"

"First, you need to understand that the Deluge was the single largest historic geotectonic, hydraulic, and volcanic cataclysmic event the earth has ever experienced. Have you ever heard of the mid-Atlantic ridge and the Pacific Ring of Fire?"

Some of the class nodded their heads and some were obviously unsure of what I was saying. On the Insta-Screen, I projected the mid-Atlantic Ridge and its volcanoes from my tablet.

"Notice with the water removed from this diagram, how the mid-Atlantic ridge goes down the middle of the Atlantic Ocean like the seam of a baseball. The one in the Pacific seems to ring the entire ocean skirting up past Japan to Alaska, and then circles down alongside California to South America. The Indian Ocean has similar ridges, also."

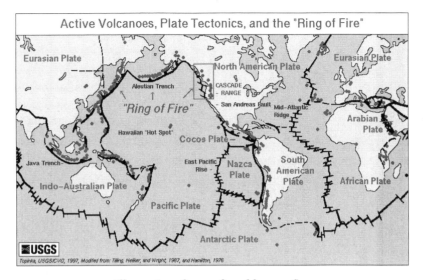

Illustration of map of world ocean floor
showing mid-Atlantic ridges
Credit: USGS

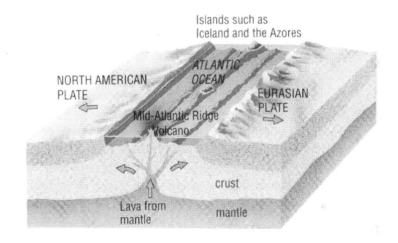

Separation of the North American Plate
and the Eurasian Plate

Matt realized what he was seeing. "Yeah, the Pacific Ring of Fire. Tremendous amount of tectonic activity: earthquakes, tsunamis, and volcanic eruptions. I'm going to buy property in the Nevada desert."

"How's that, Matt?" I ask.

"Well, when the big one hits California and drops it into the sea, I'll have oceanfront property worth a fortune. It's just a matter of time. Do you know that 80 percent of the volcanoes on earth are in the oceans? With all those tectonic plates shifting around, well, go figure the Vegas odds yourself."

Juan put his hand up. "Is Matt right about this Pacific Ring of Fire and the volcanoes? I've got relatives in Ecuador and some in Chile. There are volcanoes there."

"As a matter of fact, Juan, Ecuador owns the Galapagos Islands, which are volcanic. Does anyone remember who made those islands famous?"

Jim, still fuming, answered through gritted teeth, "Darwin with his thirteen species of evolving finches. I'm still mad at myself for being so gullible. What have these finches evolved into, or from, for that matter? They're *still* finches! I'd like to see them try to evolve into that woodpecker that Fred talked to us about. What a dumb, stupid theory, I mean model."

"Okay, Jim. Are you going to need a chill pill?"

"I'm fine. I'm fine," he said in a gruff voice.

"Now that we've had our public service announcement from Jim, let's continue." I got a few laughs from the group.

"Today's activity in the Mid-Atlantic Ridge, Pacific Rim, and Indian Ocean are leftover remnants from the rupturing of the fountains of the great deep. The current activity is only micro aftershocks of what took place forty-five hundred years ago."

"Madre de Dios!" Santi remarked. "*Only* micro aftershocks! Including the 2004 Indonesian and the 2011 Japanese earthquakes and tsunamis? Oh yeah, the Fukushima nuclear accident!"

I brought up on the Insta-Screen a YouTube video called "*Flood Initiation.*"

"This two-minute CGI representation shows how the oceanic ridges developed as a result of the rupturing of the 'fountains of the great deep'. It shows how the Flood started as a small tear in the mantle and raced around the earth in a matter of hours."

Pointing to the video on the screen, I said, "See how the pressure of the *hot* water, I repeat *hot* water, from the ruptured chambers, which were approximately ten to fifteen miles deep in the mantle, spews supersonically upward into the atmosphere before coming down on the earth as torrential hurricane-like rains. Watch and notice how the water pressure quickly erodes massive quantities of earth, as it exits the mantle, turning it into massive mudflows. It's reminiscent of the event at Mount St. Helen's. Now today, the scarred remains of that tear we call the Mid-Atlantic Ridge and the Pacific Ring."

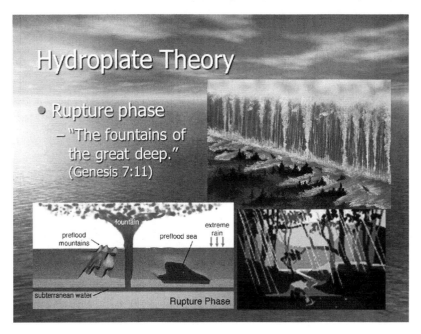

Illustration of Hydroplate Theory.
Credit: Walter Brown, PhD.

Matt was the first to notice, "Look, look the 'fountains' are breaking up the supercontinent Pangaea, and the tectonic plates are separating the land masses: South America is being separated from Africa. Wow, savage man!"

"Absolutely first-rate observation and analyzation, Matt. Hope all of you caught that. Way to go!"

Pete leaned over toward Matt and gave him a fist bump.

"Have any of you lived near a river?"

Andy and Pete's hands both went up. "Our family lives near Mobile, Alabama, and we were little kids when Katrina hit. The rivers overflowed their banks carrying massive amounts of mud in addition to water," Andy commented.

Most of the students watched the video on the Insta-Screen, and the rest viewed it on their tablets. For the remainder of the clip the class was quiet, just taking it all in.

When it ended, I simply asked, "Well?"

Then the comments started to fly from all directions at once.

"Holy crap."

"I had no idea."

"The whole earth was destroyed."

"But why did God have to kill everyone?"

"Nothing was left alive."

Jude's loud and arrogant voice dominated. "You can't *prove* there are massive quantities of water under the earth."

"Actually, Jude, there is proof of this. Go to YouTube and bring up *The Deepest Hole in the World, and what We've Learned from It*."

The students studied the video on their tablets. I heard muffled comments coming from around the room. The class was obviously surprised that the mantle of the earth contained water.

Jude commented. "Yeah, but the video *proves* this water developed under the earth billions of years ago."

Jim was all over Jude in a heartbeat. "Proves? *Proves?*" He asked angrily while looking at Jude.

Philip was leaning back in his chair, against the back wall, and looking at the ceiling. "What is the definition of science, Jude?" Philip asked, with an annoyed tone, as though Jude were wasting his and everyone's time. "The only part that was *proved* beyond a shadow of a doubt was the presence of water. The billions of years part is an unprovable assumption, not based on any evidence of long ages, may I add." He moved his eyes from ceiling to the rear doorway.

Jude just clenched his jaw tightly as he shifted his eyes briefly toward Philip who was looking out the classroom door. He felt demeaned and humiliated by Philip.

CHAPTER SEVENTY-TWO

SUSPENDED

Finally, Pete calmly raised his hand. His face reflecting that he just had an epiphany. He stood to address the class. First he looked at Jim, our ecology major. "Jim, all this water and mud encased millions of plants and animals instantaneously. That's why no matter which strata or layer we examine of the geologic column—"

"Many are all perfectly preserved." Jim interrupted immediately picking up on Pete's thought process. "Yeah, Cambrian, Devonian, Silurian, and Jurassic organisms, by and large, are well preserved."

Thad added his thoughts into the mix. "Both you guys are right. *If* each layer laid down was separated by millions of years, then why are the fossils well preserved, *regardless* of the layer—*unless* . . . this was a one-time event."

Philip then added, "We've been told by our professors that fossilization is a slow process over millions of years—grain by grain, sediment slowly covering the plants and animals. Minerals gradually replacing the organic matter over eons of time, placidly converting these creatures to stone."

Jim was getting his dander up again. "I never really thought about it. Doc is getting us to actually use our rusty brains. Ugh, all, and I mean *all,* fossils are found buried in sedimentary rock—which is *always* laid down by water. Fossils in sandstone, fossils in shale, fossils in limestone, even in coal and oil—all this caused by Noah's Deluge. Practically the whole earth we are standing on is one big graveyard!"

"By the way, you guys," I said, looking at Jim, Philip, and Pete, "do you realize that the earth's stony surface is 85 percent *sedimentary* rock? Must have been those thousands upon thousands of 'local floods' over the millennia which magically covered the land," I suggested with as much sarcasm as I could muster.

"Jim and Philip are right," Pete added. "All these mass kills of fish and plants are all impeccably preserved, including even delicate jellyfish." With that I handed Pete a plaque of completely intact and unmarred fossilized jellyfish. "All these creatures had to be covered with sedimentary mud rapidly." He exclaimed while carefully examining the jellyfish plaque. "Dead fish are torn apart and jellyfish and plants decay in short order. The slow and gradual 'millions of years' theory is a bunch of horse pucky." With that he

Photo of multiple small fossilized fish on stone.
Shutterstock

began pointing out the features on each plaque to his brother Andy, sitting next to him.

"Pete, here's another small plate with several small fossilized fish that a mudflow suffocated quickly. Examine the fine boney structure, scales, and eyes, all perfectly preserved. Please pass it around. And I'll bring up on the Insta-Screen other mass kills displayed in museums; plaques which contain hundreds of these flawless specimen fish on each plate."

"I don't know of any fish and plant burials occurring on a worldwide scale like this today," Jim announced while watching the pics on the Insta-Screen.

"Hey, Jim," I called as I passed a replica fossil to him. "Check this one out."

He looked at it only for a moment. "Oh, my lord, a fish in the act of eating another fish. It didn't even have time to finish its lunch."

Photo of fossilized fish eating another smaller fish
Photo credit: Answers in Genesis

I passed another to him, as he passed the first one over to Claudia.

"Gak! An ichthyosaur giving birth! The fry isn't even out of the birth canal. Must be one of those rare million-year gestation times," he stated sarcastically. I can figure this one out without a V-8!"

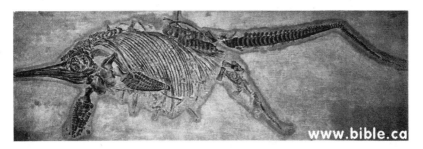

Photo of fossilized Ichthyosaur giving birth. www.bible.ca
Photo credit: Dr. Don Patton

Jim had the class in hysterics with his comments.

I waited for the class to settle down before pointing out a fossilized tree trunk on the screen, then another and another. "Anyone want to tackle this one? See anything that really doesn't make sense?"

The class evaluated the fossilized trees standing vertically through multiple layers of strata.

Photo of polystrate tree with strata
Photo credit: copyright Creation Research www.evolutionfairytale.com

Photo of man kneeling next to polystrate tree
Photo credit: David Rives at David Rives Ministry

Nate started to laugh while pointing at the screen.

"Want to let us in on the joke, Nate," Andy implored.

"Guys, look at the pics on the screen." Nate demanded.

"Yeah, so what?" Pete replied, turning to face Nate.

"So what? How long could that tree have remained there without rotting," Nate declared, forcefully making his point, "while the sediment sloooowly built up around it over millions of years? Give me a break!"

"These are called polystrate fossils," I commented, "because they traverse multiple strata."

Jim pounded on his desk again. "Nate's right. The dumb tree could no way last millions of years as the strata leisurely buried it. The Flood makes more sense. I just can't wait to have my next ecology lecture. The professor is not going to know what hit him."

Maggie appeared to want to add something to the discussion.

"Doc, I was dating an airman from Vandenberg Air Force Base for a while. He wanted to know if I wanted to see a whale on its tail. He took me to Lompoc, which was not too far from the base. And there it was, an eighty to ninety foot whale fossilized at about a forty-five degree angle in the rock."

The class looked at Maggie, not sure what to believe.

"What did you make of it, Maggie?" I asked.

"At the time, I didn't understand the significance of what I was looking at. I do now. I was dopey and immature, and more interested in *his* tail, than the whale's."

The class howled with laughter. I'll give Maggie one thing - she is honest.

The class was still in an uproar, as Nate put his hand up. In the meantime I had brought up an image of the Lompoc, California, whale.

Whale on its Tail

- The Lompoc, CA diatomite bed and fossil whale, as found excavated in 1976
- Deposit was formed catastrophically, interring the whale almost instantaneously
- Uniformitarian geologists have steadfastly maintained that such diatomaceous-earth deposits require millions of years to form

@ Dr. Heinz Lycklama   31

Illustration of whale on its tail
Credit: Dr. Heinz Lycklama

"Hey Doc, how did the whale get fossilized on its tail?"

"I'm going to force your creaky cogwheels to turn, if it's the last thing I do. Stop thinking in millions of years, doggone it."

Juan raised his hand with confidence. I nodded at him to answer.

"My grandmother made pottery from clay, which is a form of sedimentary rock, I believe. While the clay was soft and flexible, she could mold it any way she wanted, even placing carvings and other impressions in it. But once it hardened, it was easily broken—impressions and all."

"Please stop there, Juan. Let's see if the class can figure out the remainder of the puzzle."

The silence was deafening.

"Your minds are still locked in the millions of years mentality—break through it! You can do it."

Andy and Pete were intensely discussing the possible options.

"Matt! You mentioned earlier about the tectonic plates causing disastrous effects. Please read about Noah's Flood from Psalm 104 verse 8, the first line." Matt first started to read quietly to himself. He was nodding his head. "I've got it. I think. 'The mountains rose; the valleys sank down,'" as he read it out loud. "The flood laid down the sedimentary layers over a short expanse of time, burying the animals and plants, which eventually fossilized and. . . ." He hesitated a bit.

"Go ahead Matt, you're on track."

". . . and while still soft, the tectonic plate action occurred which raised those layers to the angle the Lompoc whale is in today."

"You're not finished, Matt."

"Oh, yes, Juan mentioned about his grandma with the clay. *If* the sedimentary layers had hardened *first* and then later, after millions of years, the tectonic action of raising the whale into place occurred, the whale and the layers it is in would have broken in pieces, like his Grandma's dried pottery." He gave the class his famous used-car salesman smile.

Tom then turned around to Matt. "So you're saying the strata had to be soft and pliable, like the potter's clay, for the tectonic movements to raise the whale without breaking it up." Matt nodded his assent.

Santi had turned around and was cheering Matt on. "Andale, andale!" Matt clasped his hands together and raised his arms over his head, doing a Rocky-type celebration.

I waited for Matt to settle down. Between Juan and Matt the class' brains seemed to be greased up and working sufficiently well.

Thad contributed, "I get it—the flood waters had to *first* run off the earth into the *valley* or ocean basins. What a headline story! Oh, Oh, and that's when and how the Grand Canyon was carved out."

"Way to go, Thad," Jim congratulated him as he turned around and gave Thad a loud smacking high five.

Tom turned to Thad, "Yeah, only then, with the strata being soft, could the tectonic actions of the 'mountains rising' occur without fracturing the whale."

The entire class became one big talkfest. They get it.

"Here, Jim, see if you can figure this one out."

He carefully examined the object I handed to him, turning it over and around with a puzzled look.

"Well," Jim hesitated, "it looks like a replica of a chunk of coal."

"Okay, good start. Go on."

"But there is something embedded in it. It . . . it's a metal bowl of some sort." He shook his head, totally confused. "How can that be? It takes millions upon millions of years for coal to form."

"Jim!" I almost shouted at him. "Stop thinking like an atheistic 'millions of years' evolutionist."

"Huh?" He looked up at me. The class was waiting for some kind of punch line as they looked back and forth between Jim and me.

"C'mon man. You yourself gave the answer. How did you say coal and oil was formed a few minutes ago?"

Photo of iron bowl in coal. Personal photo

"By sedimentation."

"As a result of . . . ? You said it yourself."

I watched the class closely. Some had figured it out and wanted to explode. "No one say anything. This is Jim's baby to work through."

"I'll give you a hint, Jim. It wasn't ancient aliens." Matt nodded knowingly, as he was one of the ones who had the answer.

Jim's eyes grew big and his mouth dropped open. "The flood! This metal bowl was from the cursed society that lived alongside Noah and his family prior to the flood."

"Excellent! Jim, why don't you read Genesis chapter 6 verse 5, while I show these photos to the class." On the screen I projected from my tablet a photo of a bell, and another of a necklace chain, both found in coal.

"'And God saw that the wickedness of man *was* great in the earth, and that every imagination of the thoughts of his heart *was* only evil continually.'" Jim looked up at the screen, his mind still reeling by what he was seeing.

"Oh, Jim, here's a replica of an ancient hammer that was found in a rock layer that was supposed to be 300 million years old."

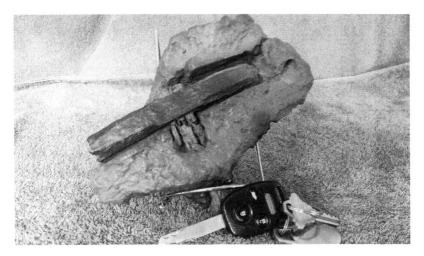

Photo of hammer in stone. Personal photo

He literally grabbed it from my hand, looked up at me as the class watched him, and said, "From the corrupt pre-flood world of Noah, I bet."

Santi hollered across the room to Jim. "Claro, hombre. The evolutionistas claim that man began to evolve around two million years ago. Only the flood makes sense of it."

Tom turned to Matt. "Either that, or it was placed in the rock by ancient aliens." He formed antennas with his fingers on top of his head, while making googly bug eyes at Matt. The class laughed, reveling at Tom's monkeyshines.

A student messenger entered the room and approached me with a note. Some students were around Jim as he was reticent to give up the hammer. I reviewed the note quickly and looked back at the messenger.

"Dean Avery would like an immediate response from you, Dr. Lucci."

The class looked up in unison, speculating as to what was going on. Thad, our journalist, was all ears.

"Tell him I will meet with him straightaway."

The messenger then turned to the students and announced that the class was suspended until further notice.

Only Santi noticed the diabolic smile that crept across Jude's face.

CHAPTER SEVENTY-THREE

O'DARK THIRTY

My alarm clock went off and I blindly slammed it. *Alarm clock— appropriate name,* I thought. *Are my eyes open?* I looked at the clock, it was o'dark thirty; no wonder I couldn't see a thing. I heard Emily rustling to get up.

"Honey, you don't have to get up at this ungodly hour just for me," I said as I turned on the light on my bedside table.

"I'll make us a small breakfast, and coffee to take with you. You're going to be on that long bus trip with the kids, so I'll pack a small cooler for you, Fred, and Cindy."

I am absolutely blessed with a wonderful wife, I thought.

"Why don't you come with us?"

"I've got too much to do around here. I have to get the garden ready for winter. Besides, you said Father Flanagan is not coming, and neither are Dorothy and Vince. And I've been to the museums with you a number of times before."

***

As I warmed up 'the tank', I took the covers off the Hella driving lights, and then hopped into the leather bucket seat, and put my coffee in its console holder next to me, behind the shifter. I've got the nine-inch mammoth Hellas bolted to a cross bar on a pair of huge police push bumpers I picked up used. With all the deer and other creatures of the night, I didn't need to be messing up my grill and front end. The seat belt clicked in place; I pulled out of the garage and slowly glided along the house-lined street of our sleeping subdivision. I noted that the dew was heavy on the lawns and mailboxes as I passed them by. There was also a low misty fog that must have come in during the night.

I hit the entrance ramp to I-81, and once on the highway, accelerated up to cruising speed. I locked 'the tank' in at seventy and flipped on the Hellas. The pair of lights cut through the patchy fog like a hot knife through butter. I settled into the driver's seat and took a sip of my coffee.

It was still completely dark out and I couldn't see any stars. *Must be overcast,* I thought. The outside temp on the dash said thirty-six degrees. The weather girl said it would be clear and should hit the high sixties.

Practically no traffic, as it was still an hour or so before rush hour began. Only ones out now are drunks, druggies, and people up to no good. I wondered which category that put me?

A vehicle approached me in the oncoming lane. I shut off the Hellas, but he was still coming with his high beams on. I quickly flashed my high beams, but he kept his brights on. *Okay, buddy, you asked for it.* I flipped the Hellas back on, and he immediately turned his brights off, obviously getting the message. Those photons of light pulsating against the back of his retina must have sent a searing message to his brain. Jerk.

As I drove along, I thought, *most people don't realize that at least half the drivers on the road have something in their systems that will impair their coordination and driving ability. Anything from sleeping pills to anti-depressants to anti-psychotics to narcotic pain meds to a bevy of illegal substances and alcohol, or a combo of all of these. And all while texting to boot. Maybe these new hands-free T-chip devices may cut down on accidents.*

We've transformed our country into a nation of zombies, and our governmental Matrix loves it. Wait until they start coming for everyone's firearms whose medical records show they popped even one Ambien. Dorothy is right. That's the excuse the Matrix will use to nullify our Second Amendment Right to bear arms; instead of incarcerating these repeat psych offenders. Whereas they look upon the law-abiding citizen as potential serial killers.

I pulled into the parking lot at ICC and saw our 'school' bus running and ready to go with the courtesy lights on inside and out. It was an impressive new monster Prevost with a tag axle. *Nice!* Immaculate Conception College was painted in beautiful script on the side, as well as our mascot—a knight on a white charger—and logo—the Crusaders. The paint job was exquisite. Brother Francis stood outside the passenger door with Fred.

"Where's Cindy?" I asked Fred as I walked up and shook their hands. Fred's hand felt like an icebox.

"She's inside at the rear, napping, where it's warm. Why Brother Francis and I are out here freezing our bippies off, I don't know."

"Let her sleep," I replied. "She probably worked both her jobs yesterday. Hey, who's watching your kids?"

"Her mom said she'd do it so we could get away by ourselves."

"Get away? Hopefully our 'kids' will not be a chore for you guys."

"Hey, Doc," Brother Francis entered the conversation, "the scuttlebutt was that the trip was going to be cancelled, and possibly your class as well. How did you turn that around?"

CHAPTER SEVENTY-FOUR

THE DEAN

"Trust me I had nothing to do with it. When I arrived at Dean Avery's office, Dietrich was there. Why did I suspect his hand was involved in it?"

"Rich Avery is a tough straight shooter," Fred injected. "I'm sure he didn't let Dietrich push him around. Do you know his background?"

"I believe he was a West Pointer. I saw his class ring when I was first introduced to him by Father Flanagan."

"He was a Heisman Trophy winner his senior year at the Academy," Francis added. "And *Ebony* magazine named him Black Athlete of the Year."

"And *Time* magazine had him on the cover a few years later as Renaissance Man of the Year. Did you fellas know that?" Fred mentioned while shivering in his lightweight Columbia jacket. "I thought it was supposed to get up close to seventy today."

"Perhaps, after the sun comes up," I chided him. "For now, it's still pitch-dark out, and we *are* on the top of a mountain; *it is* probably close to freezing." I deliberately exhaled to show my breath forming a cloud of condensation in front of Fred.

"Fred, I didn't know about the Renaissance Man thing. What's that about?"

"Doc, the guy also has a gift for languages. He is fluent in at least four tongues that I know of. And he can read and write in those, equally as well."

I started to think out loud. "I seem to recall seeing some military commendations and plaques on the wall of his office from Iraq and Afghanistan. Ah, now I see. Father Flanagan—military and CIA, Avery—military, languages . . . does Rich Avery speak Arabic?"

"I believe he does," Francis said, stroking his goatee.

"And how does Dean Avery know Father Ed?" I asked, posing the question to both Fred and Francis.

We all looked at each other and concluded that they must know each other somehow from "the Company," which must have been the common denominator.

"That explains why Avery didn't take any guff from Dietrich when I was the one suppose to be on the hot seat."

"Yeah, Avery's not going to be harassed by some pencil-necked geek bureaucrat," Francis adamantly added.

"So, what was Dietrich accusing you of?" Fred, still shivering asked. It appeared that his lips were turning blue.

"Some gobbledygook about lying to the kids in class about evolution and Mother Gaia, which is a social injustice. That I'm being intolerant of alternative lifestyles and that I claimed there are absolute truths. Dean Avery let him drone on a while about his being *personally* offended."

"I heard that Father Flanagan and Dr. Mercurio showed up," Brother Francis declared, anxious to hear the juicy parts.

"Yeah, and both of them were hot under the collar. Dorothy was standing, rocking back and forth on those sneakers of hers. Father Ed had his stone face on, standing legs astride and his arms crossed."

"Did they say anything?" Francis probed.

"Not until Dietrich started castigating me using ad hominem attacks regarding my teaching against millions of years and accusing me of personally assailing the 'heart of Mother Gaia.'"

Fred, almost dancing around to warm up, stated, "Typical leftist crap. They can never defend their points straight on and always stoop to personal insults, eventually."

"That's when the proverbial s**t hit the fan in Avery's office. Father Flanagan and Dr. Mercurio let Dietrich have it with both barrels—verbally that is. I really thought Dorothy was going to kick Dietrich in the family jewels, she was so mad."

Francis and Fred both had a good belly laugh, knowing that Dorothy was perfectly capable of doing it, too. I chuckled along with them.

"So, what did Dean Avery say?" Francis pushed for a response.

"Actually not much. He comes on like a mild-mannered Dr. Ben Carson, the cerebral type. But then he responds like a Donald Trump when either he, or one of his faculty family, is attacked."

"So, what did he do, what did he do?" Francis asked, getting very animated.

"Well, after he read him the riot act, Avery literally grabbed Dietrich by the collar and the seat of his khaki pants and 'escorted' him out of his office, under a stream of protests from Dietrich, while his Birkenstocks were dragging across the carpet. It was what Dietrich said that made me very uncomfortable."

"What did Dietrich say?" Fred inquired.

"First, Dean Avery made it clear to Dietrich that this was a Catholic institution that abided by Christian biblical principles, and that he was not going to compromise those principles for political ends, and that's when he forcefully grabbed him."

"A-a-and t-t-then?" Fred's teeth were chattering.

"As Dietrich was being escorted out, he was saying something to the effect that 'this was not going to be a Christian college much longer. That Washington would make sure of that.'"

The eastern predawn sky was just starting to lighten and the clouds were breaking up.

"Hey, Brother Francis, I think we better get Fred onto the bus, before he turns into a block of ice."

"Good idea. I see some of the students' headlights pulling into the lot now, anyway."

CHAPTER SEVENTY-FIVE

BLUESHIRTS

The Prevost is the Cadillac of buses and RVs, and the investors, again, did not spare any expense when it came to customizing that one. The seats were all akin to being in a first class cabin of a jetliner, two per row, with the aisle in-between. The seats fully reclined and had a button to inflate the headrest to create your own personalized pillow.

There was even a flat console with retractable cup holders that gave adequate room between each pair of seats so there was no bumping of elbows. The back of the seat in front of each passenger had a recessed flat Insta-Screen with a USB drive for streaming devices. The entire seat back could fold down to create a work desk, with individualized adjustable LED lighting surrounding the work area's periphery, so not as to disturb the passenger next to you.

Part of the reason for so much spacious comfort was that the unit was custom designed with only thirty-six seats. This unit had a bathroom that rivaled any high-end RV. There was even a small kitchenette with a stocked frig at the back with bottled water and soft drinks.

Tom was the last to board, as he was usually late. We crept out of the parking lot at 7:15 AM without Jude. Matt said he decided not to come at the last minute.

Fred and I were seated in the last row at the rear and were talking quietly while Cindy slept across the aisle from us with a blanket covering her. The sun's rays were now peeking over the mountaintops. Most of the students had their side window curtains pulled down and were napping. A few were playing with their cell phones.

The Prevost was rolling down the main college road toward the palatial bricked entrance of ICC. We hadn't even arrived at the entrance circle when Brother Francis slammed on the brakes, which jolted everyone from their seat. I thought maybe a deer jumped in front of the bus. Everyone was now wide awake.

Brother Francis turned in his driver seat and called to me, "Doc, you better come up here."

I walked to the front of the bus as Brother Francis was apologizing for hitting the brakes so abruptly. "They just jumped out on the road in front of me, I could have killed them."

I looked out the massive windshield to see two of Erik's Blueshirts standing only a few feet in front of the bus, one with his hands on his hips and the other like a crossing guard with his arm and hand extended demanding us to stop.

There were bushes on both sides of the road in front of the bus that they apparently had jumped out from behind. *Erik must be insane,* I thought, *willing to literally sacrifice these men for Dietrich's cause. Hoping also, that if we had injured or killed these men, the trip would have ended on the spot.*

Then, from out of the foggy shadows, on the grassy sides of the road further down the lane, Erik and his band emerged and walked toward us as rays of sunlight filtered through the mist and trees, sporadically illuminating the group as they walked.

They formed a semicircle in front of the bus about fifteen or twenty feet away. All had holstered sidearms. I've never seen that before on the campus. Five of them had, what appeared to me, to be M4 automatic rifles. Where did they get those?

Erik approached the door of the bus and proceeded to take his wooden nightstick and beat on the window. "Open up," he commanded.

I nodded to Brother Francis to open the door as I walked down the steps, but remained inside.

"And how can I help you on this bright crisp morning, Erik?"

His piercing blue eyes cutting through me with spite and malice, he stated, "Turn the bus around at the circle and return to the main campus. You have no authority to leave."

"Erik, what are you talking about? This trip has been approved by administration for over a month now. Would you care to see the papers?" I'm flashbacking to some of the old World War II movies when the Gestapo was running around demanding 'papers, papers' from everyone.

Still in his driver's seat, Brother Francis hollered out, "Let me get out and kick his butt."

"Your paperwork has been rescinded," Erik snidely remarked.

"How's that? Who has countermanded the administration's permission?" I forcefully demanded.

"The United States Government!" Erik exclaimed, almost spitting the words in my face. He stood firm with his feet apart and slowly smacking his billy club on the palm of his left hand.

Obviously Dietrich was behind it all, but I played along with Erik. "And why is the United States Government so interested in a school bus trip?"

"Because you're using this trip for proselytizing purposes. Your trip itinerary includes stops at Christian religious themed parks and museums. Is that not so?" He interrogated, continuing to beat his hand red with his stick. "You need special government permission to pull a stunt like that, and I don't think you'll get it." Erik had a devilish smile on his face.

"So if I understand you correctly Erik, with the new Freedom of Worship rules, we are free to talk about religious subjects here at

ICC or at the museums; it's just that we can't get from here to there. Am I correct?"

"That's about the size of it, unless of course, you have Scotty teleport your bus to the museums." He looked at his crew, and they all started to laugh derisively at us.

CHAPTER SEVENTY-SIX

THE SOLUTION

The students were getting a practical lesson in revised constitutional law, specifically the Bill of Rights. Most of them never understood the phrase *inalienable rights*. That these were God ordained and could never be revoked by man. But since there was no God, due to Darwin, government dictated the rights in our new Age of Enlightenment.

Tom said, "Jefferson's words have come to pass; 'When governments fear the people, there is liberty. When people fear the government, there is tyranny.'" He then subsequently turned and blindly stared out his window, apparently deep in thought.

"I'm going to make a call," I told Erik, as I walked back up the bus stairs and nodded at Brother Francis to close the door.

We all heard Erik boisterously call out, "Make all the calls you want, but don't attempt to leave. Once you cross the entrance to the public road, we have orders to shoot—and we will." He smacked his wooden baton against the door window a few more times as a final warning.

As I passed by Brother Francis, I saw the anger and frustration on his face, as well as on the students' faces. "What are we going to do?" I heard him say. Others added their embittered comments, as well.

I sat next to Fred; he looked at me depressed, shaking his head.

"I'm calling Father Flanagan at his personal number. I'm sure he'll have some solution to this mess." I had Father Ed on speed dial. His number only rang twice before he answered.

"Joe, I wasn't expecting you to call so soon. You lads get a flat tire or something?"

"It's more of an 'or something' problem we have." And I proceeded to explain the situation to him.

He was silent for about ten seconds, as I know his brain was conjuring up a viable solution. Then I heard him laughing to himself. I wished he'd let me in on it.

He then proceeded to give me the solution. "Yes . . . yes . . . good . . . excellent . . . okay then." I hung up.

Fred was all over me. "What did he say? Is the trip still on?"

Cindy was wide awake, leaning across the aisle, listening in on the action.

I told Fred and Cindy, "You guys are going to love this. Can't believe I didn't realize this myself. Piece of cake."

I got up, and walked back up to the front, leaving Fred and Cindy puzzled as to what was going to happen.

All the students' eyes were on me as I passed by them. I nodded at Brother Francis, and he opened the door again. I moved down to the bottom step. Erik was standing there at the roadside with the same devilish smile he wore when I left him. He was now rotating the club in his left hand.

"Erik, I believe we left off discussing the nuances of the new Freedom of Worship amendment and how it applies to only government-approved locations."

"Yeah, so what?" He caustically remarked, as he pounded the baton into his left hand again.

"I just had an enlightening conversation with Father Flanagan and—"

"That old sot of a so-called priest; he's all washed up." Erik rudely remarked.

I was ready to pound Erik into the ground myself at that point. I heard Brother Francis start to get up from his seat. I put my arm back behind me and waved for him to sit down.

"Anyway, the 'old sot' as you call him, mentioned that when the United States Government approved our charter as a college, it included all buildings and properties of this institution. The tractors, repair trucks, security vans, and buses were included as *property*. In this case rolling property. This bus is still ICC ground!"

Erik's eyes got as large as saucers, and his face, since his complexion was so fair, turned steamy red. His jaw tightened, as his eyes then drew down to a hostile and hateful squint.

"Oh and by the way, firing on any vehicle *outside* of the campus grounds is beyond your jurisdiction. Homeland Security would need to be notified in addition to the local Front Royal Police. Have a nice day."

Brother Francis slammed the door in Erik's face. I then proceeded to walk to the back to the cheers of the students. Brother Francis put the Prevost in gear and the massive heavy-duty Volvo diesel engine wound up as we started to roll.

The kids' faces were glued to the windows, mugging and laughing at Erik and his Blueshirts as we passed them by.

Erik's men were completely bewildered and perplexed as to what had just occurred. Erik screamed at them to let us by. Those who were not moving fast enough got a taste of Erik's nightstick.

As we rounded the circle just prior to making our escape out the grand entrance of the college, I saw Erik bent over thrashing the asphalt with his baton—still screaming.

TO BE CONTINUED....

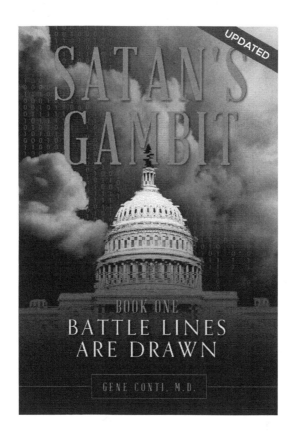

To contact the author, Gene Conti, M.D., for interviews or presentations, use the information below:

www.satansgambit.com

To order more copies of the novel, you may order through the above website or directly from Amazon.com.

Also Available:

Satan's Gambit – Book Two: The Dark Forces of Darkness Unleashed
Satan's Gambit – Book Three: Rise of the Beast